Ribbons in Time

Cathy Koon

For my recurring, childhood dream and imagination's endless possibilities to give it purpose…

Chapter 1

"The only things certain in life, each of us are born to die and everything between belongs to fate."

Sammy Jo read what was left of the weathered tombstone inscription over a year ago. More than eroded words, the faded proclamation was not only legacy of a life lost, but also prophecy of a life yet lived.

***

An open palm slapped the blaring alarm clock button, Sammy Jo dragged from the nightly images stuck in her head. Murky remains of the proverbial estate once again faded to black, mounting questions remaining unanswered. Eyes pinched, she gasped for breath in a failing attempt to extinguish adrenaline, pumping through her veins like liquid fire. The touch of cold brass was still evident on her trembling palm, remnants of the nightmare as real as shuddering goosebumps racing up both arms. Sinking into a warm silhouette of ticking and down, she waited for her flailing heart to fall steady.

For Sammy Jo Wilcox, the recurring visions began when she was a young girl, probably not more than seven or eight years old. More than a dream, the grandeur manor, was more of a familiar destination, becoming as much a part of childhood as fabled bedtime stories and the tooth fairy.

The clapboard two-story had a soothing effect on her, making each nocturnal visit feel like a welcome journey home. Images of a cobblestone walk guided her to a gleaming picket fence, where she basked in afternoon shade of a Federal style house. Two towering Elm trees flanked the veiled walk, casting a dancing filigree of sunlight through twisted branches. The trill of songbirds drew Sammy Jo's gaze to an upstairs window, where a southern, lilac kissed breeze fanned sheer lace through open panes.

But that was before shock of her grandmother's sudden death sent Sammy Jo's life spiraling out of control, slivers of life stolen away, one shard at a time. Loss of the woman who raised her left no part of life untouched. Even dreams of the night were not sacred from the long reaching fingers of death. Sense of peace once offered by the grand estate on the hill all but diminished. Tragedy and loss gradually replaced security of both night and day.

Tainted dreams transformed into an ugly skeleton of the past. For nearly two years now, nightmares left her stranded in lurking shadows of her once beloved estate.

Trapped by lucid images, she stood in the manor's shadows, sucked in a breath of stale, damp air and held it. Awakened senses prickled her hair, drawing her eyes to hazy light raining down, like the warning of a lighthouse beacon on a stormy night. White fabric snapped fiercely through an upstairs window, reflecting against a starless, black sky. Smothered sunshine faded into darkness, dancing filigree buried in ashen Earth beneath her feet. A sense of bereavement echoed in whispers of the wind, cries of loss for what once was.

Imagining an ill-fated history hidden behind the upstairs window, Sammy Jo's mind lapped hazy pictures of the nightmare through her brain. Fast moving frames sped forward with unshackled freedom. For the first time, last night's nightmare ushered her past the gate and up creaky steps of the estate, hollowed night landing her on a darkened threshold.

Swelling curiosity overpowered fear. With the brass knob clutched in her hand, Sammy Jo twisted, an imminent click of triumph echoing in her ears. But, like thistle lost to the wind, the house vanished from her mind, chased by sunny rays of reality grating her bedroom walls.

Like an intimidating bully lurking in the darkness, the nightmare taunted and teased. As much as she feared the imagined horror she sensed hidden behind the upstairs window, she felt cheated of the right to face the demon plaguing her nights.

Sammy Jo snorted at the the second annoying blare of the snooze button, fumbling for the clock angled on the side table. Tucking the nightmare back where it belonged, in a far corner of her mind reserved for childhood insecurities and fiends of the night, she flung faded quilts to the side, swinging both feet over the side of the bed. For another day, she would ponder the shrouded secret, for another night she would wait for buried truth to reveal itself.

Highland's lone diner opened well before dawn, serving enough coffee to float a boat by 8:00 A.M. Area farmers meandered in and out of the one room café like herded cattle, downing stout coffee and swapping tales, before beginning grueling sixteen-hour shifts in spring fields.

Sammy Jo angled her rust riddled pickup in one of two coveted spaces left between the bustling diner and her corner gift shop. Twisting the key in the ignition, the engine choked twice and coughed a puff of black smoke from the tail pipe before heaving a dying gasp.

Robbed of more than few hours sleep, Sammy Jo stifled a yawn and leaned toward the rear view mirror, the reflection of exhaustion peeking from puffy lids. With an inward sigh, she swiped a smudge of brown mascara with her thumb, evidence of hasty dressing and dashing out the door in record time of seventeen minutes flat.

Unfortunately, one of the pitfalls of being her own boss, two slaps of the snooze button was all the luxury she could afford on a weekday. Sacrificing breakfast for savored 18-minutes, her stomach growled like a hungry dog as an irritating reminder.

Surrendering to the persistent yawn, she cupped her hand over her mouth, reaching for the box of supplies riding in the passenger seat. Yanking the keys from the ignition, she swung the cab door open and dropped down, dragging the box of supplies with her.

Central town for business in the 1800's, the plate glass window of her gift shop reflected memories of the original mercantile. For more than two centuries, the family operated storefront catered to the small village of Highland, Tennessee, offering anything from dry goods, to food, to the latest town gossip. Egbert's fourth generation General Store closed its doors on history in early fall, a waning past resurrected as Wilcox Landscaping and Gifts two months later. Supported in part by tourist wandering the back roads of Tennessee in search of handcrafted souvenirs, the business was slowly emerging as a profitable endeavor.

Wrestling the bulky, cardboard box in the crook of one arm, Sammy Jo poked the key in the brass lock of her shop and twisted, nudging the door with a blue jean clad hip. Overhead doorbells clanged like cymbals against her pounding head as she flipped the window sign from closed to open with her free hand, kicking the door shut behind her.

Wiggling past the original cast iron stove, still taking up space in the display room, Sammy Jo shifted the weighty supplies to the other arm, nearly taking out a table of hand blown glass with her purse on the way past. Her morning had started on a sour note and the tune was growing worse by the minute. Lurching forward, she recovered the fumble, dumping the supplies and her shoulder bag on the back counter with an inflated grunt.

Tired and frustrated, gears in her brain once again kicked into high, a rendition of last night's nightmare plastered on the backs of her eyelids. Becoming increasingly life-like, images stuck in her head tailed her conscious like a stalker. She imagined the knob turning, the door swinging wide to answers of questions that had plagued her for nearly two years.

She shoved the box of supplies from the edge of the wood counter, trying to will away unnerving notions picking at her sanity like a turkey vulture. With one hand curled at the back of her neck, she pinched tense muscles, with the other, twisted for the light switch on the wall.

Fragments of her illusory dream instantly dissipated into heart stopping certainty, she was not alone. With her finger still on the toggle, ripcord tight shoulders ricocheted off her earlobes. Loud shatters of glass in the back room wiped her mind clean of imaginary threats, replacing them with real ones crashing from shadows of the stock room.

The last robbery to rock Highland was last fall, when little six years old Tommy Riley swiped a pack of Juicy Fruit from the five and dime. Word of the hard lesson spread like wildfire through the small town, after his mama hauled him in to return the unopened pack to Mr. Higgins with a sobbing apology. Loud racket emanating from the open doorway sent Sammy Jo's imagination on a rollercoaster ride of wild scenarios, none as harmless as a tow haired first grader with a sweet tooth.

Inching backward, she frantically skimmed the pine counter for a weapon. Without logical consideration of retreat, or dialing 911, clammy fingers of a feisty, red head temperament snatched the carved neck of a wooden Bantam rooster nesting on top of her supply box, hauling it over her head. Daylight flickered from menacing tips of a jagged, scarlet crest. With more reckless spirit than good sense, Sammy Jo whirled toward the stockroom door, snorting a string of short breaths out her nose, holding the last one in.

Sammy Jo's one and only physical tussle earned her a week detention in third grade after playground bully, Betsy Girdling, yanked the ribbons from her pigtails. Reciting a demanded apology with fingers crossed behind her back, she had no genuine regrets then, and listening to the commotion beyond the doorway, she would have none now.

Sneakered feet crept to the opening, echoes of a thumping heart ebbing into persistent explosions of glass. Peeking around the corner, she squeezed the neck of defense, squared both feet firmly on the floor and readied herself for a skirmish with the imagined prowler.

The stock room lights were off, her eyes automatically flitting to the back door, surprisingly, still bolted in place. Hazy sunshine seeped beneath edges of a yellowing, canvas blind, spilling a single slice of light across worn tiles, littered with glistening shards.

Fingers of one hand hugged the doorframe, white knuckles of the other clung fiercely to the rooster's neck. Steely blue eyes bounced from one corner of the room to the other. When another crash added to the mounting heap of glass on the floor, terror gushed down Sammy Jo's spine, coming alarmingly close to puddling in her shoes. Impulsive reflex drew the intimidating feathered armor higher, the quick maneuver matched with an impressive shriek that would have frightened the most brazen robber.

On cue, her startled focus swung to scuffles of a top shelf, connecting with the beady stare of the masked burglar. A broken ceiling tile overhead hinted as the obvious source of intrusion.

Partially concealed by two dangerously tottering boxes, a shaken raccoon cub cowered, sitting tighter than a Sunday morning altar boy. Black button eyes glared down, before retreating further behind the safety of a cardboard barricade.

With deflated lungs, Sammy Jo's shoulders dropped, her feathered weapon thudding to the floor, followed by a shaky giggle. Never had she been so happy to discover ten pounds of mischief wreaking havoc in her stockroom.

After a hasty analysis, she dragged a rickety step stool from the corner, wedging it to the wall shelves. Edging her weight one rung at a time, teetering toes left the top tread, stretching the few vital inches necessary to reach the impish intruder.

In slow motion, the unstable stool wobbled, and then rocked backwards, ending in a crash. With an instinctive squeal that echoed through the store, Sammy Jo clung to the shelf with a death grip; Nike clad toes curling helplessly to the one below.

Twenty miles north of Burlington, Tennessee, Grayson Wesley pulled to the curb in desperate need of a caffeine refill... strong, black caffeine. A six-hour wrestling match with a lumpy motel mattress the night before had made the last leg of his sixteen-hour journey the longest four hours of his life.

Highland was much like any other one-sheriff burgs peppering old routes of the south. Brick, two-storied buildings, symbolic of the old west, lined both sides of the street, ornate rooftops embellishing a clear, blue sky. Exactly sixteen colonial style lampposts dotted cobblestone walks of town, two lanes of Main Street punctuated by three traffic lights.

Parking his black BMW between a battered red pickup, and a gunmetal gray 4x4 with a six-inch lift, Grayson turned off the engine and slid from the seat, slamming the door behind him. He poked his keys in the pocket of tan khakis and twisted an aching back, convinced his muscles had as many knots as the innerspring ogre he left wallowing in its victory a couple of hundred miles back.

The aroma of maple-cured ham and fresh baked biscuits lured him to the lone diner in Highland where he ordered a large Joe to go and carried it outside into the warm mid-May morning. Filling his lungs with crisp mountain air, he held it for a few seconds before letting his breath slip free.

The spring weather was welcomingly sunny with not a cloud in the sky, the temperature already well above average for this time of year. The New Hampshire winter had been long and brutal and Grayson was grateful that at least Tennessee's climate was cooperating with his dreaded trip back to Thatcher Hill. His heart squeezed at the agonizing circumstances beckoning a long overdue homecoming to the family manor.

Wandering aimlessly down the walk toward his car, Grayson tipped the cup for a much-anticipated swallow of liquid momentum, his eyes following a flock of geese, jockeying for position in their rigid formation. Before coffee had a chance to wet his lips, a heart-stopping shriek blasted from the corner building, the Styrofoam cup projecting from his hand like a launching pad. Molten black splashed his green polo, turning it a menacing shade of gray, the remainder exploding across the sidewalk, drenching $500.00 Salvatore Ferragamo loafers.

Cursing a string of obscenities beneath his breath, Grayson wiped at his soaked shirt when a second shrill cry for help diluted the honk of Canadian fowl, flapping wings disappearing behind a hedge of pines lining the outskirts of town.

Instinct, fueled by curiosity drew him to the corner gift shop, cautiously poking his head inside. A strong floral scent, laced with cinnamon, wafted from cool air. The doorbell chimed overhead, the dim room still and quiet. The dark space seemed deserted, making him wonder if lack of sleep and stress from the past week had not finally taken its toll. A wrestling match with the innerspring fiend from the night before had claimed more than an aching back. He could now chuck up phantom screams to the long list plaguing him since receiving the devastating phone call last week.

Grayson shoved the door open wider, and moved inside, hiding both hands in his pockets. He tersely jingled keys and waited for the door to close behind him, before taking a slow step. Idling forward, he snaked between two linen draped display tables, quickly second thinking borrowing more trouble. His plate was already brimming without asking for a second scoop of someone else's troubles.

When another frantic squeak drifted from the back room, Grayson skidded to a halt in front of a colossal potbelly stove, the lingering smell from decades of roaring fires blending with hints of candle wax and fresh cut flowers.

"Is anyone out there?" Quivering words pleaded from the wide, arched doorway.

"Looks like I'm going to need a bigger plate," Grayson muttered sarcastically, wandering toward the opening. With one shoulder wedged against the doorframe, he folded his arms across his chest and choked the urge to laugh.

Chapter 2

A woman's hourglass figure pinned to a shelf, peered over her right shoulder through daunting blue eyes, a crown of shoulder length curls draping part of her face. The cloak of amber did little to hide the beauty's embarrassment, instead emphasized deepening crimson cheeks, peeping beneath the tightly spun ringlets.

Grayson's eyes dribbled down a tie-dyed tee shirt, to a snug fitting pair of *Daisy Dukes*. A lacey fringe of thread capped long, shapely legs, ending in sockless gym shoes.

For a long minute, they stared, sizing each other up from opposite ends of the room.

"Well, are you just going to stand there gawking, or are you going to help me down?" Sammy Jo uttered blatantly, ending the awkward silence. A lilting, southern accent trickled from pursed lips.

With a slanted stare fixed like a second skin to the stranger leaning in the doorway, Sammy Jo's heart performed a fast rendition of the fox trot in her chest.

13

Sizing up the man, felt more like an easy stroll down the dessert isle of Heckman's Grocery.

She studied her first customer of the morning and sighed inwardly, nearly forgetting her dilemma. Arms folded across his chest he looked like he had just stepped from the spring cover of GQ magazine, with the exception of a fresh coffee stain dripping down the front of his open collar shirt.

From his swanky guise, she assumed the stranger preferred golfing to cow tipping, and probably sipped olive garnished martinis at the country club, in lieu of a sudsy brew at the local tavern. Yet, the annoying flutter of butterflies in her stomach made her all too aware of the old adage, opposites can and most definitely do attract.

Tapping down a blossoming grin, Grayson made long purposeful strides across the room, and a without a word, reached up, curling his fingers just above the curve of shapely hips. Making a mental note, her hourglass figure and curvaceous hips were the reflection of wholesome country life. A physique like that was definitely not earned from fad diets or long, sweaty hours at the city gym. The touch of her tiny waist and sated hips attracted him like the secret of an exotic aphrodisiac, known only to the southern bells of Tennessee.

His fingers slid across ribs sheathed in thin fabric as she released her clutch, slowly lowering her feet to the floor. Fingers lingering for a full 10 seconds, he finally pulled them away with the persistence of a two-year-old temper tantrum, shoving both hands in his pants pockets for a much deserved time out.

With worn sneakers planted securely on vintage-checkered tile, Sammy Jo rotated in slow motion to face intimidating hazel eyes. Instinctively stiffening, she attempted to smooth the unruly locks from her forehead, only to have them spring back into place. Pausing to analyze him further, she dragged in a slow, ragged breath, unsure if the prickling hairs on her neck were warning bells of caution, or the Welcome Wagon ringing.

He was tall, easily six-three with a lean stature. Impeccably tailored khakis replaced local Levi attire, and a once green polo reflected from hazel eyes rimmed by a thin, gray halo. Neatly pressed trousers gave way to fancy leather loafers, probably costing more than her entire collections of shoes, including her new Justin's, which cost nearly two months of meager savings.

Intense scrutiny trickled from wavy, auburn hair just long enough to tickle his collar, down the open neckline where tanned skin suggested perhaps coastal life. It only took a hot New York minute to conclude he was definitely not from around these parts.

Sammy Jo's heart was thumping so hard and loud, she feared the stranger could hear the pounding. Suddenly aware of her ogling stare, she snapped her wayward eyes to the side. Hoping she was not as conspicuous as she imagined, she blushed profusely at the thoughts percolating in her head. Her attention quickly averted to the pile of shimmering splinters scattered across the floor.

"Thank you," she muttered, self-consciously tugging at her tee shirt that had inched its way up, exposing the fleshy curve of ivory skin. Remembering the frantic raccoon, a flutter of lashes gestured to the top shelf and the fretful ball of fur prancing back and forth, like his feet were on fire. Grayson followed her lead to the furry host from the peanut gallery, who stopped suddenly, hovering over the amusement from a front row seat.

"I found that little guy wreaking havoc when I came in this morning," she said, with a crisp nod. Rolling one shoulder, she acknowledged the obvious. "Looks like my rescue attempt was a bit of a blunder,"

Sensing the weight of the man's eyes, she unconsciously jerked at the frayed hem of her jeans. "Lucky thing that you came along when you did mister." she said, not daring to make eye contact. "Both of us may have ended up spending our day stranded on a shelf."

Grayson's inner conscious could not agree more, today was not only lucky for her and the nosey trespasser; his impromptu stop for coffee had spun him an unpredicted win on the roulette wheel. After the week he'd had, it was about time that lady luck smiled on him.

"One down, one to go." he said, instead. Righting the step stool with a wink, his eyes locked on her.

Stunning, her beauty was pleasantly distinct. Porcelain skin with a splash of freckles gave her a girlish glow, yet the hourglass curves of her figure shouted anything but childlike. Her eyes were the bluest he had ever seen, the color of her hair, cinnamon kissed autumn.

Trying his best not to drool, or at the very least, stare, his eyes darted around the room. "Got a pair of gloves?"

She was right. The man's deep, masculine voice, tinged by a strong New England accent, implied he was definitely from up the coast. Watching his lips move, she was intrigued with the way the words rolled from his tongue. Feeling her cheeks warm beneath the fascination, she turned snatching a pair of canvas gloves from the workbench. With an outstretched arm, she dangled them between two fingers. After he took them, she politely extended her right hand. "Sammy Jo Wilcox. I own the place."

Gripping her hand, his grasp was firm yet gentle, certainly not the hands of a farmer. His palm was smooth, not calloused, and his nails well cared for, like a doctor or perhaps an attorney.

"Grayson Wesley," His grip lingered and she did not mind a bit.

"So if you're the proprietor, then I guess you'll be the one responsible if I'm attacked by a rabid coon," he surmised, his eyes rolling menacingly to the top shelf, before returning to meet her questionable gaze.

An attorney...without question...

It was only after he smiled did Sammy Jo realize he was joking. She let the breath ease from her lungs, along with the slow slip of his hand.

She watched from a safe distance as he up righted the stool and climbed it, skipping the bottom two slats all together. His tall physique made an easy reach for the stranded cub. Lifted from the shelf with a gloved hand, the furry, gray ball squirmed briefly, but quickly responded to his soft, hypnotic voice as he carried it down the ladder by the nape of its neck.

Turning to Sammy Jo, the wide-eyed animal dangled in mid-air between them, finally giving up on an attempted escape. "Now what?" A definitive shrug rolled from Grayson's shoulder.

Sammy Jo pointed to the back door. "His mama's probably wondering about him. I'm sure he wandered in from the woods." Her voice was low, tempered by a slow southern drawl. Hurrying ahead, she unbolted the back door, swinging it open ahead of him.

Leaning against the doorjamb with her thumbs hooked in the front pockets of her jeans, Sammy Jo's eyes trailed the stranger's confident strut, as he made his way to the woods edge. Releasing the cub at the bottom of a soaring oak tree, he waited for it to scamper out of sight before spinning around with a bemused smile. She stepped to the side when he approached the door, peeling the glove from his right hand.

"I'm impressed, what are you, the raccoon whisperer?" she teased, with an outstretched hand.

"It's a talent," Dropping the glove in her palm on the way past, one rogue brow drifted confidently into his hairline with a jiggle, making her wonder what other macho talents lay hidden beneath his suave exterior. "I'm a natural born charmer," he cajoled.

Pushing the door closed, Sammy Jo slipped the dead bolt back into place, not quite sure how to respond to such an audacious admission. "Well thank you for getting the little fellow out of here before he bankrupted me,"

"You're welcome," Grayson poked both hands in his pockets, checking out the small, dark paneled stockroom. Shelves of meticulously arranged planters lined the wall, the top three ledges reserved for vases, most of which lie in a glistening heap on the tile floor.

"A floral and gift shop huh?" he asked curiously. "I don't remember the place being here the last time I was through Highland."

Suddenly feeling self-conscious over her captivation with the stranger, Sammy Jo tucked a loose strand of hair behind her ear and flipped the fluorescent light switch on the wall. Eager for a distraction, she practically lunged for the coffee decanter on the counter, filling it at the sink.

"Can I offer you a cup of coffee?" she asked, over her shoulder.

Motioning to the dark, menacing stain on his shirt, three zigzags creased his forehead. "No thanks, I think I've had plenty. I had just left the diner next door when I was summoned."

Color traveled up Sammy Jo's neck, deepening the blush of her cheeks to a bright, cherry red. Her ivory complexion was a curse when it came to embarrassment, a tall tell sign of unspoken feelings. She could feel heat creeping from beneath the neckline of her tee.

"I'm sorry if I caused that. I'd be glad to pay for the shirt." Sammy Jo flinched when cold water spilled over the sides of the pot, splashing her hand. Twisting the faucet closed, she reached for the coffee maker.

Waving a hand through the air, a husky laugh replaced Grayson's mischievous grin. "It's fine. Really...I'm just teasing."

After dropping a coffee filter in the basket, followed by four scoops of coffee, trembling fingers poured the water through. Slipping the decanter in place, she turned to him, eager to engage her mind with more rational thoughts than the ones causing her to tremor like an anxious puppy.

"To answer your question, I've been here a little over a year. I also do landscaping," She tucked her thumbs in her back jean pockets, shifting her weight to one foot. "You must not come through often," she surmised.

Grayson's shoulders drooped, as if he had just been heaved a hefty burden. A lingering grimace suggested anything but a leisurely visit to the great state of Tennessee.

"No," he offered regretfully, gripping the back of his neck with a twist that crunched like dominos down his spine. "Unfortunately, it's been awhile since I've been through these parts."

Following Sammy Jo to the front room, he waited for her to switch the light on, watching her move a supply box from the counter to the floor. "Well welcome back to Highland," she said, avoiding tantalizing eyes like the Bubonic plague.

"You have a nice place here," Head bobbing from side to side, he took a slow step forward. Surveying the room, several white, linen draped tables surrounded a potbelly stove. Sauntering to a display of hand quilted throws; he dragged his fingers over patchwork fabric before wandering to the other side. Stopping at a colorful spread of glassware, he sunk both hands in his pockets, inspecting the delicate shapes. "Surprising though," he added, his tone fringing on flippant.

Sammy Jo squared both shoulders and chased the comment around her head trying to figure if his remark was supposed to be a compliment or an insult. She waited for him to finish and when he didn't, she circled from behind the counter, her brow wrinkling at the question. "What's so surprising about it?" Her intense stare challenged a rational reply.

Grayson moseyed to the other side of the table and picked up a crystal candleholder. With it pinched between two fingers, he raised it to morning sunlight streaming through the plate glass window. Cocking his head a bit, he twisted the glass, eyeing dancing blue and green prisms.

One shoulder rolled precariously. "I wouldn't think there's a market in Highland to keep you in business with pricey knick-knacks, that's all," His rash observation sounded a bit more like a snicker in Sammy Jo's ears, his persistent grin as irritating as fingernails on a chalkboard.

A chill descended on the room. Icy blue eyes widened with offense, in what Sammy Jo intended as a threatening glare. Spine straightened, her open expression was easy to read and it was screaming outrage, all in capital letters.

Insult brought the hairs on her neck to attention with a rigid salute. Any infatuation she might have had with the stranger died a sudden, quiet death. Not sure if he was her knight in shining armor, or the rear end of the horse he rode in on, she cleared her throat and asked with one fist digging into her hip, "And just what's that supposed to mean?" Her brows dented deep furrows in her forehead, fingers of her free hand drumming the counter. Searing him with a look that suggested he was just about to lock horns, the tempo in her fingers amplified.

He nodded nonchalantly, carefully replacing the candleholder to the table, his gaze shifting to the floral cooler lining the adjacent wall. "It's simple, from a keen business perspective, Highland's a small town. I wouldn't think you would sell many flowers and frills around here." A glance in her direction told him he had raised Sammy Jo's hackles to an all-time high. Trying to rally with a crooked smile, he did not quite succeed, not even close.

"You pompous ass," She muttered the words so quietly, only she could hear the razor sharp sarcasm. Tightening her face, a ripple of anger raced to balled fists at her side, her feisty temperament flaring as bright as fireworks on July 4. The way she felt at that moment, she never figured she would see the drifter again, so why bother holding back.

"Oh, so what you're saying is that you don't think us *Tennessee hicks* can afford flowers and candles," Craning her neck, she added dryly, "Or is it our *hillbilly* taste that leaves you wondering?" The stranger's words stuck in her crawl like a pine needle under her thumbnail.

Grayson pulled a frown, knowing instantly that he had struck a raw nerve. His mind froze, along with his tongue that suddenly felt accurately close to a size 12 shoe. Both hands in the air, he automatically retreated with a quick step back, surrendering to hostility shooting from the other side of the room.

"No need to get all riled up lady. No one said *hick or hillbilly*."

Bulging eyes flashed cool disdain, informing him that he had clearly crossed the line. "You implied!" she snarled. Sliding her glare from Grayson, she focused on keeping the rage within manageable measures, her heart one beat from exploding.

"I most certainly did not," Opening his mouth to speak he stopped short. The little vixen looked locked and loaded and he didn't figure it would take much for her to pull the trigger.

"A sensible observation, that's all," he added, through tight lips. Back paddling, he felt like he was quickly drowning in a torrential flood of poor words.

"Not that it's any of your business, but I happen to do very well for myself," she spat defiantly. Her head jerked with a snappy tilt, nostrils flaring like a prodded bull. "The shop and my landscaping business give me all the work I can handle…" Quickly tacking on, "And then some…"

Maybe a tad over the top, her business checkbook was teetering on a sandy edge this month, but there was no way she was going to let *Mr. Goody Two Shoes,* poised arrogantly in his high fluting loafers, think she was anything but successful.

His rude assumptions made her feel as ignorant as a bottom-sucking catfish, and just as useless. Folding her arms over her chest, she wasn't sure, if she was angry because of how he made her feel, or because she lent him the ability to do so. Usually confident and poised, his raw notions chipped at her composure.

Sensing a red bullseye plastered to his forehead, Grayson considered a quick escape out the door with no looking back, but gave a terse nod instead. In the most empathetic voice he could muster, he made a purposeful attempt at mending fences.

"I can see you're passionate about your business, and I'm sure you're very good at it. I meant no disrespect," He waited in the long silence for a reply, shuffling from one Italian leather clad foot to the other. His face drooping like a scolded child, he painted on his most pitiful expression before making a final plea, "Please accept my apology,"

Chewing on the pout of a bottom lip, Sammy Jo briefly considered it. When her eyes drifted up from the floor, she cracked a smile and lifted one shoulder in a half-hearted shrug.

Playing it safe, Grayson quickly shifted gears on the subject, moseying to the refrigerated display case along the wall. A lavish spray of yellow roses and daisies immersed in a plastic bucket of water caught his attention. He pointed to the bouquet. "Do you think you have a vase left from your little buddy's escapade to make a sale?" His attempt at humor earned him a thin smile.

"I'm sure I can probably rummage something up."

After taking the bouquet from the case and arranging them in the back room, Sammy Jo carried the finished product back to the front counter, fidgeting with the final sprigs of baby's breath until she was satisfied with its placement. "Will you need a card?" she asked, finding her curiosity of the lucky recipient vexing.

Grayson stood on the other side of the counter, digging for his wallet. "No, the flowers will be fine," he replied.

Sammy Jo pushed his hand to the side as he fished through a stack of bills. "There's no charge. Consider the bouquet an exchange for your rescue services. We'll call it even." Her smile was genuine.

Swiftly dismissing thoughts of refusing her generosity, he slipped his wallet in his back pocket, avoiding casualties of a second offense. "Thanks, I appreciate it."

Sammy Jo pulled a daisy free poking it beside an unopened bud, squirming beneath the unsettling assessment of hazel eyes. She was just about to ask how long he was going to be in town when the doorbell clanged, breaking the silence between them.

Lettie Mae charged through the door like a jackrabbit, babbling midway through a sentence. "Sorry I'm running late Sam..." Skating to a halt, both brows shot to her blonde hairline, eyes ricocheting from Sammy Jo, to graze the heart-stopping customer leaning against the counter.

"Well, hello there…" A strong southern accent dripped like honey from her tongue. Tossing a golden braid over her shoulder, pink glossed lips bowed, deepening the dimple in her left cheek.

Sammy Jo ignored Lettie Mae's interruption, tipping her chin with a haphazard attempt at a professional tone. Scooting the crystal vase towards Grayson, she smiled politely. "Thanks again Grayson. Enjoy the flowers."

Taking his cue, he picked up the vase tucked safely in a cardboard box, smiling at Lettie with the tip of an imaginary hat as he walked by. "Good morning," he said, dipping his chin.

With a pretended shrug of indifference, Sammy Jo watched the brawny swagger of khakis exit through the door.

The door had no sooner clicked closed, the last chime fading, when Lettie Mae leaned elbows on the counter, rattling assumptions that all ran together in one jumbled sentence.

"Wow…and just who the heck was that…did I interrupt something…he sure wasn't looking at you like a customer…" Her gaze shot back over her shoulder and out the plate glass window. The heartthrob opened the passenger door of a black BMW, sliding the boxed bouquet in the seat with one last glance through the shop window before closing the door.

A pink flush crept over Sammy Jo's cheeks, tight curls sticking to tiny beads of perspiration speckling her forehead. Swiping damp hair with the back of her hand, she made an ill attempt at sounding nonchalant.

"There goes that wild imagination of yours again Lettie," she said, rolling her eyes to the ceiling. Snatching her purse from the counter, Sammy Jo tucked it under her arm. "I have to run,"

Sidestepping further interrogation, Sammy Jo hurried to the door for a quick escape, spouting over her shoulder as she pulled the door open, "We had a little critter make a visit in the stock room this morning. He created quite a mess ...if you wouldn't mind..." Throwing a hand in the air, she waved, leaving disappointed Lettie to fill in the blanks.

Sammy Jo yanked open the door of her 1964 Chevy pickup. Primary shades of rust red and primed metal was a chastening contrast to the shiny, black BMW disappearing down Main Street. Slinging her purse across the seat, she scooted over the worn, tweed fabric and slammed the door so hard the glass rattled the back window.

Clammy hands gripped tight to the wheel, Sammy Jo growling through clenched teeth. She stared out the windshield and replayed the last twenty minutes in her head, rewinding and pausing on 6' 3" of pure intimidation.

Sammy Jo could not remember ever feeling intimidated by a man, any man, and the thought of

Grayson Wesley's effect on her made her fighting mad. Even the recent breakup with her longtime boyfriend of 5 years came surprisingly easy.

The thought of sweet Harley whizzed through her brain. If you looked up "country boy" in the dictionary, wholesome Harley Wiesenborn's picture would be staring up from the page, a piece of fresh straw wedged between teeth of a perfect, snowy smile.

She and Harley, an item since High School, he was more like her best friend. Sharing teenage memories, from senior prom to Honky-Tonk Texas 2 stepping, the romance just wasn't there. Everyone in town expected him to pop the question soon, but the last year with Harley left Sammy Jo more fearful than anticipated of the outcome. The only thing she could imagine her life being with Harley was a brood of kids outnumbering hens in the coop. Not that there was anything wrong with marrying and having a large family, she just pictured life with more possibilities than milking cows and gathering eggs with one kid on her hip and another in tow.

Growing up in the confines of a small town where the biggest excitement came from the annual fair's bull riding competition, Sammy Jo dreamed of another life, one of romance and adventure. She imagined traveling to big cities where every day bared new discoveries. But, not once did she imagine awkward or inadequate as a part of that picture, which was exactly how Grayson Wesley made her feel.

With a second snarl, she twisted the key in the ignition and pumped the gas pedal. Shoving the clutch to the floor after the engine fired, she crammed the gearshift in reverse with the thrust of a boxer's right jab. *"Hillbilly…"* she muttered aloud, dropping her arm over the back of the seat. With a quick glance out the back window, Sammy Jo backed onto the two-lane road, worn rubber chirping dry pavement.

Chapter 3

Grayson passed the Burlington city limits sign, slowing well below the speed limit. Taking in unchanged scenery and businesses lining the town walks, memories of his childhood crept from each street corner. His mind reeled as he passed the old-fashioned ice cream parlor, four faded, black bistro tables and chairs arranged in the same staggered pattern along the front walk as when he was a kid. The five and dime, carrying anything from cold medicine to hand dipped milk shakes; still sported the same washed-out green, canvas awning, and he wondered if they still sold locally made peanut brittle that he loved as a boy.

Stopping at the second of town's five traffic lights, he slowly filled his lungs with the familiar roasted aroma of hot dogs and brats from the food wagon, angled along the East corner. Grayson slowed and poked his hand out the window with a wave to Mr. Marcella, setting up for lunch regulars. Receiving an expected friendly exchange from the hunched, silver haired man, Grayson was sure the old merchant did not recognize him as Rosaline Worthington's grandson.

It had been almost ten years since Grayson visited the lunch wagon with his Gram, diving into one of Mr. Marcella's oversized wieners, better described by townsfolk as pork on steroids. His mouth watered at the thought of mustard slathered hot dog, topped with sweet relish and an extra sour pickle on the side.

Spending most childhood summers on Thatcher Hill, regular visits to the lunch wagon became routine, although his grandmother labeled wieners as nothing more than discarded meat scraps. Remembering her selfless surrender of not only nibbling at one of Mr. Marcella's delicacies, but also pretending to enjoy it, a sudden pang of guilt erased the fond memories. Replacing the warm recollection with thoughts of the grim task at hand, he accelerated, watching town dwindling in the rear view mirror.

Grayson drove a few miles along snaking curves, slowing to turn onto the familiar dirt lane of his late grandmother's estate. Twisting up the steep grade, soaring pines darkened rocky cliffs on both sides, gravel crunching beneath the tires. The car bounced on the rutted path in obvious disrepair, lurching from one side of the road to the other, nearly bouncing him out of the seat with a sudden jolt.

The memorable scent of fresh pine blowing through the open window helped banish the despondency of his impromptu visit, offering a sedating effect. With the accelerator half throttle, the steering wheel twisted hard left beneath his palm into the clearing at the top of the ridge. Bright sunshine rained down on the once grand estate known to locals as *Thatcher Hill*.

The weathered, two hundred and fifty year old structure contrasted against a towering backdrop of emerald Pines, and Chestnut Oak trees in early bloom. Ropey vines twisted up one of the four white columns. Creeping across a sagging porch roof, a leafy waterfall of foliage cascaded down the other side. His eyes automatically shot to a black wreath reflecting from the massive front door, a long-standing southern tradition and reminder of death calling.

Grayson parked before a rickety gate, opening to an overgrown lawn, shoving away heartache of what once was. Twisting the key in the ignition, he gripped the steering wheel, dragging in a slow, shallow breath.

Through the windshield, he peered with a smile as Martheena struggled, pushing up from one of four southern staples lining the sprawling porch. With one hand still gripping the arm of the rocker, she paused for brittle joints to settle into place, before taking a slow, wobbly step forward.

The beaconing smile, radiating from ebony skin, had not changed much through the years. Once coal black locks had long turned silver, twisted into a tight bun on top of her head. Watching Martheena shuffle toward the steps, Grayson swore she was wearing the same blue and yellow plaid housedress and white apron he remembered from when he was a kid.

With her hand pressed to a wildly beating heart, she blinked twice at tears forming on her bottom lash.

Grayson swung open the car door and pulled the flowers to him, twisting from the seat. Bumping the door closed, he stood silent and drank in the sight of her.

"You're sure a sight for sore eyes," Martheena called out, after finally finding the strength to speak.

Martheena was Rosaline Worthington's housekeeper for nearly 60 years, more of a companion than she was an employee. Residing in the second largest of five bedrooms and treated like family, Martheena cared for Rosaline's every need, including a broken heart lugged through life like a ball and chain. The pudgy woman with a gentle smile became as much of Thatcher Hill's legacy as the grounds itself.

Cherished memories kept tucked safely away bubbled to the surface. Grayson could almost smell fresh blueberries of many years ago when he scrambled on a step stool in Martheena's kitchen, a wooden spoon in hand, eager to help. More of a hindrance to her than a help, not once did she complain of his unintentional sabotage, when he dumped a whole cup of salt in the cake batter instead of sugar. Pitching the full porcelain bowl of lumpy blueberry batter in the garbage, Martheena insisted was their practice batch; she reached for the flour bin of the Hoosier cabinet, humming as she went. With a slight smile, Grayson's breathing steadied and his tense muscles relaxed. The fond memory awakened an earlier time when life was steadfast and simple.

He stepped past the car, shoving open the squeaky gate, a nostalgic grin playing across his face. "You look great Martheena."

She swatted at the air, a blush deepening the swell of rounded cheeks. "Get on up here and give me some *huggin'* boy," she said with outstretched arms. "It's been way too long."

The targeted words pierced Grayson's heart like a dagger. He had intended to visit, but the timing never seemed right after the accident. His grandmother came to New Hampshire for the memorial services, spending a couple of weeks with him before he returned for fall classes. After graduation from NHU, his energy focused on a budding writing career, which quickly escalated into more of a mental escape than a profession.

Rosaline visited twice after his parent's funerals, never playing the trump, guilt card. Always strong and independent, the last thing she wanted was for her only grandchild to dote over her like an inherited responsibility. He had his own life to live and she reminded him during weekly telephone calls, how important that was to her.

The bottom step squeaked, waning beneath the weight of his foot as he stepped up. Grayson's eyes flitted across worn boards, whitewash fading beneath years of neglect.

"Been *meanin'* to call someone about that darned step," Martheena declared, noting the curl of his lip. "I just added it to my long list of *to dos*, there's always tomorrow." Martheena fretted over very little and obviously, maintenance on the old homestead was not on her scanty worry list. The roof was still standing and that was good enough for her.

Grayson ignored the second and third squeaks climbing the last two steps. Sitting the vase of flowers on the porch, he stood and wrapped his arms around the one woman who felt more like family than friend... the only family he had left in this world.

Martheena even smelled the same, like a bouquet of spring wildflowers, splashed with peppermint.

Martheena's stout frame gently rocked Grayson from side to side, filling the void that Rosaline's death had left in her heart. She patted him on the back and took a slow step back. Her eyes clouded, sensing regret trickling from hazel eyes. "You know, she was very proud of the man you've become."

Ignoring the words, Grayson squatted and picked the vase up from the porch, handing it to her. "I picked these up for you in Highland."

Cradling the box in stiff hands, Martheena turned to the rocker and shuffled back. After sitting the meticulously arranged spray on a faded, rattan table next to the chair, she dropped back into one, the breath gushing from her chest as she did. Inhaling deeply, she let it slowly seep from her lungs.

"Thank you, they're real *purdy,* but you shouldn't have wasted your hard earned money on this old woman." She patted the arm of the rocker beside her. "Come sit with me."

Grayson slumped into the rocker next to her, leaning folded arms across his knees, his eyes following gray paint chips of wood porch planks. "I should've been here Martheena, I'm all she had left …and she had to die alone."

"She wasn't alone Scamper, I was with her." Martheena reached over and patted his knee with fingers warped by passing years and hard work. "Your Gram was a stubborn ole' cuss, she did it her way."

Grayson blew out a ragged breath with the force of a slug in the gut. He knew his grandmother as well as any, but could not help but wrestle with guilt, squeezing his heart like a vise. His last conversation with Rosaline nearly two weeks ago rang in his head and he wondered if she sensed the end was near. When he promised a visit to Thatcher Hill soon, she reassured him that the time they had spent together was her most prized memory, reminding him one last time of how proud she was of him.

Martheena slowly rocked, the chair squeaking each time her foot scuffed the floor. "You know your Gram wouldn't have wanted you here fussing over her. She was far too proud of a woman for that."

Grayson winced, dark brows denting. He thudded an open palm to an empty chest. "I hear what you're saying, but that's not how this ache feels." Clambering from the rocker, he walked to the edge of the porch. With a shoulder leaned against a pillar, he stared across the waist high meadow of wildflowers, washing over the hillside like a waterfall of spring color.

Behind him, the rocker creaked, as Martheena wrestled from her chair. When she stepped up and put her hand on his shoulder, he automatically brushed a tear from his eye with the back of his hand before turning to her. "Tell me again," he said. "Are you sure Gram didn't suffer?"

"No *darlin'*...she didn't suffer." Martheena's gaze followed Grayson's back to the meadow. Hooking her arm through his, she paused, recalling details of the day Rosaline left this world.

"We had a nice afternoon, mostly sitting right there in those two rockers." Martheena dipped her chin to the chair she left, still gently swaying, glazed eyes reflecting the memory. "I think instinct warned your Gram that her time was close." Her attention returned to the wave of color rippling in the warm breeze. "We talked a lot about you, reminisced about your mom and even talked some about your Grandpa Isaac, God rest his soul." With her right hand, she slowly traced the cross of the trinity over the swell of her chest. When she turned back, scuffling slippers against the floorboards, Grayson followed. After dropping into the chair, she began a slow, leisure rock, her soft southern tone resonating in the warm breeze filtering across the porch.

"She wanted rolled dumplings and apple pie for supper. Chicken and buttermilk dumplings were her favorite, you know. And that was the best darned pot I ever made, if I must say so myself." The corners of her eyes crinkled beneath a gentle smile. As she replayed the day Rosaline died, Grayson had a clear picture of his grandmother happily reliving the joys in her life. He joined Martheena in a gentle rock, her words reassuring.

When Martheena reached over and patted the arm of Grayson's rocker, he sensed an uncanny presence, as if his grandmother was standing right beside him. He took in a slow breath and held it, afraid if he moved the comforting closeness would vanish.

"She was sitting right there in that very rocker." With her fingers curled over the arm of Grayson's chair, Martheena continued to rock, her eyes following a flock of starlings taking flight from a cap of pines, their wings filling the air with rhythmic flutter. After watching them disappear behind the ridge, she continued. "It was a beautiful evening, the sky clear and the moon full. The stars wrapped around the mountain and felt so close you could reach out and pluck *em'* right out the heavens." She took Grayson's hand and squeezed it before softly adding, "Rosaline leaned back and closed her eyes Scamper, just like that." With her eyes closed, Martheena paused, her chin trembling at the image in her head. When her eyes opened again, she found Grayson staring at her, heartbreak reflecting in the depths.

"I thought she'd dozed," Martheena pressed an open palm across her breastbone in attempt to calm the pain of a throbbing heart. "She nodded a lot in the last days; rattling on one minute and snoring like a winter bear the next." A sentimental smile smoothed the deep etched pain from her face. "But she was gone Scamper, quietly and peacefully gone,"

Chapter 4

Sammy Jo shoved the quilt to the side and swung both legs over the side of the bed, early morning temperatures leaving the wood floor cold beneath bare feet. Delicate, pastel sheers fluttered at the partially open window, a late May chill seeping in, bringing with it the scent of Earth and pine. Morning shadows streaked Street's over dated peach and teal floral wallpaper, slices of golden light angling across worn farmhouse planks.

Drawn to the window, Sammy Jo stared out at amber hues peeking above Hackberry Ridge. Dawn burst over the mountain, shades of fluorescent orange preceding a sunny day. Her eyes automatically fell to the chicken coop near the barn, the shrill of barnyard roosters crooning their diurnal wakeup call from wire fence, strung between weathered posts. Sliding the wood frame window open a few more inches, she pinched her eyes closed and breathed deeply, the sedating pine breeze scattering any remaining effects of a restless night.

The small town of Highland laid nestled in the Tennessee foothills, less than forty miles from the Georgia state line. Sammy Jo predicted typical warming temperatures, compliments of the high southern sun, already seeping over the ridge like a fiery, orange ball.

Digging a pair of cutoff jeans and her favorite Brad Paisley tee shirt from the bureau drawer, she dressed, padding bare feet down the steps. The pungent wakeup call of fresh brewed coffee beans permeated the early hour, Pop's first order of business after feeding the livestock.

Leaning a shoulder against the door facing, she crossed her arms over her chest and watched her grandfather sitting at the table, the morning newspaper spread across the table. In the milky glow of a dangling light fixture, he tipped the last drop of coffee, his cup hovering while he skimmed the newspaper's front page over the rim. Only glancing up briefly, he nonchalantly returned his attention to small town headlines, announcing the area's first Walmart grand opening, in bold, black print.

Although construction of the super store was nearly thirty miles away, it was still the biggest news to hit Highland, Tennessee since Main Street got its third traffic light a year and a half year back. One of the few American towns left untouched by golden arches or tacos served out a drive through window, it was a twenty-minute drive, to wrap your hands around a greasy burger done your way.

Walmart would definitely be the talk of the town for
months to come.

"Looks like Ashland County finally made the cut,"
her grandfather muttered.

Sammy Jo ambled over to him and draped her arms
over his shoulders. Peeking at the headlines, she smacked
a good morning kiss to the top of his head.

Without comment, she went to the cabinet and
pulled down a mug, filling it from the porcelain percolator,
perched on the stove burner. Adding a spoon of sugar, she
gave a quick stir, watching her grandfather from the
corner of her eye. He still looked lost. Each day over the
past two years, she watched him regress, imprisoned by
grief. Loss of her grandmother had left a huge gaping hole
in his life, eroding away at the man he once was.

After popping a slice of bread in the toaster, she
turned to her grandfather. Blowing across spiraling steam,
she took a slow sip from her mug. "Did you take your
blood pressure pills this morning Pops?" she asked, getting
the halfhearted grunt and nod she expected. "And I hope
you ate something first," she added, knowing darned well
from experience that he had not.

Death of his partner had taken a toll on James
Edward Wilcox. A stoic, handsome man with the lean build
of a man half his 74 years, silver threads coursed through a
full head of dark hair, high cheekbones emphasizing his
father's Cherokee Indian heritage. Commonly mistaken for
a man twenty years his junior, a map of grief now etched
new lines into his forehead. Sorrow's mark tugged at
deep-set eyes the color of polished onyx. With his wife of

nearly 5 decades gone, Sammy Jo feared the hands of time were catching up with him.

As with most, it was the early years that defined the calloused man Jim had become. Growing up on an Indian reservation in the late 1930's, life was hard for as long as he could remember. The frequent growl of an empty stomach lulled him to sleep most nights, spending his teen years working cotton and tobacco fields to help support six younger siblings.

Life's early lessons were both a blessing and a curse to Jim, a blessing because he learned to be self-reliant, independent, a curse because they molded him into a doubting, suspicious man, trusting of few people.

Although his late wife, Emma, was the love of Jim's life, Sammy Jo always suspected she was not his one and only. Imagining an early heartbreak added to molding the reserved man he had become, he wore proof in fading ink of a thorn-snared rose on his left arm.

Curiously asking him about the tattoo once, he quickly dismissed it to spirited hormones and a beer fed weekend in Nashville with buddies. It was the following caution that made Sammy Jo speculate if there were more to the tale. "Let it be a lesson, even the most beautiful things in life cause pain," he warned. Something akin to bitterness and regret stitched his words.

When the bread popped up in the toaster, Sammy Jo pulled a knife from the drawer and began buttering it. Sliding it across the table on a saucer, she propped a hand on her hip, sounding more like his mother than granddaughter, "Who would watch after you if I weren't here Pops?"

Jim plucked a corner from the toast, ignoring the obvious. "Do you have a busy day?" he asked, poking the bite between his lips.

Pushing down another slice of bread, Sammy Jo turned, coffee cup perched at her lips. "Lettie Mae's coming to sit the shop for a bit this afternoon. I have a landscaping estimate to make for Doc Bowens." Blowing at steam rising from her cup, she took another sip. "What about you?"

He nodded, his eyes never leaving the newspaper page. "Yep, a witching appointment in Jonesburg this afternoon..."

A tobacco farmer and dowser by trade, Jim inherited the gift of willow witching from his father. Using the branch of an old willow tree, he owned bragging rights for the highest success rate of finding water in all of Ashland County, Tennessee, as well as well as three adjoining counties.

Leasing sixty acres of his land for tobacco crops the past couple of years, he gave up the demanding task of farming, immersing himself with dowsing appointments instead. Originally intending to slow his pace, the demand for the lost art of willow witching was more plentiful than he had expected. Most mornings began before dawn, seldom finishing until after sunset.

"Will you be home in time for supper?" After topping off his cup, Sammy Jo sat the pot back on the stove, slanting a glare when he did not answer right away.

Jim's gaze flicked upward, brows pinched. "I'm a big boy Sam, I don't need a babysitter," he snapped, the definition of grumpy plastering his face. Returning his focus to the newspaper, he added in a slightly softer tone, "Why don't you find something to do with your friends tonight, I'll just grab something on my way home."

Sammy Jo rolled her eyes grunting a breath. After sliding the creamer in front of him, she hooked her thumbs in her font jeans pockets. They had beaten the topic to death like a dead horse, it always finding a way to resurrect itself.

Sounding harsher than intended, she replied in a stern, steady voice. "Pops, I know you don't need a babysitter and I'm not a kid anymore. I am 23 years old and have more important things to do these days than play with my friends." She watched him absently thumb the page as if he hadn't heard a word she'd said.

"Supper will be ready around 6:30. If you're not home, you can warm a plate when you get in." She turned and reached for the toast when it popped up, ignoring the lopsided frown from across the table.

Grayson splashed cold water in his face, glancing at blood shot eyes staring from the bathroom mirror. It was near 3:00 A.M. when he last glimpsed at the neon numbers on the bedside clock. Sleep eluded him; good intentions, wrapped in insignificant excuses of the past ten years, chased one another in his head the entire night.

Details lost to time, he repetitively replayed his last visit to Thatcher Hill a hundred times over, the memory now nothing more than cloudy images and voices he could no longer hear in his head. His brain was numb with exhaustion. The only thing he could feel was an ache in his chest, more crushing than anything he had ever known.

Deep baritone notes reminiscent of his childhood, drifted from the kitchen downstairs, drawing Grayson from the bathroom. Anchored in memory, he started down the steps, following the swell of soulful blues from past generations. As a boy Martheena's voice made the hair on his neck ripple to attention. The chill working its way up his spine reminded him that not all things in life are victims of change.

Rounding the corner, he crossed his ankles and leaned folded arms against the doorframe. With a smile, he watched Martheena flip a flapjack, her stout, apron clad hips swaying in perfect rhythm. Conducting her final note, with a spatula turned conductor baton, she held it for several beats. Going unnoticed, Grayson cleared his throat. "Good morning..." he said.

The extended note Martheena held, pitched to an all-time high. Her shoulders jolted, grabbing at her chest with a gasp. "You scared me half to death Scamper, I didn't know you was up," Dropping the spatula on the stove, she picked up her coffee cup and washed down fright, grating her throat like a cat in water.

Grinning, Grayson sauntered into the kitchen. "I've got a lot of work to do today, figured I'd best get an early start." Reaching for the empty mug sitting next to the sugar bowl, which he assumed was for him, he filled it from the pot on the stove. "I'm not sure how much I'll get done though if you plan on me eating all of that," He arched one brow with a grin and nodded at a breakfast fit for Sasquatch warming on the stove.

"Can't work on an empty stomach," Shooing him to the side, Martheena wiggled around him, moving a platter of scrambled eggs and bacon to the table. "What cha' plannin' on doing anyway?" she asked, the scuff of fuzzy slippers toddling back to the stove for a second trip.

"Mowing that hayfield of a yard for starters," Pouring cream in his coffee, he pulled out a chair from the table and sat down.

Martheena opened her mouth, but snapped it closed without reply. She knew Grayson had the same stubborn blood coursing through his veins as his grandmother and did not figure an argument was worth the waste of valuable breath. Hoping he would spend the next few days relaxing, she knew better.

Tilting past his shoulder, she sat a stack of buttermilk flapjacks in front of him.

Snatching a piece of bacon from the plate, he poked it in his mouth, scooping a spoonful of eggs with the other hand. "My appointment with the attorney isn't until Wednesday, which should give me time to get a few things done around here," Picking up his fork, he speared a pancake.

"It's gonna' be sad seeing the old place on the auction block, been in the family for nearly 200 years."

Martheena's back was to him lowering the oven door, but Grayson could hear the quiver in her voice.

He sat the fork back down next to his plate and reached for his cup. With hot coffee balanced at his lips, he thought about it. It was disheartening to think of Thatcher Hill filled with strangers, but there seemed no reason to keep it. There was not much of a rental market for a rundown, 100-acre mountaintop estate, and he had no interest being a landlord even if there was.

"Are you still planning on moving to Atlanta with your niece?" he asked, before washing down the remorseful thought with a hot drink of coffee.

Blinking back tears, Martheena turned with a pan of hot biscuits, bringing them to the table. "I don't know what she wants with an old woman under her feet, but I guess that's the plan," Filled with every emotion but enthusiasm, Martheena joined him at the table with a sigh, reaching for a pancake with her fork.

Conversation ceased as Grayson reclaimed his fork. Pushing a scoop of eggs across his plate, he took a slow a bite.

After tightening hinges on the screen door, repairing a leaky faucet at the kitchen sink and nailing the last porch step in place, Grayson got in his car and headed to Highland.

About 2:00, the bell chimed overhead as he ducked inside the shop at the corner of Elm and Main, a southern drawl calling out a cordial greeting from the stock room. Both hands shoved in the pockets of grass stained jeans; he wandered through the display tables. With his heart hammering in his chest like a drum, he recalled their last encounter, his reaction mirroring a junior high boy with a crush on his English teacher.

Slightly awkward and extremely forbidden…

Sammy Jo stepped through the doorway carrying a crate of scented candles, nearly dropping them when they made eye contact. Feeling both stunned and secretly thrilled at the same time, she stuttered a hello.

The heavy crate clattered as she sat it on the counter. "Didn't think I'd be seeing you again," She subconsciously combed fingers through a mane of tousled curls. Her eyes dripped from a fashionable bit of stubbles shadowing a strong jaw, down a thin tee shirt stretched over brawny shoulders and chest. His hair more unkempt than when she had last seen him, Grayson's dirty clothes made him look more like a local ranch hand than the city slicker he portrayed the day before. The only thing missing was a camo hat, slightly tipped over daunting hazel eyes. She shivered at the picture in her head.

"I actually have a business proposal for you," Grayson admitted with a wary step forward.

Sammy Jo's heart slammed to the pit of her stomach like a lump of coal. Snatching her eyes to the side, her shoulders drooped with unanticipated disappointment. Exactly what was she expecting, perhaps a date proposal? After their last chance meeting, he obviously thought she was beneath him, nothing more than a *hill jack.*

A pink flush crept over her cheeks and she prayed he didn't notice. "What kind of business proposal?" Forcing a professional tone to her voice, she pulled a candle from the box, moving it to the counter.

"You mentioned yesterday that you do landscaping design?"

A satisfied smile replaced tightly pressed lips. "Yes and I'm pretty darned good at it, if I must say so myself." She raised a defiant chin and began unpacking the crate of candles one by one.

Moving closer, Grayson's voice was lost in the clatter of glass. "I lost my grandmother last week. I'm actually in town to settle her estate and sell the family home." Watching her focus on the dwindling candles, he took another step towards her and blew out a breath. "The old place lacks maintenance and there's only so much one person can do. I could sure use help getting the grounds in order before putting it on the market." One brow drifted into auburn wisps falling randomly across his forehead. "That's where you come in." He leaned elbows on the worn counter, peering up with an annoying and intimidating stare. "I could sure use your help," he repeated.

"I'm sorry to hear about your grandmother," Silence filled the three feet separating them as she recalled the sting of such loss. Two years was not nearly long enough to dull the pain of losing Grandma Wilcox.

Removing the last candle, she shoved the empty crate to the side. "Where is your grandmother's home?"

"About twenty miles south of here, Burlington,"

Sammy Jo nodded recognition. "I was down there a month or so ago to make a delivery, nice town." she added.

"Ever heard of *Thatcher Hill*?"

Drawing a quick blank, her head twisted.

"I spent nearly every summer there when I was a kid." He looked past her, the air draining from his lungs. "It breaks my heart to see the old place in such disrepair. It was once majestic. Not anymore," he added regretfully, tucking his hands in his jean pockets.

"I'm sure it can be again, you'd be surprised what a few shrubs and annuals can do," she declared, with professional optimism.

Grayson's shoulders relaxed; unaware he had been tensing them. It was important to restore the old place down to the slightest detail. Rosaline's final request in her letter of instructions was cremation with no service, her ashes scattered over the meadow. This would be Grayson's last opportunity of tribute to the special woman in his life.

Sammy Jo flinched when Grayson reached out touching the back of her hand. "You don't know what this would mean to me," he said.

Instinctively pulling back, she picked up the empty crate from the counter, dropping it to the floor. "It's my business," she added, curtly remembering his offensive assumption from the day before. She nudged the box to the side with her foot. "I'll have to check my schedule of course, make sure I'll have time."

Her scanty calendar appointments for the next two weeks scribbled her brain in red ink, reminding her of the quickly approaching mortgage payment. A surprise leak in the original galvanized plumbing had trickled an entire weekend, damages putting a substantial dent in this month's account budget. Brushing her finger instinctively across a twitch in her nose, she suddenly feared Pinocchio's fate.

Climbing the ladder of business success, Sammy Jo had encountered more than her share of broken rungs along the way, setting her back from time to time. She really needed the work and did not have the luxury of being persnickety about who she accepted as clients. Grayson's money was as green as anyone's was.

Grayson's back went stiff as her unequivocal message bellowed in his ears. He was a paying client, nothing more, nothing less and that was how she wanted it.

"Do you think we could get started Thursday morning?" Lips pressed tight he picked up a pen and scrap of paper from the counter, jotting down the address of Thatcher Hill and his cell number. "I'll be tied up all day tomorrow."

She rolled her eyes pretending to run a mental inventory of her work schedule. "Thursday should work."

"Great, see you then," Dropping the pen and scrap of paper on the counter, Grayson hesitated before tucking his wounded ego under his arm, pivoting on his heels towards the door.

"Oh, how did the lady like her flowers?" Sammy Jo quickly tacked on with one hand perched on her hip. Annoyed for asking, the question popped out of her mouth before she had a chance to reconsider. Too late to retract, she feared sounding like a jealous little girl with a schoolyard crush.

Stopping mid stride Grayson tamped down a blossoming grin before turning around. "She loved them," he replied simply with a wink before leaving through the door without another word.

Perhaps Miss Wilcox was not so transparent after all...

The orange sun was sinking behind rocky cliffs like a giant jack-o-lantern, a hazy halo of gold surrendering to creeping night. Sammy Jo and her grandfather gently rocked on the front porch of Wilcox Farm, bowls of homemade ice cream cupped in their hands.

Returning home early from his witching appointment, Jim brushed dust from the old ice cream maker wedged on the back room shelf. What was once a summer tradition, had become a faded memory, tucked away on a pantry shelf since Emma's passing. He churned a gallon peace offering of Sammy Jo's childhood favorite, peach with fresh cream and a dash of cinnamon. With each crank of the churn, he hoped for clemency in Sammy

Jo's heart. Like an old junkyard dog, he bit first, and then looked at where he sank his teeth. Sammy Jo did not deserve his cranky attitude.

"You're awfully quiet tonight," Jim raked his spoon through soft ice cream, the rocker steadily squeaking in unison to chirping crickets as he awaited her response.

"It's been a long day Pops," Sammy Jo sat her half empty bowl on the side table and walked to the porch rail, staring across the front field, alive with glints of yellow.

Jim sat down his bowl and joined her. His eyes followed her gaze to the dashes of lightening bugs flickering over the meadow, sensing a struggle inside. "Is everything alright?" he asked, fearing a bucket of ice cream fell a bit short of earning her forgiveness.

She thought about his question. The truth was it had been some time since everything felt normal. Maybe it was the time of year, springtime, her grandmother's favorite, or maybe it was Grayson's earlier reminder of loss that made it all feel raw again. Her lips parted with a reassuring smile when she looked up, recognizing worry lines tugging at Jim's eyes. Reaching out she brushed a wisp of dark hair from his forehead. "Everything's fine Pops," She hooked her arm through his. Leaning her head on his arm, she covered a yawn. "It's getting late, I think I'm going on up to bed,"

Jim squeezed her against him and pressed his lips to the top of her head with a lingering kiss. "Sleep well honey," he said. "See you in the morning,"

Chapter 5

Sammy Jo's eyes popped open, the night wrapped around her head like a seamless, black cloak. Beads of sweat dampened her upper lip and forehead, her heart pounding hard as a jackhammer in concrete. Squirming to sit up, she clutched the sheets to her neck, choking the scream wedged in her throat.

Night after night, the dream summonsed her to the estate on the hill, ushering her to the darkened doorway, but never allowing her inside. Tonight was different. Staccato frames of the nightmare clicked through her head, the steps, the pitch-black porch, the door, and the cold knob; the twisting knob that changed everything.

She seized a breath and held it, recalling the creak of the heavy door. For years, she wondered, stepping inside, wonder circled to terror. With a will not of her own, she found herself in the foyer, halting at pitch-black stairs. Staring up into a haze of the unlit corridor above, a resounding thud echoed in her ears, each deafening thump growing louder.

Her heart thrashed in her chest as she clutched waded sheets in her fists, the nightmare replaying like a cheesy late night horror film. In her dream, dim moonlight from the landing window rained recognition on what once was, what will never be again. A broken porcelain doll shattered across the manor floor, a glassy, lifeless stare piercing the night.

Pressing balled fists to the sides of her head, Sammy Jo tried to erase the frightening vision from her head but failed. All she could see were black eyes, the blank, empty stare of death.

Retreating to the corner of her bed, she drew her knees to her chest, hugging them against her, her mind trying to make sense of the revelation haunting her like a crime scene.

The sun had had barely crested the ridge when Sammy Jo was ready to leave the house. Shoving open the back screen door, she skidded to a stop when Jim stepped onto the porch after morning rounds of feeding the livestock. Pulling a red and white handkerchief stuffed in his coverall pocket, he stepped past her while dabbing sweat from his brow.

"You're out of here a bit early this morning," He poked the hankie in his pocket and glanced at the coffee pot on the stove. "Did you even get a cup of coffee?"

She let the door ease closed, her palm still in place on the frame, raising a thermos cup in the other. "I'm taking a cup with me. I have a couple of stops to make this morning, figured I may as well get an early start."

"Didn't sleep well?" he asked, inching past her.

"No not really," The last thing she wanted was to get in a long-winded conversation with her grandfather about a nightmare that made absolutely no sense. All she wanted to do at that point was forget the dream, the house and the emptiness nipping away at her insides.

Pulling open the refrigerator door, Jim grabbed a bottle of water, twisting the lid. "I heard you rattling in your sleep about four-thirty this morning. You must've been dreaming, and from the sounds of it, it wasn't a good one." Tipping the plastic bottle, he chugged a long swig, studying her over the container as he did.

With a forced smile, she offered a curt reply. "That should be a good lesson not to eat peach ice cream before going to bed," Without giving him a chance to pry, she pushed through the door and left, the wooden screen frame slapping shut behind her.

She had only shared the house from her dreams once with her grandmother, hoping she could help make sense of the repeating details. Convinced she had perhaps visited as a child, the place seemed as much a part of her past as the house where she grew up. No, was her grandmother's brief reply. There was nothing remotely familiar about Sammy Jo's description of the two-storied house with white columns. From that day on, Sammy Jo kept the dreams to herself, the house on the hill becoming her secret refuge from reality. After last night, she questioned her safe haven, wondering if it were more of an illusion hiding a horrific secret.

Driving to town, visions from the dream and uncertainties it left spun a mangled maze of confusion in her head. The house on the hill and the shattered doll sickened Sammy Jo with mystifying feelings of loss and bereavement. Last night's revelation left her with more unanswered questions than ever before.

After an ill-fated attempt to organize stock in the back room, Sammy Jo pressed her aching back against the wall, steady breath pumping from her lungs. Sleep deprived and a pounding headache to boot, she still brooded over yesterday's meeting with Grayson, not sure which needled her more, his arrogant confidence, or her lack thereof. Pinching the bridge of her nose, she stomped to the medicine cabinet above the bathroom sink and reached for a bottle of aspirin, pondering today may be a good day to hang a *gone fishing* sign on the door, and do just that.

After three frustrating attempts at loosening the childproof cap on the bottle, she sprinkled two tablets in her hand. Triggered by raw nerves, she fumbled them, nearly dropping the pills down the sink when the doorbell jingled out front. Growling through clenched teeth, she called out a greeting in her best facsimile of pleasantry. "I'll be right with you,"

"Take your time." With Grayson's voice, she quaked in her shoes, the answer to her earlier question focusing crystal-clear in her head. Something about the man both irritated and intrigued her, her anchoring confidence slammed rock bottom.

Washing down the aspirin with a swig of water, she craned her stiff neck, stretching tense muscles that corded all the way down her back. She swallowed hard and smoothed her composure before stepping through the doorway.

Grayson stood at the counter holding a box of salted, caramel cupcakes with buttercream frosting from Bella's Bakery… confident, drop dead gorgeous and a mind reader to boot.

Salted, caramel…her favorite…

"What are you doing here?" she asked, pretending not to notice the box of seduction cradled in his hands.

He cleared his throat mocking her in a dainty voice, "Well good afternoon Grayson, how very nice to see you again,"

She could not help but splutter a giggle. "I'm sorry. It's just that I didn't expect to see you this afternoon. I thought you said you were tied up all day," Pretending to busy herself, she straightened a stack of invoices next to the register, shoving the neat pile to the side.

"Yea, I thought so too. Ditching all the big city bureaucracies from the mix, details with Gram's attorney were not as complicated as I feared. A few scribble signatures and it was done," Switching subjects, he inched the bakery box toward her and leaned his elbows on the counter with the waggle of one brow. "Thought I'd drop a little bribe off to the boss before heading back to Burlington,"

"Bribe?" She screwed her head, her eyes falling to sugary enticement staring through the cellophane window.

"I'm afraid when you see the jungle growing on Thatcher Hill; you may change your optimism…"

"I'm sure it's not the worst I've ever seen," Lifting the lid, she raked her finger through buttercream icing, poking it between her lips.

Grayson's gaze stuck like glue, her painfully languid movements…her finger sweeping over her tongue in slow motion. His eyes settled on a smudge of frosting at the corner of her mouth, biting the urge to swipe it.

Never had buttercream frosting seemed so erotic, so seductive…

Feeling searing heat of a tawny gaze settled on her mouth, Sammy Jo automatically wiped the back of her hand across sticky lips, a blush creeping over her cheeks.

"Are we still on for tomorrow?" With a gulp, Grayson straightened, trying not to sound as hopeful as he felt.

She swore she could hear the lump in his throat rake all the way down as he spoke. "Tomorrow…" Sammy Jo's mind went white, her eyes pinning on his.

"Yea, the estimate…for landscaping," he reminded.

"Oh, yea...tomorrow..." Nearly choking on her words, she blinked away forbidden thoughts, wiping clammy palms on her jeans. "How about 9:00?"

"Perfect,"

Ten minutes early for her appointment with Grayson, Sammy Jo shoved the clutch to the floor and downshifted, flipping on her right turn signal. A gravel drive slanted next to a lopsided wood sign, remnants of faded black letters marking the estate of Thatcher Hill.

Curling up the pitted road, she swerved her battered pickup, avoiding craters deep enough to swallow a Volkswagen. A lacey veil of ivy blanketed the treetops, dimming the morning sunshine. Misty slivers of sunshine sliced through a dense cover of pines. Damp, heady air from bordering woods blew through open truck windows, fanning Sammy Jo's hair. Accelerating up the steep grade, she twisted the wheel sharp left and then leveled the truck towards the sunny clearing at the top.

An icy chill shivered up her spine, freezing her hand to the wheel. Snatching her foot from the gas pedal, she slammed the brake pedal to the floor. The truck skidded to a stop in the shade of two towering Elm trees, gravel pinging against the undercarriage like buckshot. Fingers of both hands drummed the steering wheel in steady rhythm to a pounding heart. Sammy Jo stared out the windshield. The monstrous house trapped in her head for decades stared back.

No longer white and pristine, the estate was a haunting vision of decay, an empty shell of the past. Instinctively dropping the truck in reverse, her foot held tight to the brake. She contemplated a quick escape when Grayson appeared in the doorway, throwing a hand in the air.

Too late for an undetected retreat, Grayson had seen her, but more significant, she had seen the house, *the house*... the house that had grown a part of her since childhood.

Grayson was down the steps, pushing open the rickety gate when Sammy Jo finally found the courage to throw the truck in park, turn off the engine, and slide from the seat. Her darting gaze shot from the gate to the porch, settling on the heavy wood door, marked by a black wreath. The same door she had pushed open in her dream only hours earlier.

Hand on his hip, Grayson noticed her incredulous stare and tipped his head towards the house. "See, I told you, pretty bad, huh?"

Ringing her hands, Sammy Jo chewed on her lower lip, a traumatized gaze roaming the deteriorating estate as if she were identifying a corpse.

You have no freaking idea...

A loud gulp preceded her shaky reply. "Needs some work..."

With a cackle that sounded cynical, Grayson rolled his eyes at the gross understatement. "Work...more like a complete overhaul," Spinning back to the house, he motioned for her over his shoulder. "Come on in, there's someone I want you to meet."

Sammy Jo retraced her steps from the night before, following Grayson to the gate. Stopping, she brushed a finger over rough wood, feeling a little Da Ja Vue and a whole lot of crazy picking at her composure. This could not be happening. Wishing she could just pinch herself and wake up, the curdling in her gut told her that was not an option.

Waiting with his foot on the bottom step, Grayson turned over his shoulder. "Are you coming?"

She nodded and stepped through the gate, trailing him up the steps and through the front door. A familiar creak welcomed her inside. Standing in the entry, she clenched her teeth and prepared for a resounding thud on the stairs.

The same cold, eerie presence haunted her that had shadowed her from the night, her eyes automatically drawn to the stair landing. Expecting the shattered remains of a porcelain doll strewn across the wood floor, she blinked twice at the bare landing.

The only spot of color in the dim foyer was the arrangement of yellow roses on a marble-topped parlor table, a bouquet that suddenly seemed like a fitting tribute of mourning. A sweaty sheen covered Sammy Jo's forehead, the remainder of blood draining from her face, along with her courage. With one small step forward, she tucked quivering fingers in her back pockets.

Grayson pushed the door closed behind her. "Are you okay? You look like you've seen a ghost." He chuckled, although she did not find his remark the least bit humorous.

She opened her mouth to speak but smacked it closed again when nothing came out, nervously tugging at the hem of her tee shirt.

Tucking his hand under her elbow, he followed the hum of a southern tune to the kitchen, just off the foyer, where a stalky woman with a plump middle stood at the stove, stirring a pot of soup. Martheena turned, casting a toothy grin over her shoulder when they entered.

"Martheena, this is Sammy Jo, the landscaper I was telling you about," He smiled at Sammy Jo. "Sammy Jo, I'd like you to meet Martheena, Grams housekeeper...best friend and partner in crime," He corrected, winking as he said it, knowing all too well, how truthful the account was. The two were thick as thieves, a force not to reckon with.

Sammy Jo took a step forward, politely extending her hand. "Nice to meet you mam,"

Martheena's eyes flickered over Grayson's guest, a gradual smile sharing obvious approval. She tapped the wood spoon on the side of the pot, dropping it on the stove, before taking a step forward with wide arms. "We're huggers around here darlin'," she said, before wrapping her arms around Sammy Jo with a bear hug that nearly choked the breath from her.

Sammy Jo looked over the pudgy housekeeper's shoulder at Grayson, colorful amusement deepening the brown of hazel eyes.

"Can you stay for supper?" Whirling back to the stove, Martheena sniffed at the simmering steam, before angling a lid on the cast iron pot. "I just put on a pot of pintos and ham hocks to cook this mornin', they're one of Grayson's favorites,"

"Thank you, but I need to take a look around and get back to town. I have to place some orders this afternoon, I'll take a raincheck though," she tacked on politely.

"You don't know what you're missing," Grayson coaxed. "No one makes ham and beans like Martheena,"

"I'm sure," Sammy Jo agreed. "But we have a lot of work to do and the sooner I get the plants ordered, the sooner we can get started." What she really wanted to say was, *"I'm sure, but the sooner I make this estimate, the sooner I can't get the heck out of here..."*

Grayson motioned for Sammy Jo, crossing the kitchen to the cellar door. "That reminds me, I have something I want you to see,"

Winding down a set of narrow, uneven stone steps, Sammy Jo followed Grayson to an increasingly pungent smell of damp soil. Swatting a spider web from her face as she stepped from the bottom step, she breathed in thick, musty air, waiting for him to find the light.

The chain clicked on the singe bulb hanging from a low rafter, glints of light swinging across the dirt floor like a pendulum.

Waiting for her eyes to adjust to the dim light, she focused on Grayson, already making his way across the cellar floor. Wedged next to a tall wood cupboard lined with dusty, vegetable filled Mason jars, were two large, stone urns. One toppled urn added soil to the dirt-covered floor, the other standing tall, like a tribute from the past. Drawn to them like a magnet, Sammy Jo crossed the room and ran her fingers reverently over the rim of one. "These are magnificent. They must be at least 100 years old,"

Grayson smiled proudly. "I was hoping we could use them in your design. I remember them from when I was a kid,"

Sammy Jo dared not mention that she too remembered the urns from her childhood. The image stuck in her head was like a snapshot of the past. Stone urns sat on each side of cobblestone steps, alive with color, brimming with vivid blooms of bright red geraniums and cascading ivy. For the first time she touched what was once an illusion in her head.

"Of course we'll use them, they'll be beautiful," she muttered.

"So many reminders fill this basement," Grayson ambled to a rusty metal wagon leaned on end against the wall. "This was my mother's; I loved playing with it when I was a boy." Dropping on one knee he gently rolled the wheel, mentally spinning happier times in his head.

Sammy Jo's heart clenched, sauntering over to rest her hand on his shoulder. "Memories are good,"

Grayson flinched and stood. "Yea, memories..." He stepped away, his posture suddenly becoming steel rigid. "That's all I have left of her, memories..."

"She's passed?"

He nodded, reflective eyes becoming distant, his mind clipped to memories of not so happy times. "Yea, died when I was 19," He shook his head. "Sometimes it feels like it was yesterday though, the pain I mean,"

"I'm sorry Grayson,"

He rolled one shoulder. Shrugging the memory, he dismissed the thought. "Yea, me too,"

Meandering past his obvious reluctance to talk about his mother's death, Sammy Jo walked over to a blanket chest on the opposite side of the room, brushing years of dust from the top with her finger. The slow, swinging light shadowed intricate carvings. "There are some beautiful antique pieces down here,"

With a grunt, Grayson joined her. "I don't think Gram ever threw anything away, always figured she or someone else may need it someday."

Sammy Jo laughed recognition. "My grandfather's like that. I think he still owns his first pair of work boots."

Grayson drew a long breath; his eye veering around the room, from dust-covered pieces of furniture, to boxes filled with God only knows what. "Well let me know if you see anything you're interested in because it's all going on the auction block. There sure as hell isn't anything down here I need or want,"

Detecting sadness in his words, Sammy Jo saw something profound in his eyes, concluding that perhaps his needs were deeper than even he believed.

After assessing the grounds and scribbling figures on a note pad that she took from the truck, Sammy Jo tallied the estimate, hesitantly accepting the job. What choice did she have? The lid was off that can of worms and there was no putting it back on. Decades of answers awaited her like undiscovered artifacts. She could no more turn away from this opportunity than she could will dreams of the night to stop.

On the drive back to Highland, Sammy Jo turned up the radio in attempt to drown earlier events playing in her head like a fast-forwarding cassette. The house from her dreams, the creepy presence shadowing her entire inspection of the estate and Grayson.

Oh yes, Grayson Wesley...

Chapter 6

Grayson stood just beyond the gate watching Sammy Jo turn her truck around, throwing his hand in the air as she disappeared down a shadowy tunnel of spruce. Shoving both hands in his pockets, he blew a breath of relief, pleased that she agreed to take the job... and not just for the sake of curb appeal. Although improving the grounds would increase real estate value dramatically, Sammy Jo seemed to understand his attachment to Thatcher Hill and share his desire to restore the old girl to her former glory.

Before dust settled in the lane, Martheena came out the front door, a black, patent leather purse swinging from the crook of her bent arm. "I have to run to town, plum out of buttermilk, can't make cornbread without buttermilk," she rambled. "Need anything?" she asked, pulling the door closed behind her.

Grayson pushed back through the swinging gate, stopping at the bottom step. "No, but I'd be glad to make the run into town for you."

Martheena waved her free hand through the air. "Nah, going to stop by the butcher's too. Mr. Lankan looks forward to my weekly visits you know," she teased, with an indicative wink that made Grayson's toes curl in his shoes. He remembered as a kid that the old widower trembled like a goat in heat when Martheena came into his shop to place her weekly order. The butcher's idea of a romantic gesture was discounting a fresh beef tongue or adding an extra half pound of liver to Martheena's order at no charge. Thoughts of the blood-smeared apron knotted at the man's portly waist revived the overactive imagination of an eight year old.

Climbing the steps two at a time, Grayson stopped, pecking Martheena's plump cheek. "Well, we certainly wouldn't want to disappoint Mr. Lankan, would we?"

"Nope, not if I want him to save me the best chitins'." With a playful grin, she stepped around him, slowly maneuvering the steps, her purse swinging from her arm.

Grayson's mouth watered, forcing him to swallow spontaneous nausea gurgling in his throat. If there was one thing that could make his stomach churn more than the thought of liver and onions, it was an intestine on a plate. It dumbfounded him how Gram could sit down to a bed of chitlin' and rice over eating a hot dog. The notion made him shiver.

Martheena interrupted the sickening visualization. "Oh, would you keep an eye on the beans darlin'?" she called out in afterthought, stepping down from the last step. "Give them a stir every now and then. They're on low, but we don't want them scorchin',"

Standing in front of the vintage O'Keefe and Merritt stove sporting its original mint green paint; Grayson adjusted the burner down another notch and gave the beans a second stir with the wooden spoon. His head was full of notions of Sammy Jo. Something about the southern beauty fascinated him like no other female he'd ever known. He could not shake the memory of his hands sliding along curvaceous hips as he lifted her down from the stockroom shelf or the fiery glint in her eyes when he stepped on her toes with his remark about her shop trinkets. The last thought brought the slip of a smile.

After a tap of the spoon on the side of the pot, he dropped it on the stove, poured a cup of coffee and started for the front porch, trolling thoughts of Sammy Jo lagging through his brain.

His feet spontaneously froze to the floor halfway across the kitchen, hot coffee sloshing from the full cup. Startled by the sound of scuffing wood behind him, he stood in the silence, waiting for a second scraping, at last convinced the noise was not his imagination.

Kitchen boards squeaked beneath a slow pace as he crossed the room, creeping up on the muffled sound, leaching from beneath the cellar door. The closer he got, the more unmistakable the scraping. Sitting his cup on the table, he gripped the porcelain knob to the cellar and twisted. The door edged open a couple of inches and the noise ceased. He leaned his ear towards the thin gap and listened ... nothing but the low creak of hinges.

Gradually pulling the door wider, Grayson's eyes fixed on the narrow passage. A dim ray of light slowly swayed, shadows creeping back and forth across stone walls. Mentally replaying his earlier visit to the cellar with Sammy Jo, he swore he'd turned off the light. Maybe Martheena had gone down for something after they came up he reasoned.

With one foot on the top step, his heart pounded, feeling ten years old again. The cellar was always dark and creepy, hiding ghostly images of a little boy's imagination. It was still dark and creepy and his imagination was still as intimidating as it had been all those years ago.

Cinching his big boy pants, he started down, stopping halfway, with one foot on each step when he heard the scratching again. This time it was more muted and distant. His final three steps ended in the damp basement, the single bulb flickering twice before snapping back on.

His eyes darted to each corner of the room, landing on the blanket chest, evidence of Sammy Jo's finger trailing the dusty lid. His shoulders sagged with a relieved breath when he heard scraping of wood from inside the box. "Damn rats," he muttered, with a slow approach.

Tapping the toe of his shoe against the wood side of the trunk in attempt to scare the rodent away, all was quiet inside. Again, he kicked, a little harder this time but heard nothing.

Curiosity lifted the lid, his eyes settling on the contents. Shadows of the drifting light spilled recognition over random contents. Filled to the top with tattered quilts, a wadded swath of yellowing silk that seemed out of place lay nestled in the center. Grayson lifted the bundle just as the light flickered overhead, the room flashing black.

Tucking the find under his arm, he carried it with him. He shuffled his feet against the dark, uneven ground, finding his way to the dim haze of the stairwell, making his way back to the kitchen.

Laying the fabric on the kitchen table, he slowly pulled back the corners like gift-wrap, revealing a neatly folded baby swaddling in the center, the corners lovingly palmed in place. On top of the swaddling, were a small leather binder and a gold pocket watch.

Grayson picked up the antique timepiece, winding it before putting it to his ear. Flipping the crystal face with his thumb and finger before listening again, he presumed the piece had spent one too many years in a damp basement, tiny gears frozen in time. Dropping the watch on the table, he picked up the binder and thumbed through the pages, a journal he quickly recognized as kept by his late grandmother.

Fanning through yellowed pages, a dried flower dropped to the floor, crumpled, orange petals flatted in place. The slightest tinge of peach had survived the years, the floral scent lost to the decades. He gently moved the fragile flower back to its resting place between pages, thumbing to the first scrawled entry.

Absorbed by the pages, he dropped in a kitchen chair with a slow, disbelieving shake of his head, eyes flitting across the first account. Rosaline's story began shortly after his grandfather's death in the year 1952. Faded ink stared up at him, a cracked door leading to another dimension creaking open. Revelations of a past life awaited in the brittle pages of the journal. He could almost hear the quiver of his Gram's soft mountain drawl as he began reading.

March18, 1952

"Andrew runs the mine now my love, keeping me comfortable in finance. Payment from the single thing that took you from me somehow feels like a betrayal, although I have Cora to consider. She is all I have left of you. I miss you so much it hurts Isaac; I awake every morning feeling empty and alone. I cannot believe you are truly gone. The pain is more than I can bear at times. I cannot imagine continuing life without you... "

The coalmine of Pine Ridge had been in the Worthington family for more than two generations, many lives claimed by harvesting of black gold, mostly from suffocation. Most men succumbed to pneumonia and fever of Black Lung, while dozens were lost to shaft collapse. Either way, the mine determined when and how workers would die, most fathers and husbands never knowing how it felt to grow old.

Rosaline never wanted to think of how her years with Isaac would end, praying he would be the first to beat the odds of Pine Ridge and the Worthington legacy.

Isaac seemed invincible. The year prior to his death, he worked unrelenting for three days and three nights next to his men to free twelve workers, held captive by a collapsed shaft. Regarded as a hero, he insisted to be the one to crawl through the narrow, unstable opening, aiding weakened and injured men's escape.

Rosaline's prayers went unanswered. Pine Ridge spoke and Isaac's fate determined. His last breath was lost to a silent, darkened grave of coal and dust in February of 1952.

Grayson leaned the chair back on two legs feeling a physical ache in his chest, pain for his grandmother's loss of a husband, pain for his mother's loss of a father, pain for the grandfather he would never know.

Slapping the journal closed, he tucked it and the watch along with the baby swaddling into the piece of fabric. Remembering Martheena's strict instructions, he gave the pot of beans another stir and carried the journal upstairs to his bedroom. After dropping the swaddling and watch on his dresser, he settled in the velvet, indigo colored chair angled next to the fireplace, propping his feet on the ottoman. With the open journal spread across his lap, he stared at the pages, sensing emotion his grandmother had written decades ago.

For the next two hours, he read, riveted by his grandmother's loneliness and struggles of widowhood. He struggled to imagine the facet of a grandmother he never knew. To him, Rosaline had always been unwavering and independent, a woman who feared nothing. Pages from her journal revealed a broken soul, afraid and alone.

Friday morning Grayson sat in a rocker on the sprawling porch of Thatcher Hill, paint samples ranging from subtle gray to bull charging red fanned at his feet. A full minute before spying Sammy Jo's truck, he looked up to the clunk of her engine bounding up the road, an eruption of dust hovering above the lane.

Rolling to a stop in front of the house, Sammy Jo cut the motor and waited for the notorious, final cough before climbing from the seat. The cab door slammed behind her, as she pushed her sunglasses on top of her head and started for the house. A smile that rivaled the early June sunshine embellished porcelain skin, a white ribbon gathered her hair into a knot of copper curls.

Grayson's eyes dribbled down Sammy Jo's standard work attire, jeans that hit several inches above mid-thigh, a John Deere tee shirt and sneakers.

"Hey there," she called out, wiggling through a gap in the creaking gate.

Grayson shoved the paint samples to the side with a sandal-clad foot, sprung from the chair and waited for her at the top step.

"I brought a few plants to get started. The shrubs I ordered will be in Monday, but I think I have plenty to keep me busy until then," With the unbridled spirit of a Tennessee filly, she barely took time to breathe. Replacing questions of her nightmare with hope and new insight, her spirit felt lighter than it had in months.

"A few?" Grayson glared past her and chuckled aloud. Filled with everything from vibrant geraniums to dusty purple petunias, colorful crates lined the rusty truck bed, blooms peeking over both sides

Ignoring his accurate observation, she climbed the stairs, stepped past him and hooked her thumb in her back jean pockets. "What cha' got here?" Surveying the fan of color spread across the porch, her interest zoomed in on two particular shades.

Grayson leaned his shoulder against a column with a grin, noting her infectious smile, her very presence energizing.

He dipped his head to two painters dressed in spattered coveralls, straddling scaffolding. Putty knives chipped fervently at flaking paint, the ground dusted in a snowy blanket of faded chips.

"Trying to pick paint colors and not doing a very good job I might add. As soon as they finish, I need to have two colors picked out, one for the house, one for the trim." He looked back to the daunting choices spread across the floorboards and puckered. "Any suggestions?"

A glint from the past ignited Sammy Jo's imagination in living color. Her mind flashed to earlier dreams of the grand estate, sporting stark white paint and contrasting coal black shutters, her choice an easy one.

"Black and white it is," he said, gathering the paint samples into a neat pile.

With a crisp nod, her lips bowed with contentment before retracing her steps down the stairs and back through the gate, Grayson trailing her.

Tugging a large fern from the dropped tailgate of the truck, Grayson deposited it to the ground, waiting for Sammy Jo to drag a second fern to the edge.

When Sammy Jo bent with the pot, Grayson tried his best not to stare. Unfortunately, the frayed edges of her cut off denims offered way too much temptation. When she turned back for a tray of geraniums, he snapped his eyes to the side like a guilty kid caught with his hand in the cookie jar. After a couple of cool off seconds, he turned back, her cheeky grin saying his quick diversion was not nearly quick enough.

Sammy Jo hoisted a flat of annuals to her shoulder with a smile, holding his gaze long enough to make him squirm worse than if his sandals were padded with hot embers.

Mid-day, Grayson carried Sammy Jo a glass of fresh squeezed lemonade, clanking the side of her glass with a toast after she took it. "Don't you think it's about time you break for lunch? You know, this job doesn't pay by the hour?"

After taking a long, satisfying swig, Sammy Jo blew a wisp of hair from her forehead and plopped down in the tall grass. Sitting crossed legged, she carefully positioned her glass in a bushy clump of chickweed and tugged at her garden gloves, one finger at a time.

"I can't believe it's time to break for lunch already," She wiped the back of her hand across her forehead, leaving a dirty smudge in its wake. Looking up at him, the bright afternoon sun shielded the expression from his face but she sensed the weight of his eyes.

Grayson squatted in front of her and rubbed at the smear with his thumb, grateful for an excuse to touch her. "I can't believe everything you've gotten done this morning. The flower bed looks great," Tearing his focus from satin skin, he checked out dotted red geraniums lining the front gate.

"Thanks," she said proudly. "You'd be surprised what a little playing in the dirt can do,"

Dropping to the ground beside her, Grayson sat down his glass and leaned back on palms with a chuckle. "You call this play? If this is your notion of recreation, I'd sure hate to see what you consider work,"

Sammy Jo studied the results of her labor before smiling. "I love what I do for a living," Picking up her glass, she chased a droplet of water down the side with her finger and asked, "What do you do for a living?"

"An author," he replied.

It was good thing she was sitting down. Grayson's bombshell reply would have knocked her flat on her fanny. She would have guessed a doctor, maybe… a Wall Street banker more likely… but a writer. A bark of laughter filled the warm breeze. "A writer, huh?"

"What's so funny?" he asked, through widening eyes, one brow drifting to the middle of his forehead.

"You just don't strike me as an *author kind of guy*,"

"And just what's an *author kind of guy* supposed to look like?" Unsure if he should be impressed by her hasty assessment or offended, he remembered his shrewd opinion of her gift shop and the snappy reaction it received. The gander got just what he deserved, an unintentional poke from the goose.

Pushing up from the grass, Sammy Jo pulled her foot out of her mouth and dusted her dirty jeans. "I think you're right, it is time I break for lunch,"

He peered up at her, the sun outlining her face. "You're not going to answer?"

She shrugged one shoulder, her head rocking from side to side while she searched for a clever reply. "I don't know, just not like you," Dropping her sunglasses from her head to her nose, she twisted and ambled towards her truck.

Grayson struggled to his feet, falling in step beside her. "What are you doing for lunch?"

She nodded to the rickety pick up while tucking her gardening gloves in her back pocket. "My specialty, I packed a peanut butter and banana sandwich,"

Tugging her by the arm, he snapped her quick departure to a stop. "I have a better idea. How about I take you to lunch?"

"Like this?" she laughed, brushing a layer of caked dirt from her knees.

"Just like that," he agreed. "The place I have in mind has no dress code and some of the best food in Burlington," He did not give her a chance to say no. "I promise, it'll be a whole lot better than any old peanut butter and banana," He waited impatiently, shifting from one foot to the other.

She took a drink of lemonade and hesitated, but only for a few seconds before answering. "Can I at least wash up first?" she asked, handing him her empty glass.

Forty-five minutes later, Sammy Jo and Grayson were sitting cross-legged on a faded quilt in Burlington Park, eating sauerkraut-topped franks from the lunch wagon and sharing a bag of potato chips.

Sammy Jo uncapped her water bottle taking a drink before sucking in a deep breath, letting it leisurely seep from her lungs. She leaned back on one hand, her gaze following puffy clouds drifting overhead, before focusing on the budding leaves of an ancient Oak, rustled by the warm, afternoon breeze. A pair of squirrels chasing one another from one branch to the next in a caper of tag pulled a smile to her lips.

"Was I right?" Grayson puckered, crunching on an oversized sour pickle.

Her attention went from scampering squirrels to hazel eyes with a satisfied sigh. "You're right; it sure beats peanut butter and banana. This is the nicest lunch I've had in a long time,"

Swallowing, Grayson dabbed a paper napkin at the corner of his mouth. "I hope you're not just talking about the hot dog," Crossing one ankle over the other, he dropped the napkin on the blanket beside him, eying her skeptically.

Sammy Jo snatched a chip from the bag with a cheeky grin, poking it between her lips. "It is a pretty darned good hot dog,"

Grayson exaggerated a pout, holding his hand out palm up. In the silence, he attempted his most pitiful expression and waited for her to add more.

"And the company was nice too," she added, dropping a potato chip in his open, palm along with the compliment he was fishing for.

Crumpling the empty potato chip bag, Grayson reached for Sammy Jo's hand helping her from the ground, before gathering the remains of their picnic and quilt into the crook of his arm. Dropping the blanket at the car, they wandered down the hiking trail, neither ready for lunch to end.

Steeped in memories from the past, Grayson stopped at the bubbling creek, flowing full with spring rains. A pair of turtles sunned on a log on the far side, a Bluejay shrieking from the top branches of a century old Maple.

"I've really missed this place," Grayson admitted. Shoving both hands in his pockets, he toed at loose soil along the bank with his shoe. "Makes me feel like a kid again, Gram use to bring me here a couple of times a week when I came for summer visits. We'd have lunch in the park and take a walk along this same creek bed."

Sammy Jo could hear the melancholy and sense of sadness in his voice. "Memories keep our loved ones alive," Reflecting on her own loss, she thought about the long talks with her grandma and the special closeness she would never feel again.

"I guess," he said. "But I'm sure going to miss her," he admitted, with a step forward.

Sammy Jo nodded, relating more closely than she wished, convinced her life would never be the same after burying her grandma.

Grayson took another step, wandering along the bank and Sammy Jo followed. "After losing my folks, Gram and I were all each other had," The account to Sammy Jo came surprisingly easy.

Chastened, she remained stoically quiet as he began purging hurtful memories.

It was not often Grayson spoke of his parents and never did he expose deep seeded thoughts in conversation, particularly memories tied to a painful past.

In previous relationships, he guarded the core of the man he had become, yet here, he stood sharing something so personal with a woman he barely knew. Thinking back, he could not remember the last time he had openly mentioned his parents to anyone, although their memory and demise haunted him every day of his life. He was not sure what made him want to talk about them now. Maybe it was Sammy Jo, or maybe it was the setting, taking him back to happier times. Whatever the reason, he dredged up distant memories, the words flowing without effort.

"My parents died in a sailing accident when I was 19. They were cruising along the coast and got tangled in a brewing storm." He stopped, bringing a shaky hand to his forehead, brushing away stray strands picked up in the breeze. Eyes pinched, he tried imagining their last moments for the thousandth time, feeling the same suffocation that stifled his breath every time the thought crossed his mind.

"Still not sure what happened, Dad and Mom were both seasoned sailors," When he opened his eyes, he looked ahead with a glassy stare, still trying to make sense of the tragedy. "They found Dad's body in the boat wreckage along a rocky reef, but..." His words trailed and he swallowed hard before taking a slow step forward. "They never found Mom's body,"

"I'm sorry Grayson," Sammy Jo took two steps ahead and stopped him with her hands on his chest, looking into the painful memory, still raw in his eyes.

His mouth twisted with a swift shrug, hazel eyes suddenly turning as dark and cold as the sea that had stolen his parents. "It is what it is…"

Like the drop of a black curtain, Sammy Jo watched sadness turn to anger as he held his chin high, his back stiffening. "Anyway, I was their only child, all the family Gram had left," Moving past her, he straddled a fallen log facing the creek. "What about you, do have brothers or sisters?" he asked, patting the log next to him.

Sammy Jo sat down, plucking a tall blade of grass at her feet. "Yes, I have a younger brother and sister,"

"Don't see them much?" he assumed from the regret in her words.

"No," she answered, offering nothing more. Tearing the blade of grass into pieces, she tossed it along with the bleak reality creeping to the front of her mind.

They sat for several minutes, neither speaking, watching the burbling creek. When a frog leaped from a moss covered rock, sending ripples along the gentle moving current, Grayson's quiet gaze shifted to Sammy Jo. He stood reaching down an open palm. "I guess we should probably head back to the house. There are still a lot of plants in the back of that truck of yours," With a smile that seemed artificial, he dragged himself from ancient history, sensing sadness lingering between the lines in both stories.

Sammy Jo left Thatcher Hill just before 6:00, the sun barely brushing the treetops of the western ridge. Grayson sat on the porch step for about an hour after she disappeared down the lane, appreciating the splash of color along the fence, brightening the lengthening shadows of dusk. He flipped through memories of their lunch and stroll, the intimate details he shared of his parent's death and the peculiar closeness he felt to a woman who was not much more than a stranger.

After drying the last dinner plate that Martheena washed, Grayson bid her goodnight with a peck on the cheek and retired to his bedroom. Clicking the door closed behind him, his eyes automatically landed on his grandmother's journal lying face down on the nightstand. Drawn to it like a desert watering hole, he thirsted to learn about the newly discovered details of his grandmother's life.

Taking the diary with him, he sat in the fireside chair, propped his feet on the ottoman and opened it. Flipping the pages, he stopped where he had last left off, his eyes flitting to the first paragraph. Riveted to the pages, the more he read, the more his insatiable appetite craved. Reflective words not only revealed a multi-faceted insight into his Gram's past, but also a new understanding of his mother. He saw her life in a way he never imagined.

The sun faded into the western sky, replaced by deepening indigo. Lengthening shadows stretched across the bedroom walls. Grayson slapped the journal closed and crossed the room, switching on the table lamp. He slid the window closed to cooling temperatures blanketing the mountain with a misty fog and settled into the bed.

Back rested against the headboard, he reached once again for the journal and opened it. Thumbing to the next page, he continued reading,

January 9, 1953

You have been gone nearly a year Isaac, the longest year of my life. I leave the house very little these days, my world imprisoned by this mountain. Part of me died with you in that mine, leaving me only half-human. I find it more difficult to deal with life, deal with being a woman, a mother. I know Cora does not understand. In some ways, she lost us both that fateful day. I have tried and failed you both. I know you would have expected me to be stronger and for that, I am sorry. I have done the best I can and realize far too well, that is not good enough. I have made a decision tonight Isaac. Cora has turned four and needs a mother. More importantly, she deserves a mother. She needs someone who can nurture her to become the strong, caring woman I know she can be. I only have weakness and frailty to offer. I want more for her. I am sending her to Indiana to live with my sister and her family. I pray this is only temporary. Bell can be the mother that I cannot.

Please forgive me Isaac, I am only thinking of our Cora and what is best for her...

Folding together pages of the past, he dropped the journal on the bed next to him. For the first time, pieces of his mother's life fell into place. He began to understand the wall of silence she had erected around memories of her early childhood and the simmering tension between her and his grandmother. As the words settled in his head, his mother came into focus as never before, as a survivor.

Shortly after midnight, Grayson showered and crawled between the sheets. His head had no sooner settled into the pillow, than trickling accounts from the journal began a feeding frenzy of distant memories. His mind conjured images of a young girl frightened and alone, ripped from the only home she had ever known.

Grayson was in his teens before hearing the story of how his grandfather died. Although Rosaline never spoke of the day that forever changed her life, Grayson's mother had reluctantly pacified his curiosity after several prodding attempts. Her voice quivered and she fought tears at the recollection of the day her father's best friend and business partner, Andrew, appeared at the door, coal dust covering his body like a black mask. Even a young girl could recognize the unspoken horror reflecting in his eyes.

Entombed by a silent grave of rock and coal, Isaac Worthington perished along with several other men on the fateful day. Ink scrolled over brittle pages, painted a vivid picture of the curse his untimely demise left on the family, a curse left to filter from one generation to the next.

Grayson too became a victim of the mining collapse. His mother's childhood left torn, the grandmother he had admired as strong and confident, now exposed as weak and broken. He questioned every detail of his life, a history clouded by deception. The two most important women in his life were gone now, images from the past shattered.

Driven into the horizon, the moon surrendered to sweeps of violet and lavender brushing the morning sky. Grayson stared at a blank ceiling, early dawn chasing nightly shadows from the walls, as well as haunting images circling in his head. Relinquishing any hope for sleep, Grayson threw the wadded sheet to the side and swung his feet over the side of the bed. He wrenched his aching neck from one side to the other, his head pounding in steady rhythm to his beating heart.

Slipping into a pair of jeans and tee shirt, he dressed shortly after 7:00, went downstairs and put on a pot of coffee. Drinking two cups on the front porch, he carried his third with him down to the meadow of wildflowers, yellow, pink and lavender bursting in the bright sunshine and bursts of bright orange poppies waving in the gentle breeze. Warm air blew up the hillside, swells of blooms rippling at his feet. Despite the early hour, the air was warming with just enough humidity to leave a dewy finish on his skin.

Surprised by the clunking of Sammy Jo's truck engine bounding up the lane, he turned in time to see her rusty grill and faded red hood popping over the top of the hill. She waved a hand out the window when she spotted him, skidding to stop in front of the house.

Swinging the door open, she dropped down from the cab, slamming the door closed behind her. "Hope you didn't mind me stopping by so early," she called out. Moving to the back of the truck, she lowered the tailgate, squeaky hinges echoing down the slope. "The shrubs I ordered came in early so I thought I'd drop them by,"

Grayson wandered up the hill, downing his last gulp of coffee. "Of course I don't mind," Sitting his empty cup on the side rail, he gripped the woven mesh securing the root of one shrub and dragged back an evergreen.

Sammy Jo noted dark circles ringing his eyes, and stubbles shadowing a rigid jaw. Something had changed in the strong, confident man from the day before.

"Rough night?" she asked.

"Something like that," The evergreen thudded to the ground, Grayson jerking at another. "Nice looking bushes," he said, ignoring her prodding.

"Don't want to talk about it?" Reaching past him for a boxwood shrub, wedged behind the wheel well of the truck, she watched him from the corner of her eye.

"Nothing to talk about, just a restless last night,"

"After clearing that thicket of honeysuckle from the back of the house, I would've thought it would have been lights out for you before your head hit the pillow." The boxwood pot thumped the ground. Sammy Jo brushed the dirt from her hands and turned to him, tucking her thumbs in her hip pockets.

"I have a lot on my plate," he admitted, giving her only half the truth. "It's a bit overwhelming."

"All work and no play are not good for a man's soul. I think a break from all of this would do your heart good," she patted the dirt from her palms.

"Oh you do huh?"

"Yep," Hoisting her foot on the bumper, she crawled into the bed, shoving the two remaining shrubs towards him. "How about joining us for Sunday dinner tomorrow evening? I'd like you to meet my grandfather."

He thought about it and paused long enough for her to add, "I make a mean pot roast."

"I do like pot roast," he grinned.

"Good, how's 6:00 sound?" Not waiting for a reply, she climbed down from the bed, darted to the cab and began rifling through her purse for a pen and scrap of paper. Jotting down her address with directions on the back of a nursery receipt, she turned, holding it between two fingers.

With a step forward, Grayson took the address, dropping it in his shirt pocket. "Tomorrow at 6:00 sounds good,"

Chapter 7

The sidewalks of Highland folded on the Sabbath, all area businesses closed, with the exception of Franny's Diner on Main Street. Homemade meatloaf lured parishioners from the only church in town every Sunday evening, packing booths with early diners before worship.

Grayson's fingers drummed the steering wheel, slowing to a stop as a family of four crossed the street in front of the diner. After the father stepped up on the curb, towing a wavering toddler by the hand, Grayson returned his friendly wave and accelerated.

Catching a glimpse of Wilcox Landscaping and Gifts at the corner, he recalled his first encounter with the spirited Sammy Jo and smiled. Her beauty likening to no other, he pondered the hazard hidden beneath her simple splendor, like the alluring lavender Autumn Crocus, with a masked toxic bloom capable of cardiac arrest.

Reminded of Sammy Jo's simple nature, he gave a second thought to his choice of dinner attire, tugging at the navy blue tie looped around his neck, which suddenly felt more like a noose. Yanking the tie free, he tossed it in the passenger seat, unbuttoning the first two buttons of his freshly starched, white shirt. With one hand on the wheel, he cuffed one arm of his shirt to the elbow before changing hands.

The missing tie may look less formal, but the squeezing in throat remained. No amount of self-talk could convince him this dinner was no big deal; the two fisted clench of his stomach was quickly winning the debate.

About five miles north of town, Grayson spotted the narrow gravel road on the left, a crooked wood road sign with Pine Hollow Road etched in black letters. Making a left at the sign, Sammy Jo's directions precise, the mailbox marking Wilcox Farms was the first lane on the right.

Slowing, he twisted the wheel beneath his palm, gravel crunching under the tires. Unlike Thatcher Hill, sunshine rained down on an open snaking lane, bordered by rows of early tobacco plants.

A covered bridge, the color of crimson, spanned a bubbling creek, the house visible from the other side. Set in a valley of waving green grass, the white two-storied, clapboard farmhouse closely resembled a Norman Rockwell spring scape, down to ferns swaying from the porch eaves. Sunny orange zinnias and velvety purple petunias peppered a bordering flowerbed.

Just to the east of the house, two horses grazed in a slanting pasture, enclosed by rough-hewn split rails. The slowly sinking sun reflected slivers of shimmering light from long spikes of Orchard grass and Fescue swaying in the breeze.

A black lab shimmied beneath the fence, barking as it bolted down the hill towards the idling car. Grayson veered his attention back to the house just in time to catch sight of Sammy Jo, pushing her way through the screen door, wiping her hands on a yellow twill apron. If anything could make this scene more striking, it was the woman ambling towards the steps, her hair pinned up, loose tendrils spilling around her face. For the first time, he saw her wearing something besides blue jeans, a transformation that made his heart do a quick summersault in his chest. A dusty blue sundress tied at the neck leant a feminine edge, bare feet enhancing her simplistic nature.

When he pulled to a stop in front of the house and cut the engine, Sammy Jo stepped down from the porch calling the dog. "He won't bite," Patting both hands on her thighs, her whistle went ignored.

The dog planted four paws firmly in the dirt. A swiftly wagging tail rocked ninety-pounds of muscle and fur.

Grayson tugged the keys from the ignition and poked them in his pant pocket before opening the car door and sliding from behind the wheel. Offering a sniff of his hand to the black pooch, he dropped down on one knee. Without hesitation, a wet tongue slapped the back of Grayson's hand, a swishing tail beating his dress khakis in perfect rhythm.

A vigorous buff behind both ears of the squirming dog, won Grayson a string of low, satisfied rumbles. "They say animals are the best judge of character," Grayson teased, glancing up at Sammy Jo with a laugh.

Sammy Jo wandered down the cobblestone walk. She joined in the chuckle of the grateful Lab, twisted to the ground with his bottom poked up, soliciting one last scratch to his favorite spot.

After a final pat, Grayson stood and poked his head inside the car door. Pushing the discarded tie out of the way, he retrieved a bottle of red wine from the passenger seat. He stood and turned, nearly bumping into Sammy Jo, standing right behind him.

"For dinner," he said, cupping a pricey bottle of Sangiovese in his palm. "You said you were preparing pot roast, this should pair nicely,"

Tucking a stubborn curl behind her ear, Sammy Jo reached for the bottle with the ghost of a smile. "Thank you," she said. "I'm not sure what pairs with pot roast, but I do know that cold beer goes real nice with cheeseburgers,"

Shuffling from one foot to the other Grayson's ears flared red, regretting the wine nearly as much as the abandoned tie lying in the passenger seat. Fidgeting with the top button of his shirt, the illusory noose was tightening. "I would've brought you flowers but..."

"I'm teasing," She nudged him with a grin, taking the wine from his hand. "Lighten up. You look like you're here for a root canal instead of dinner," Bumping the car door closed, she looped her arm through his, ambling towards the house with him in tow.

"Come on Stewart," she called to the pooch planted next to the car. Stealing a glance from the corner of her eye, she recognized the questionable, raised eyebrows. "Don't ask," she added. "I know... I've heard it before. Who names a dog Stewart?"

When they reached the porch steps, Grayson spotted a man for the first time, gliding in a faded white porch swing, hidden from view by a leafy Boston fern.

The proverbial dentist...

Cherry scented pipe tobacco smoke circled the man's head, blending with the savory aroma of roasted onion and pot roast.

"Grayson, I'd like you to meet my grandfather Jim," Bumping her shoulder into Grayson, she added, "Pops, this is the new friend I was telling you about. Grayson is visiting Burlington to settle his grandmother's estate,"

"Sir..." Stepping onto the porch, Grayson left the safety of Sammy Jo and leaned forward. Offering his right hand, Jim left it dangling mid-air for a full ten seconds, as if it held a hand full of poison oak. Jim's reception and less than friendly demeanor had all the warmth of a three-day winter storm, suddenly making the balmy seventy-eight degree evening feeling chilly.

Not bothering to stand, Jim pushed his foot against the floorboard, stopping the swing. After a painstaking few seconds, he leaned forward and shook Grayson's hand mechanically before pulling back. Black eyes scrutinized the chump dressed to impress in a white shirt and perfectly ironed trousers, before swinging his attention to the dog, following onto the porch.

Grayson swallowed hard thinking that maybe a root canal, minus the Novocain, would be more comfortable.

"I'm just going to run in and check the potatoes. Can I bring you something to drink Grayson?" Gripping the screen door handle, Sammy Jo flashed a dubious grin over her shoulder.

A double shot of Scotch sounds good...

"No thanks, I'm fine for now," Grayson answered instead.

"Pops?"

"I'm good," her grandfather replied, a black, steely glare raking over Grayson like the final inspection of a stockyard hog purchase.

After the wooden screen door slammed shut, Jim motioned to an oversized white wicker chair opposite him and asked Grayson to take a seat, which clanged more like an order. With a soft, quiet before the storm tone, Sammy Jo's grandfather expressed how special she was to him, a discreet warning understood loud and clear.

The two men sat in silence, staring over a well-manicured lawn, waiting for Sammy Jo's return. After several painful, fastidious minutes, she appeared at the door announcing dinner.

Supper was as tense and quiet as a southern wake. Although Sammy Jo was an exceptional cook, more than once, Grayson washed down a wedged bite of pot roast, one gulp short of requiring the Heimlich maneuver. He struggled to swallow; certain James would allow him to choke blue, right there on the kitchen floor if the need for help should arise.

Feeling a bit like a lock ward patient in a one-sided chitchat, Sammy Jo fell reluctantly into added silence, after several ill-fated attempts at conversation. She shoved her plate to the side, grateful when her grandfather swallowed his last bite of potatoes, dropping the fork on his plate.

With the finale of one of the most grueling dinners in history in sight, Sammy Jo scrambled to her feet and cleared the meat platter and vegetable bowls from the table. She returned balancing a lattice topped blueberry pie in her hands. Jim wiped a napkin across his mouth, dropping it next to his plate, not so surprisingly declining his favorite dessert. The cold stare in Grayson's direction declared that he had a belly full.

Shoving his chair from the table, Jim stood and bid Sammy Jo and her dinner guest goodnight, pecking his granddaughter on the cheek. Before retreating to his bedroom, he cast one last glare in Grayson's direction; three deep furrows carved his forehead as a caution reminder. Jim's room was at the top of the stairs, buckshot loaded, his gun propped conveniently beside the bedroom door.

After her grandfather disappeared upstairs, Sammy Jo reached for Grayson's plate, carrying it along with hers to the sink. She did not hear him step up behind her, but sensed his nearness before he leaned around her with the last plate.

She stretched for the window above the sink, heaving it several inches to the evening breeze. The blush in her cheeks reacted to the sudden rise in temperature his closeness brought. Her eyes fell to the red barn, nestled at the base of the hillside. Last hints of daylight gleamed from the metal roof.

"It would be a nice evening for a horseback ride to the pond," she said, trying to occupy her mind with anything but the emotions fanning a smoldering fire inside her.

Not exactly a seasoned horseman, Grayson figured anything that put distance between him and her grandfather sounded inviting. After all, straddling a horse could not be any more challenging than sitting across the table from a grunting bull all evening.

"Sounds great," Brushing her arm with his hand, he sat the plate in the sink. The only thought more inviting then putting distance between him and her grandfather, was being alone and close to her.

"Just let me run up and change," Twisting, she found herself so close to Grayson, she could feel his breath against her cheek. With a managed smile, she slipped from between him and the counter and skittered across the room with the agility of an anxious cat.

"I'll meet you out front," she uttered over her shoulder before disappearing around the corner.

Elbows leaned on the porch railing and his chin resting in his palms, Grayson's eyes flitted across the grassy meadow where two horses grazed in waning light. The sky had changed to orange, and finally a golden yellow, as the sun melted from the sky. A burst of cool mountain air lowered the daytime temperature by several degrees, colorful hues of sunset reflecting in the gentle sway of budding trees.

When the screen door creaked open, Grayson turned to Sammy Jo, dressed in blue jeans, sweatshirt and boots; a brown hoody draped over one arm. "The evenings here still get pretty chilly. I brought you one of Pop's sweatshirts."

"Sure it's ok?" Offering a poor excuse for a smile, one side of his mouth curved, dimpling his right cheek.

Sammy Jo pitched the sweatshirt across the porch, Grayson snatching it midair. "Don't be silly, of course it's ok." She crossed her arms over her chest and waited for him to slip the sweatshirt over his head.

"Please excuse my Pops, he's a little overly protective, that's all,"

After Grayson tugged the snug fitting hoody over his head, Sammy Jo looped her arm through his, pulling him from the steps, ambling towards the barn. Fearing

Grayson judged her grandfather on his insolent rudeness, he surprised her with praise of Jim instead.

"Your grandfather shouldn't have to be excused for being protective. It's obvious how much you mean to him. I'd have probably run me off the property if I were him," he teased.

Sammy Jo smiled, their steps falling in rhythm as they silently made their way down the winding, gravel lane.

When they reached the barn, Sammy Jo pulled her arm from Grayson, unbolted the latch and dragged the wide door open. Inside, the horses from the meadow had retreated to their stalls. In one, a golden red mare with a flaxen mane whinnied, moving towards the swing gate, obviously happy to see Sammy Jo. Beside it, a less observant, reddish brown Bay Stallion lackadaisically lashed its tail while munching on hay, oblivious to their presence.

Buffing an open palm over the mare's nose Sammy Jo shot a glance over her shoulder. "Have you ridden before?"

"Of course," he lied, remembering sitting atop a guided pony at the fair when he was eight, and the one time his Gram took him riding with experienced guides through the National Park Forest. Resting folded arms on the wood slats of the gate, he peeked at the stallion that had finally decided to take interest in them. "Are they friendly?"

"Do they look friendly?"

"Makes a man a little nervous when you answer his question with a question," A jagged brow floated into his hairline.

"They're friendly," she giggled, motioning to a brown saddle tossed over an empty stall gate. "There's Bolts tack, you can ride him."

"Bolt huh?" Twisting towards the saddle, Grayson hesitated and asked the discernible question, "Any particular reason you call him Bolt?"

"Just saddle him," Sammy Jo chuckled and swung open Sadie's stall gate. With her riding merits shining like a polished trophy, she dragged the leather gear down from a walnut saddle rack, heaving it over Sadie's back in one swift swing. Peeking at him from the corner of her eye, she swallowed the urge to tease.

Grayson stared from the saddle to Bolt then back to the saddle, looking as uncomfortable as a man dragged on a mission through the woman's lingerie department.

"Do you need help?" she finally asked, after several seconds of watching him squirm.

"I think I can manage," Following her lead, he lugged the saddle into Bolt's stall, tossing it effortlessly over him, and then secured it in place. Tugging the rigging tight, he wedged his left foot in the stirrup and gripped the horn with his right hand as if he had done it a hundred times. The horse clopped sideways, Grayson hopping on one foot. "Whoa! Whoa!" he shouted, warranting a chuckle from Sammy Jo, already mounted on her horse.

"Been awhile huh?" Tamping down her amusement, she feigned a sober expression without success, breaking into a belly laugh when his foot slipped from the stirrup, sprawling him across a buffer of strewn hay with a thud.

Springing to his feet like he'd just fallen into a hill of fire ants, Grayson brushed the dirt from the back of his Khakis. "Just give me a minute, I'm a little rusty, that's all..." His second attempt was successful, his chest inflated, his chin held high.

Shifting in the saddle, he trailed Sammy Jo through the doors, into fading daylight. Stars lit a purple horizon, the cap of a full moon visible from the hilltop. The earthy scent of pine from dew kissed mountain air filled his lungs.

Sammy Jo nudged Sadie with her heels, an easy canter picking up to a full trot. Rounding the fenced meadow, she snapped the reins and sprint up the hillside, a trail of dirt kicking the air. Underestimating Grayson's male resolve, she heard the steady pound of Bolt's hooves quickly gaining.

Grayson gripped the reins in both fists and leaned forward. He could not remember the last time he felt this kind of freedom, the endless of night wrapping around him and the wind in his hair. Suddenly forgetting the sadness in his trip to Burlington, he heeled his horse and bolted past Sammy Jo, leaving his grief in the valley below. Capping the ridge, he snapped back the reins and twisted in the saddle. Sporting a smug grin of victory, he winked when Sammy Jo joined him a few seconds later.

Breathless, she halted her mare and tightened her hair clip tucking a few loose strands behind her ear. "Looks like it all came back to you cowboy. You surprise me."

"Let me take a wild guess," he said, scratching his head with one finger. "Didn't figure this green city slicker could ride?"

"Something like that," Casting her focus past him, she nodded to Fern Valley below, where glints of young moonlight caught on gentle pond ripples. She heard him suck in a breath.

"Beautiful huh…" Her mare snorted with a clop forward, nudging Bolt to the side with her nose. Sammy Jo shifted on the leather saddle and could sense Grayson's eyes moving from the pond, lighting on her.

"Very…" he replied simply. The low-pitched bellow of a bullfrog echoed from a distance, nearly drowning his soft reply.

Easing forward in the saddle, Sammy Jo clicked her tongue and led the way down the uneven path, ending at the water's edge. The first to dismount, she tossed leather reins over a low hanging tree branch.

"Pretty amazing, isn't it?" Taking a seat on a rock at the pond edge, she picked up a pebble and skipped it over the water, watching dashes of moonlight across the black surface. "I use to come here a lot when I was a kid. I'd start off fishing but always ended up taking a dip,"

Grayson sat on the ground next to her, wrapping his arms around bended knees. He stared over fading shimmers of light until the water went still again.

They sat quietly, the steady croak of the frog growing faint. Sammy Jo looked up at the rising moon, chasing twilight into the night sky. Slipping behind a cloud, the glow grew hazy, then bright again. "I'm glad you came to dinner tonight," she said, watching the moon inch from behind the cloud, casting a silvery sheen over the pond.

"Me too," Twisting to face her, the emotion on Grayson's face was blurred. The corners of his mouth bowed gently with a concealed a smile, but his eyes frowned with sadness. "I'd really dreaded this trip to Burlington you know,"

She nodded a reply.

"Meeting you has been the silver lining." He paused for a second. "Do you believe in fate Sammy Jo?" His eyes fell to his a finger drawing lines through powdery dirt.

She shrugged, picking up a second stone, skipping it across the still surface of the pond, she asked, "Do you?"

Thoughts of the morning he found her stranded on a shelf snapped through his head. "I don't know if its fate or coincidence, but I don't believe me stopping in Highland for coffee was by chance."

Silence filled the space between them as she looked out across the water.

Just like her recurring dreams of Thatcher Hill were definitely not chance...

Grayson stood and shoved his hands in his pants pockets, snorting a breath. "I'm sorry," he said. "I'm rambling," Creating distance; he walked several steps, palming his hand down Bolt's neck. The horse clopped to the side, nudged against him and whinnied.

Sammy Jo clambered from the ground, brushing dirt from the back of her jeans. When she stepped up from behind, touching Grayson's shoulder, he flinched to attention.

"To answer your question, I believe life is two sided. On one side, God takes control and offers us choices. On the other, we decide what to make of those choices."

She felt Grayson's shoulder stiffen beneath her touch, as if her words had sliced open an old wound. When he turned, she saw his brows gathered in pain.

Her hand slipped from his shoulder. "Things happen in life that we don't understand Grayson. Maybe it is God's doing," she lifted one shoulder. "Or maybe we made the wrong decisions."

He looked away from her, then back again with a confession. She could see both anguish and confusion reflecting in his eyes. "I've been reading Gram's journal,"

She waited.

"There's a lot I didn't know about my Gram, choices she made."

Her eyes narrowed as she waited for him to explain.

"I knew my grandfather died in a mining accident when my mother was very young. What I didn't know, was that Gram sent her away to live with an aunt in Indiana. I guess she was falling apart emotionally and couldn't care for a young child." He toed at a loose stone with his shoe, focusing on the ground.

"I always admired Gram, believing she was strong and independent." Jolting the stone loose with a final kick, his tone became blunt, brimming on sarcasm. "Guess I was wrong on both accounts." His teeth clenched, flexing his jaw. "Now I understand why Mom never spoke of her early childhood and why there always seemed to be tension between her and Gram." His voice lowered, not much more than whisper. "I don't think it's fair to blame God for that one. Maybe that was one of those decisions Gram screwed up."

Sammy Jo flattened both hands on his chest, and could feel the kick of his heart beneath her palm. She dropped her hands along with her gaze, considering her own reasons for not understanding. She had decided years ago not to question fate and just accept it. "Or maybe you're looking at it all wrong."

His lips pinched tight as Grayson gave Bolt a final pat. "Not too many ways to look at it Sammy Jo,"

"Sure there is. It took a petty strong woman to make a decision like that, do what's best for her child, no matter how badly it hurt her."

Continuing with a confession of her own, Sammy Jo scrubbed an open palm across Bolt's nose, her eyes following the slow movement of her hand. "I told you that I have a brother and sister." She caught a quick breath and blew it out. "What I didn't tell you is that they are my half-brother and sister. They live in California with my mom and step-father," She chewed at her lip before going on.

"Mom got pregnant in High School, too young to raise me, so my grandparents did. I grew up thinking of her more as a sister than my mom."

Grayson inhaled sharply. "I'm sorry," he said, his voice going flat.

"Oh, don't be. I had two wonderful role models who brought me up to value everything in life, even hard lessons."

"What about your father, ever meet him?"

She shook her head. "No, he and his folks moved away shortly after they learned mom was expecting. I never really felt like I was missing anything though, I had Grandma and Pops,"

He waited for her to say more, but when she didn't, he smiled and took her hand. His fingers laced with hers, the feeling nice.

Strolling along the banks of the pond, they circled to the other side, talking about anything and everything, the conversation trickling, until it stopped completely beneath a starlit sky.

"We should probably be heading back," Grayson said, pulling her to a stop as they neared the grazing horses. "It's getting late and if we're gone too long, your Pops may send out an armed posse," he added, with a crooked smile, only halfway joking.

When she looked up at the gauging moon, the milky glow cast a flutter of lashes across her cheek. Trying unsuccessfully to keep his feelings on tight leash Grayson's eyes settled on full lips, aching to kiss her. His hand slipped from hers, the back of his fingers stroking a porcelain cheek. His back went ram rod straight with desire, leaning closer. The feel of her quick breath against his skin sent his heart racing. Slipping his arm around her, he tugged her to his chest, inhaling the sweet scent of jasmine on her skin.

Sammy Jo's knees went weak as he touched her, hazel eyes unlocking doors to the most private part of her soul. Her heart hammered her ribs, blood rushing through her veins like molten remains of a melting heart as his lips drew close. She folded easily into him, their bodies a perfectly tailored fit.

The stealth swoop of an owl broke from the treetop, skimming tall grass near the pond before vanishing up the hillside, the frantic squeal of a field mouse squirming futilely in its clutch. Sammy Jo's body leaped forward, bumping noses with Grayson, before breaking into a laugh.

"Talk about a mood changer," she giggled, rubbing her hand over the tip of a red nose.

"Yea..." Grayson watched the owl flagging from sight. He wasn't sure if he wanted to laugh with her, or sit down and cry over opportunity loss to the food chain.

The ride back to the barn was quiet, each wrestling with their thoughts. The bungled kiss left them both more frustrated than irritated, although Sammy Jo could barely hide the amusement of Grayson's exasperation when the owl broke loose from the treetop. The last time she saw that kind of targeted focus, her grandfather's hunt brought home a dozen plucked quail.

A silvery moon hovered overhead when they returned to the barn, casting a ruddy glow over the green metal roof. Moths darted in hazy glow of security lights, crickets growing silent as the steady clop of hooves approached.

Once inside, Grayson threw his leg over the saddle, his feet landing in the dirt with a jolt. Reaching for Sammy Jo's waist, she leaned into him, slipping to the ground. With his hands still clasping her waist, all he could think about was how beautiful she looked in the moonlight, full lips that seemed to lure him like water to a thirsty sponge. He searched her eyes for any indication of feelings, but she quickly looked away.

Eyes darting to the side, Sammy Jo refused to look at him, afraid he could read heated thoughts swirling in her head. Not accustomed to wearing her heart on her sleeve, her obvious attraction to Grayson plastered her forehead in neon letters. Life was complicated and the last thing she needed was restraints of a new relationship, yet the host of sensations tickling her insides, argued otherwise.

As if sensing the tussle inside, Grayson cupped his palm to her cheek with an emerging smile. "I had a great time tonight Sammy Jo."

Without thinking about it, her hand covered his, their gaze finally locking. "Me too," With a blink, she drew a long breath and knelt on one knee next to Sadie. Busying her hands, she began loosening the girth on the saddle, before she was tempted to finish what he had started at the pond.

Grayson watched her loosen the cinch, before standing to remove the saddle completely, along with the red, wool blanket beneath. Unbridling Bolt, he pitched the saddle across the empty stall rail as the horse wandered inside, behind Sadie. Patiently, the pair of horses turned in wait for the pail of oats Sammy Jo had already begun scooping from the bin.

"See you in the morning?" he asked.

"Yea, about 9:00?" she answered, focusing on emptying the galvanized bucket. Still refusing to look at him, she tapped the side of the bucket against the wood feeding troth.

"9:00 it is..." Backing through the open barn door, Grayson waited until she was out of sight before he turned and made his way towards the house. Stewart rushed from the dark shadows, lapping at his hand as he walked.

Chapter 8

The next morning, Sammy Jo cranked the volume knob on the truck radio, in attempt to drown the one-sided chatter in her head. Only making matters worse, a sappy love song blared through the speakers and once again, she pictured the enticing desire reflecting in Grayson's eyes. Once priding herself as a reasonable, sensible woman, the uncensored pictures flicking through her head were anything but.

Highland Tennessee was not exactly dating central, and even if it were, Sammy Jo did not have free time to squander on socializing. Running a business, and trying to spend more time with her grandfather since her Grandmas passing, sucked every ounce of energy she could muster. Dating just did not take precedence in her busy life. At least that was before Grayson Wesley showed up in her stockroom. "Damned owl," she growled though gritted teeth, flipping off the radio knob.

Tapping the turn signal, while twisting the steering wheel hard right, Sammy Jo turned onto the gravel lane, the front tire clunking into one of Thatcher Hill's notorious potholes. Unpredictable spring weather flipped the morning forecast like the flick of a light switch since she had left Highland, gusty winds blowing through open cab windows. Sammy Jo leaned into the windshield peering up at tumbling gray clouds, threatening a short workday. The temperatures were already well above average, lending even more instability to the front swooping in from the northwest. Settling in, the breeze brought with it the damp scent of rain.

Coasting to a stop in front of the house, crisp white paint and glistening coal shutters transported her to an earlier time, when shade from the towering Elms offered a sense of peace and security. She threw the truck in park and turned off the engine.

The estate was already buzzing with workers; two painters straddled scaffolding, their brush strokes rhythmic, a third putting final precision touches on window frames. Roofers nailed shiny metal sheets in place, each strike echoing through tall timbers of the ridge. Even the rickety fence surrounding the house was reborn, sporting a fresh coat of white paint.

Sammy Jo's mouth went dry when Grayson bolted through the front door and down the steps carrying a cup of coffee, wearing a thin sleeveless tee that left little to the imagination. Her eyes dragged across him like a Jack mule with his heels dug in the mud. Thinking he was handsome before was like comparing flat beer to champagne. This morning he was definitely a perfectly chilled bottle of vintage French Krug Brut.

Wide shoulders gave way to flexing biceps, threading muscles wrapped by a ring of inked barbwire. Her jaw dropped like a frog waiting on a fly. There it was… the flipped side of a shiny coin. A bet she would have surely lost if she were a betting woman. Never in a million years would she have imagined a tattoo hidden beneath a pricey polo. One hand frozen to the door handle of the truck and the other to the steering wheel, she was still wedged behind the column when he came through the gate.

"Good morning Sunshine," he said, leaning a folded arm on the open truck window. "Coffee's on, want a cup?" he asked, holding up his mug before swigging a drink.

"Thanks anyway," she replied, slapping closed a drooling gape. "I've already had more coffee this morning than I should've," Grabbing the first excuse that came to mind, she hoped he didn't notice her trembling death grip on the steering wheel, blaming it on caffeine overload, instead of the girly hormones pumping through her veins at warp speed.

"Well, sit with me on the porch while I finish mine," he said, swinging the door open.

Dragging a covered plate of blueberry pie from the passenger seat, she handed it to him. "You didn't get desert las night."

"Thanks," He smiled, the memory of full, moist lips flanking his definition of desert.

Hoping she was not as translucent as she feared, Sammy Jo dropped down from the cab, slammed the door and followed him onto the porch, taking a seat in the rocker next to him.

Avoiding his searing gaze, she watched a roofer drag a box of nails from the tailgate of his truck. She made and ill attempt at replacing the "R" rated images raking her mind, with more rational, sobering thoughts.

"I must be keeping banker's hours," She nodded at the roofer, heaving the heavy box of nails to his shoulder. "Looks like everyone else got an early jump on me this morning,"

Grayson sat the pie on the table and drank down the last swallow from his cup before resting it on the rocker arm. "Yea, they were here about 7:00, rain's coming," His eyes trailed menacing gray clouds, rolling over swaying tips of distant pines.

"The painters are almost finished." He lifted his chin, studying the classic haint blue ceiling paint of the porch. Keeping with southern tradition, a coat of the original dusty shade reflected daylight, believed to ward off everything from evil spirits to pesky insects.

"They finished the porch ceiling early and are just touching up some of the under trim," Moving his cup to the side table, he exchanged it for the journal, thumbing through the yellowed pages.

Sammy Jo followed his gaze to the ceiling before returning her focus to the diary lying open in his lap.

"Been doing some more reading from your grandmother's journal?" Grazing the leather bound diary spread across his legs, she stole a glimpse from the corner of her eye, a six-pack, rippling beneath taught tee shirt fabric.

Stopping, he flipped a couple of pages back, running his finger over an entry. "I've got to admit, Grams journal is a hell of a lot better than anything I've ever written. I was up half the night, couldn't put it down,"

I was up half the night too... She confessed inwardly, brushing her eyes shamefully to the side. Her tongue swiped her bottom lip, her eyes following the wood planks at her feet with all the guilt of a kid caught in the Christmas candy. Sammy Jo thought about the restless night she'd had tossing and turning until the wee hours before dawn. With her mind on autopilot, thoughts flew from one forbidden destination to another, always crash landing on Grayson Wesley.

"Looks like Gram had a bit of a romantic side," Looking down his nose, Grayson's eyes skimmed the page.

Shifting in her seat, Sammy Jo's eyebrows squished together. Her mind locked on the words Gram and romantic. Trying to sink the words together in her brain was like sinking a round peg in a square hole. Her aging grandparents seldom displayed open affection. She could only remember witnessing one kiss, which elicited her grandma's cheeks deepening three shades of red when she realized they had an audience.

Drumming one foot against the floor, Grayson's heart picked up pace, eager to share the shocker he had uncovered the night before. His focus shifted from Sammy Jo, to the open page of the journal in his lap. "Listen to this," he said, picking at her curiosity.

May 2, 1954

"Heavy spring rains washed out the lane making travel to town nearly impossible. With the well muddied, and the roof leaking, I feel even the weather is conspiring to destroy me. Not knowing where else to turn, I've once again called Andrew for help."

He thumbed ahead a couple of pages. Sammy Jo watched his finger trace mid-way down the page before stopping.

"Andrew was co-owner in the mine my grandfather operated," he explained. "From what I understand, he and my grandfather were as close as brothers," He glanced at her from the side before adding, "He was there the day my grandfather died," Grayson's eyes scuffed the page and he continued reading.

May 9, 1954

"Andrew arranged for workers. Today they came to Thatcher Hill, bringing food and supplies. He is a good friend Isaac. I know I can always depend on him…"

"Maybe I was quick to judge Gram," Laying an open palm on the journal, his thumb gently swiped the scrolled words. "I cannot begin to imagine how tough life must have been for her Sammy Jo. She was all alone with a daughter to raise and no one to help her."

"Obviously your grandmother was stronger than even she realized," The graze of Sammy Jo's toe on the floorboard picked up momentum, the gentle rock of the chair creaking on wood. "Can I hear more?" she asked, her curiosity boosted.

Grayson's eyes dropped back to the page. Clearing his throat, he continued reading.

May 11, 1954

"The workers began repairs on the roof today. It also seems I need a new well. A crew began digging at the new sight this morning, just past the barn. It is refreshing having folks around, even if they are laborers hired to do a job. Life feels somewhat normal with people here,

reminding me that the world still turns with each sunrise and sunset. I had all but given up my love. This proves that hidden blessings come at the most unimagined times."

A misty drizzle began falling from a single gray cloud that had stalled over the house. Painters and roofers scurried from ladders and scaffolding, snatching up tools and scurrying in every direction as the impending storm crept closer.

A potbellied painter, his jaw lined with scruffy gray stubbles, made his way up the stairs. With one foot on the top step, the leaden cloud ripped open, rain pouring like water through a sieve. He scowled at the downpour, pulled off his cap and buffed an open palm over his balding head. Replacing the white cap, he dug a pipe and match from his shirt pocket. He struck the match and wedged it in the wood bowl, puffing on the stem until the tobacco glistened red.

"Looks like we're done for the day Mr. Wesley," he said, after blowing a ring of nutty and vanilla scented tobacco smoke that smelled more like a fresh baked dessert. "We'll finish up tomorrow if that's ok,"

Grayson thanked E.C. for his work, watching past him, at men scampering for cover like a washed out anthill. Already filling with water, gravel lined potholes of the lane, spattered with torrential raindrops.

After E.C. sprinted for the truck, and slid in beside the other two already inside, Sammy Jo tucked one leg under the other, swiveling in the seat to face Grayson. "You can't stop now,"

"No, this is when things really get interesting," With a sly wink, he thumbed to the next page.

May 16, 1954

"The workers have been here nearly a week now. The roofers finished up today, but the well is going to take a little longer than expected. It turns out that the spot near the barn is not a good location after all. Grateful to one worker who has a nose for finding water, they began a successful dig near the meadow this morning. I made sandwiches for the labors, obliged for a purpose. Approaching the youngest man of the crew, he seems to know his business well, pinpointing the exact point of excavation. I laughed aloud when he rose from his knees, covered in mud from head to foot. He had enough dirt caked to him to plant a small plot of potatoes. After dropping his shovel and wiping muddied hands on his trouser legs, he introduced himself, but I playfully nicknamed him Digger. After brushing encrusted soil from his knees, he grinned, sunshine reflecting from eyes as black as coal. An unexpected blush filtered into my cheeks, his smile somewhat tantalizing. It has been quite some time since I have felt that kind of fascination with a man.*

Wind lashed across the porch, bringing with it, a showering mist. Sammy Jo scooted her rocker closer to Grayson, heavy rain pinging from the metal roof. When Grayson asked if she wanted to go inside, she pulled her feet up, resting her chin on one knee, and rejected the offer, asking him to continue reading instead. Grayson resumed with a detailed depiction of the spring, 1954, Sammy Jo's attention dangling on each word.

After about an hour, it was obvious that rain had settled over the mountain with no end in sight. When Sammy Jo stood and started to leave during a lull in the storm, Grayson invited her to stay for dinner. Attempting a polite decline to the invitation, Grayson dug in his pocket for a quarter balancing it in the crook of his thumb and finger. "Heads you stay, tails you go home." Flipping the coin, he caught it mid-air with a quick glance at the shiny silver sitting in the palm of his hand, before shoving it back in his pocket.

"Martheena scored a pork loin from her weekly visit to the butcher yesterday. You won't be disappointed in her pork and dumplings, I promise," His slanting smile suggested self-assurance that made Sammy Jo wonder if the dinner menu was the only thing pumping Grayson's confidence.

"Hey, how do I know it was heads?" she asked, listening to the winning coin jingle in his pocket.

"Because it was," he replied, with a wink.

Rocking her head, she rolled her eyes, pretending to ponder, but quickly accepted his invitation. It had been awhile since she had taken time for herself and with her grandfather out of town, anything sounded more tempting than an evening of sitcom reruns.

Sitting back down in the rocker, she crossed one leg over the other. "That actually sounds wonderful. Pops is out of town on business so I'm on my own this evening." Her smiling eyes met his. "You saved me from the likes of a frozen Salisbury steak dinner. You know... those things with mushy meat that looks more like dog food and gritty mashed potatoes?"

Attempting to help clear dinner dishes from the table, Sammy Jo and Grayson were shooed from the kitchen, flitting fingers jostling them through the doorway. Martheena obviously ran a tight ship, making it clear that she was in charge and any extra hands in her galley would be in the way.

"It'll take me ten minutes by myself and twenty if I have help," Martheena teased. "You two go enjoy the evening while I put on a pot of coffee,"

Sammy Jo hooked her arm through Grayson's, matching strides onto the front porch. The rain had ceased, replacing the air with a pine and lilac scented breeze, taking her back to days of earlier dreams, when the house seemed happy and full of life.

Wedging against a white column, she wrapped her arms at her waist, and stared out at the meadow. Water drops glistened on a kaleidoscopic of wildflower petals, finishing rays of the setting sun glittering like diamonds.

She turned and followed the lulling creak of a rocker, joining Grayson in one of the four chairs. They rocked in quiet unison, watching the last golden hint of daylight settle behind the mountains. A purple sky pushed forward, followed by a starlit horizon. In the distance, near the barn, the call of a nightingale whistled, harmonizing with the steady chirp of crickets.

"It's been an amazing evening Grayson," Sammy Jo's eyes never left the meadow, her thumb drawing imaginary circles on the rocker arm. "You were right about Martheena's pork roast."

She felt Grayson's hand slip beneath hers, his entwining fingers giving her heart a giddy beat.

"And I hope the company was equally as pleasing," he prodded. His rocking slowed as he waited a hopeful response.

She squeezed his hand and smiled. "The company was good too,"

"Just good?" he asked, one brow rose quizzically.

"Exceptional," Easing from the rocker, she walked to the edge of the porch, her gaze drawn to stars climbing higher into the night sky. Earlier storm clouds were lost to glinting flickers of starlight.

"It looks like the rain has passed. Hopefully we'll have a good work day tomorrow." She had not noticed him walk up behind her and startled when his arms encircled her waist. Resting his chin on her shoulder, he followed her gaze to twinkles of overhead light.

In the silence, she could feel his warm breath on her neck. A swirl down her spine made her think about the near kiss from the evening before, an interrupted moment that left her admittedly brooding the entire night.

When his fingers curled over her shoulders and spun her to him, she sucked in a breath, her eyes frozen to his.

In slow motion, Grayson leaned closer, brushing his lips softly over hers. Arms tightened at her waist, he drew her against him, his slanted mouth kissing her long and hard.

A kiss exceeding anything her fantasies could conjure during the long, restless night before.

When Grayson pulled back, Sammy Jo ran her finger over tingling flesh of her lips, the kiss leaving a lasting passion. A quick gasp for air, she realized she had been holding her breath. A single kiss had never left her feeling so wanting, so needy.

A welcoming gust of cool air swept copper curls across Sammy Jo's face. She swiped at a ringlet brushing her forehead. Suddenly feeling flushed, heat traveled up her neck, turning her cheeks a rosy red in the dim light.

Grayson's lips drew apart gently, before blossoming into a broad smile. Admittedly, he had not felt that much simmering testosterone since his first date with Pat Quincey back in high school, and just like then, it left him aching for more.

"The best part of the night," he said, trolling for a reply. When she said nothing, he looped a finger around a strand of hair lifting in the breeze and tucked it behind her ear. Pinning her with a look capable of conning a winter squirrel out of its stash of walnuts, his passion filled eyes turned a deepening shade of gray in the moonlight.

Drawn like a magnet, Sammy Jo's finger swiped his bottom lip, tracing a warm trail down his neck and across his chest. Settling on the tattoo ringing a bulging bicep, her eyes followed the feathery strokes. Her finger outlined sun kissed barbed spines, flexing beneath her touch. She looked up with the ghost of a smile.

"Let me guess," he said, sensing her thoughts. "Not the tattoo type."

She tightly tucked her chin, her smile widening. "I must admit, you have me stumped Mr. Wesley. I'm not exactly sure what type you are,"

"Is that a good thing?" he whispered, leaning closer.

"It's not a bad thing," She picked at an imaginary thread on his tee shirt, thinking that maybe it was time for a quick retreat while she had control of the ball game. Her heart was thumping like a giddy teenager with a schoolyard crush, and her knees were rubber weak. Second base felt uncomfortably close, and she feared a home run in the near future was not out of the question if she did not get in her truck and head home.

"I probably should be getting home, dinner was great but I still have livestock to feed,"

"Ah, the livestock..." Reaching for her hand, his chin lifted, his eyes never leaving hers.

She slipped easily into his clasp, their fingers intertwining. Pulling him with her, she stepped to the stairs and into the night, away from the golden glow of the porch light. An cobalt sky replaced the last threading clouds, a pearl moon peeking above the pines.

Grayson followed her to the truck pulling open the door, rusty hinges impeding on the quiet night. After she slid behind the wheel, he leaned in with a kiss that made them both pause. "The livestock..." she reminded him. Disappointment dented the space between his eyes.

"The livestock," he repeated. The groan was so soft she barely heard him.

Reaching for the handle, she pulled the door closed, propping her elbow out the window. "I'll see you in the morning though," she said, twisting the key in the ignition while pumping the gas. The motor turned slowly at first before stubbornly firing, spitting a puff of gray smoke from the exhaust pipe.

"See, even the truck doesn't want you to leave," he said, fingers of both hands curling the door.

Sammy Jo rolled her eyes playfully and put her foot on the brake. "I'll be here early, about 8:00, so have coffee ready."

Stepping back with a mock salute, he winked. As she dropped the old red pickup in reverse, he took a step forward throwing his hand in the air, stopping her. "Is your grandfather still going to be out of town tomorrow?"

She nodded a reply. "Until Saturday,"

"Want to barbecue? I grill a pretty m

The words were out before she could

"I'll bring clean clothes if do you don't mind me

after I finish work?"

He patted the door with a single nod and

step back while Sammy Jo turned the truck around. She eased down the gravel road watching him disappear in the rear view mirror, both hands shoved in his pockets, the moon outlining his lean silhouette.

On the drive back to Highland, Sammy Jo's mind pinged like a pinball machine, from the morning Grayson swooped her off the ledge in the stockroom, their horseback ride to the pond, ending with the kiss on Thatcher Hill.

Thatcher Hill...

The thought brought a needling shiver, raking her spine. It had been a week since she last dreamed of Thatcher Hill, the ruins of a glassy, lifeless stare seared into her memory. As frightening as the nightmare had been, she could not help but sense a great loss, as if the final, tragic scene had played, the curtain dropped on a finale she may never know. A repeating dream since childhood seemed to vanish, and with it, any hope for closure.

Sleep would not come easily tonight; both anxiety and fear would surely feed a restless night; anxiety she would never understand the implication behind the dreams, fear that she may.

Chapter 9

Grayson sat on the porch after the last glint of red tail lights disappeared down the lane, the sound of the rocker scuffing worn floorboards. He watched the moon make its slow climb over the mountain until it was high in the night sky, casting liquid silver over the pines. He could not stop thinking about the taste of Sammy Jo's lips, the smell of citrus and jasmine on her skin, or her breast squashed to his chest as they kissed. Lapping through his brain at double time, one thought chased another leaving him breathless. Captivated by the little Dixie temptress, a yearning for more tied his stomach in one giant knot, finishing with a neat bow in his loins.

Thatcher Hill had long gone quiet, the moon high in the sky when he went inside to the kitchen and pulled a nearly full bottle of Merlot from the cabinet. Pouring a long stem glass two thirds full, he took a sip followed by a hefty swallow that emptied the crystal chalice. He refilled the glass, carrying it upstairs to his bedroom.

A long, cold shower did little to relieve the desire simmering in his veins, every muscle in his body gone iron clad rigid with tension. He found himself back downstairs in the kitchen refilling his wine glass but decided to take the half-empty bottle back up with him instead. It was undoubtedly going to be along night.

Pulling his bedroom door closed, Grayson's eyes drew to Gram's open diary lying face up on the bed. He leaned against the closed door, the open pages as luring as squirming bait on a hook. Swirling blush colored wine against the sides of the crystal glass he waited for it to go clear again before taking a drink.

Dragged to the bed by an overwhelming sense of curiosity, he sat the crystal glass and dark bottle on the nightstand. Propped against pillows wedged at the iron headboard, he reached for the leather bound diary next to him. With the stem of the balloon shaped goblet poised between his fingers, he took a sip before resting it on his thigh. Ankles crossed, his body relaxed into the mattress, his Gram's words luring him to another time.

Latter entries revealed an obvious change in his grandmother's demeanor, a progression of the woman she would soon become. Rosaline began the journal as an escape from reality, a way to connect with her late husband. Lonely and desperate, there were times her tone sounded forlorn, nearly suicidal. Had Grayson not known the ending of his grandmother's life, he would have bet his last dollar that she died a ghastly death, broken hearted and by means of her own hand.

That was all before a young man she affectionately referred to as Digger, shed new light on a desolate future. Lost to darkness, a ray of hope appeared when Rosaline needed it most. At 18 years old, Digger was nearly 10 years her junior, described as striking, with dark hair and even darker eyes that peered beneath a fringe of black lashes. The young chap quickly became more than a laborer to the lonely widow of Thatcher Hill, a story of love, lust and betrayal began to unravel from yellowed pages of his grandmother's past.

May 26, 1954

The sun is blazing hot today and the air is so dense you can cut it with a butter knife. The new well is nearly finished and everyone has left for the day, with the exception of Digger and one other fellow who stayed behind to avoid going home to a cantankerous wife and eight children, all under 10 years old. I know this to be true because he talks of nothing else. Makes you wonder how a man that miserable ended up with eight kids.

As the scrawled text led Grayson along his grandmother's twisted journey, he imagined a graphically vivid picture of the day that changed Rosaline's life forever. Written words faded from yellowed pages, an unusually hot, sunny day in 1954, coming into clear focus.

May 29, 1954

I awakened this morning just before dawn, to humid air stirred by the rhythmic whirr of fan blades. I stood at the bedroom window just in time to watch golden rays peek above the pine tipped ridge. Beyond the windowsill, the air was still and stagnant, a thick haze blanketing the mountain like a shroud. Tight ringlets sticking to my neck foretold of another hot, sticky day. Rain and humidity always send my ginger curls spring tight, a forecast as accurate as the rain crow.

After a long, cool bath, I clipped my hair high on my head with a barrette, a few loose tendrils brushing my shoulders. Digging in the back of the closet, I pulled out a yellow chiffon dress with taffeta waist that I have not worn in over a year. The fabric's golden color deepened the green in my eyes, the fitted bodice complementing my petite figure. For the first time in many months, I feel like woman.

I was sitting on the front porch sipping a glass of sweet tea when the truckload of workers came bounding up the lane. Scattering over the sides of the truck bed, it seemed the foreman had brought enough men to promptly finish two jobs, a thought that suddenly made my heart sink. I am sure it will not be long before loneliness returns to Thatcher Hill.

Scanning the crew, I searched for Digger, the last to hurl over the side; I watched as he tipped his hat and greeted me good morning. It has become ritual to carry water and sweet tea to the laborers during the day, and I must admit, I look forward to breaks and spending time with the young man that I am finding myself strangely attracted to. Many of the workers share pleasantries with me, a few stepping to the blurred line of flirtatious, but it is only the youngest of the crew to earn my fascination.

It was nearing noon when most of the men piled back in the truck leaving only two workers behind to finish with final details. I watched from the porch as a trail of dust capped the lane, the truck bouncing from one side to the other, gradually disappearing down the rutted road.

I prepared two sandwiches, wrapping them in cheesecloth before capping a Mason jar of sweet tea for the two remaining workers. Making my way down the grassy slope, I spotted Digger scooping from a mound of loose dirt with a shovel, tossing the weight of muddied soil to the side. His shirt pitched over a nearby bush, his dark skin shimmered in the afternoon sun, sweat glistening from flexing muscles.

As if sensing my approach, Digger was the first to look up. Leaning on his shovel, he wiped his brow with the back of his hand, concentrating on my every step. Eyes as deep and dark as refined granite reflected in afternoon rays.

I stopped in front of him, a clenching in my throat making it difficult to speak. His smiling eyes made me feel like a silly girl. I presented the sandwiches, trying my best not to stare at his sprawling chest, a constant effort on my part.

Snapped from an intense daze, Digger suddenly became aware of his shirtless chest, grabbing tattered cloth from the bush, dropping it over his head. He thanked me, taking the sandwiches I held in a trembling hand.

The second worker scurried from behind and snatched a chicken salad on rye from Digger's hand. Stuffing a bite in his mouth, he acted as if he had not eaten in days. Complaining that his wife did not take such good care for her husband, he chomped like a cow chewing its cud. Enthralled by the sandwich, the worker thankfully did not lapse into one of his lengthy and explicit tales of a neglectful wife, but rather found a rock to devour his lunch.

Digger's chin went high with an apology, as he glared at the rude scallywag sprawled over the rock stuffing his face.

I politely excused the discourteous behavior with a chuckle, remarking on the obvious approval and enjoyment of my chicken salad recipe.

Digger offered an excuse, stating the scamp would eat a shoe sole if he got hungry enough. Quickly recanting, he feared his warranted defense sounded more like an insult of my recipe, his face lighting in a tinge of pink.

Pleasantly surprising me, Digger dug a flick knife from his pocket and cut the remaining sandwich in half.

Handing me a wedge wrapped in the cheesecloth, he asked me to join him for lunch.

My hand brushed his as I took the sandwich, sending an unexpected tingle to my fingers that ended in my chest. It was at that instant I knew there was so much more that I wanted to know about this man, so much more I needed to know.

After finishing lunch on a fallen log, I received praise and appreciation from both men, before gathering the cheesecloth and empty Mason jar. Turning with a step up the hill, Digger called from behind. When I turned, he had the bloom of a delicate Pink Fringed flower between two fingers. Without a word, he held it out to me. I took the blossom, pressing it to my nose. In that moment, something clicked between us, like the movement of time.

Trailing back up the hill to the house, I could sense the weight of Digger's eyes following the swish of my full skirt, a gratifying feeling I had not felt since losing my dear Isaac. It has been nearly two years since feeling like woman, feeling this alive.

After stepping onto the porch, I turned for one last glimpse of the dark haired chap, his chin resting on the shovel handle with an expression as dazed as a midnight deer in the headlights.

It was near suppertime when I heard a tap at the front door. Drying my hands on a paisley apron tied at my waist, I stepped from the kitchen, into the foyer. I saw

Digger beyond the screen; both hands poked in muddied pants pockets. His eyes cast on shifting feet; he looked like a boy dreading a trip to the woodshed with the schoolmaster. When he looked up, I motioned for him to come in, which he quickly declined, followed by the excuse of being too dirty.

He pulled off his cap and ran his fingers through black, wavy hair before twisting it back in place. There was no mistaking the sense of regret etched in deep lines of his forehead, or the sadness in his tone when he announced that they were finished with work on the well. Obviously, he too was not anxious for the job to end.

Meeting him at the door, I shoved it open ahead of him and insisted he come in. When I peeked past him to the deserted porch, I asked about his friend.

"I don't know if you'd call me and Fred friends' mam. We don't always see eye to eye, more times than not, we don't even come close." He heaved a breath to stop the rambling. "Anyway," he went on. He has a brother just down the road, gonna' hitch a ride home with him,"

The door hinges creaked as I swung it wider, offering to fix him a cold drink while he washed up in the washroom off the kitchen.

He hesitated before crossing the threshold, easing the door closed behind him. Again, the rusty hinges creaked. Digger noted the need for a good oiling.

I confessed how much I depended on my late husband for such repairs, adding to the long list of changes in life since becoming a young widow. Turning back to the kitchen the mention of Isaac suddenly made me feel sad and awkward. Passing the washroom on the left, I paused in the doorway with a nod before returning to the stove.

Absorbed into the past by the wooden spoon swirling in a pot of soup, I flinched back to the present when Digger appeared in the doorway a few minutes later. I turned and found him leaning against the doorjamb, face and hands clean and his expression serious.

As if sensing sadness in my thoughts, he asked about my late husband, "You miss him, don't you?" A question I had answered in my head a million times over.

I nodded a reply, tapping the spoon on the side of the pot. Reaching in the cabinet for a glass, I motioned to the long farmhouse table, taking a glass pitcher of sweet tea from the icebox.

Digger took off his hat dropping it on the table before pulling out a chair. "Thank you mam," he said, reaching for the glass I offered.

With a cheeky grin, I propped a hand on my hip. "I really wish you'd stop calling me mam, it makes me feel like your Sunday school teacher," I said. "How about Rosaline?"

He took a long, steady drink from the glass watching over the rim before smiling. "I like Rosaline, it's a pretty name."

The mundane tasks of everyday living are something I took for granted before Isaac's death, the loss leaving a huge gaping hole, once filled with dreams of the future. I miss having someone to share morning coffee with and small talk of daily tasks over evening meals. It was not until all was lost and my husband gone did I *realize how empty life was without a companion, how time becomes the enemy, nothing more than empty hours leading to long, empty days.*

Pouring a second glass of sweet tea, I joined Digger at the table where he asked about Isaac and the circumstances of his death. Expecting the tranquil candor with another man to feel like a betrayal of the heart, it did not. Instead, I found it surprisingly easy to talk about the mine collapse and my beloved's sudden death. The conversation felt somewhat cleansing, as if saying it aloud helped it all make sense. When I finished with my sad story, I leaned on folded arms and asked about his life.

Digger's story was also surprisingly sad, or maybe shocking would be a better fitting word. I found him to have an old soul, far beyond his years. I never would have guessed a young man only 18 years old earned my captivation. Already living an existence of seclusion and hardship, he seemed much wiser than his years on this Earth. Traveling from town to town, he followed where work took him. Without a place to call home, he slept where he could find a safe place to lay his head, sometimes a co-worker's barn and sometimes the dark alley behind a storefront.

After about an hour, our conversation trickled to a halt. Digger thanked me for the cold drink and stood, twisting his hat back on his head. My reprieve from loneliness was reaching its final moments, an anchoring heart reminding me of reality's cruelty. Carrying his empty tea glass to the sink, he paused before turning around. With a heavy sigh that made me wonder if there was something on his mind, he turned and politely told me to call his boss if I had any problems with the new well.

I assured him that I would call and after a slight hesitation, thanked him for staying. I am sure my pained expression drew a vivid picture of my lonely and isolated life without painting the details. It was all I could do to blink back hot tears stinging my lids.

Digger opened his mouth to reply but snapped it closed with a second thought. Headed for the foyer, I trailed him, stopping as he pushed open the door to the familiar slice of creaking metal. Without turning to me, I heard only every other word of his muffled offer to fix the hinges before leaving. With the excuse of being helpful, it was obvious that he would do anything to stall, to postpone the inevitable. He dreaded leaving Thatcher Hill as much as I dreaded him leaving.

I could not disguise the joy of having him stay, even if for a short time. I agreed to his charitable offer, but only if he would allow me repay him with supper. Not giving him a chance to decline, I quickly added the temptation of buttermilk cornbread to go with the pot of beef barley soup simmering on the stove.

A wide grin dimpled both cheeks when he thought about his last visit home over a year ago, and the honey his Ma would serve with her fresh baked pone.

I found myself holding my breath in anticipation of his reply when I added the enticement of honey and a pound of fresh churned butter.

His lips curved gently and he could not ask fast enough where he could find the oil can.

It was dark when we finished dinner, Digger eating two bowls of soup and nearly half of a skillet of cornbread. I would never have believed he could stuff that much food in his lean physique.

We took coffee on the porch and watched the sun settle behind the mountain, a blue sky replaced by shades of violet. When Digger rose to leave, I worried about him walking into town at the late hour and instinctively offered him the tack room in the barn for the night. The shiplap sided room is nothing fancy but is dry and has a ticking covered down cot. I figured anything would be better than the alley behind a general store or sharing a stall with a mare.

As Grayson turned the pages of his Gram's journal, he learned that Digger agreed to sleep the night in the barn, and the next and the next. Earning his keep with long overdue maintenance on the house and barn, the arrangement served both the young laborer and Rosaline equally. Digger had the best food and board he'd had in two years and Rosaline no longer felt empty and alone in this world.

Not bothering with the glass, Grayson reached for the gangly bottle sitting on the night table. Gripping the neck, he swigged the last drink of Merlot, the liquid warming his throat. After slapping the journal shut, he sat it on the nightstand, along with the empty bottle, heavy lids dragging him deeper in bed.

      The bedside table lamp was still on when Grayson bolted upright in bed as if he'd been shot. Gasping for air, sweat trickled down his face and neck, dark hair coiled across his bare chest. Trying unsuccessfully to focus on the dimly lit room, his eyes frantically searched for the hands that roughly shook him from a sound sleep. He pushed up in the bed and leaned against the headboard, his heart nearly exploding from his chest.

      Squinting past the glow of the table lamp, Grayson's attention veered to the tall gentleman's bureau, more precisely, the chain from the pocket watch dangling loosely over the side. He squeezed his eyes tight and then opened them again, aiming a cold stare on glints of lamp light reflecting from the gentle sway of gold links. He listened to the steady scrape of gilded metal and wood, as rhythmic as a ticking clock.

      In slow motion, he twisted in the bed and dropped his feet to the floor. Sucking in a breath, he brushed sweaty palms on his thighs and stood. The swaying chain drew him across cold wood planks, the resonating scuff growing louder with each progressing step. Staring at the backside of the golden disc, three inscribed initials stared back at him, three initials he had not noticed before.

Picking up the watch, he ran his finger over the mystifying scroll before flipping the timepiece in his palm. Halfway expecting the steady tick of the late hour, the hands of petrified time reflected from the crystal face.

Chapter 10

Sammy Jo beat the chickens out of the roost, her head a hodgepodge of thoughts. As with every other night over the past week, she did not dream of Thatcher Hill, although that did not keep it from encompassing her mind the entire night like a dense fog. Her thoughts darted from the manor to her dreams, then from the irritating city slicker who rescued her, finally ending on unnerving temptation from the night before.

It was 7:50 when Sammy Jo topped the gravel lane of Thatcher Hill. The sun had climbed past the tips of the pines, bathing the mountaintop in shades of orange and yellow. Music rattled the speakers as a welcome distraction, cool mountain air blowing through the open cab window.

Sammy Jo glanced in her rear view mirror at the bed, chocked full to the rails of plants needed to finish the landscaping job. The front tire thudded in a pothole, bouncing the truck to the other side of the lane, a flat of red geraniums and ivy shifting to the other side. She twisted the steering wheel hard left, dodging a second crater, her mind swinging to the two urns Grayson had returned to their original post on either side of the steps. She smiled and accelerated up the steep incline.

The afternoon proved productive, despite Sammy Jo's wandering thoughts. E.C., along with two of his sons, finished with a few paint touch ups and pavers replaced the walkway to the porch with terra cotta bricks in a familiar herringbone pattern. By days end, the house closely resembled the grand manor from Sammy Jo's childhood dreams.

The sun began a slow decent behind the foothills of Tennessee, casting lengthening shadows across the ground. Kneeling at the base of the proch, Sammy Jo was finishing up with ivy in the last urn when Grayson stepped through the front door, ambling down the steps on bare feet.

Smelling like soap and musk, he held a glass of sweet tea in each hand. His auburn waves were still wet, a single slip of dark hair drifting onto his forehead. A tee shirt clung like skin to his damp chest, revealing ripples of muscles beneath. He had not shaved, the shadow of a ticking, 5 o'clock stubble airing more on the side of sexy than scruffy.

Sammy Jo's gaze trickled over him ending on naked toes. She could feel warmth traveling to her cheeks, a flush admittedly not from the southern heat.

"Don't you think it's about quitting time?" Moving towards her, he offered a glass. "The boss may not be happy with your overtime."

Sammy Jo scrambled to her feet, the ground spinning beneath her as she did. Stumbling forward she plopped down on the bottom step, wiping a dirty glove across her sweaty forehead.

"Hey…you okay there?" Grayson sat both glasses of tea to the side and knelt on one knee, smoothing damp curls from her face.

The haphazard excuse came easily. "I'm fine, just got up too fast," she said. Snatching a glass from the step, she swigged half the contents in one drink, wishing it were something stronger than sweet tea. When she pulled the glass from her lips and looked up, Grayson laughed.

"What's so funny?" she asked, tugging pink dyed leather from each finger, tossing her gloves to the side.

With his thumb, he swiped at the dirty smudge across her forehead, left behind by a soil covered garden glove.

Instinctively retracing his thumb's path, she wiped at the remaining dirt. "I must look like a hot mess,"

Grayson remained silent, but the smile teasing his lips said she looked anything but a mess.

Hot definitely… a mess, not even close…

Squirming beneath a hazel gaze, she struggled to her feet, fiddling with two sprigs of ivy to busy unsteady hands. Pulling a leafy vine over the side, she stood and took a step back, assessing her finished creation like an artist scrutinizing her final brush strokes.

"Did you remember your clothes?'" he asked.

She nodded a silent reply, suddenly wondering if staying for dinner a second night was such a good idea after all.

After Sammy Jo finished fussing over the urns, she retrieved a small, black canvas bag from the truck, slinging it over her shoulder. Trailing Grayson inside, she paused at the stair landing, her heart thumping double time in her throat. Memory of the disseminated doll suddenly felt uncomfortably distinct, shattered glass, the empty, lifeless stare. Moving her bag from one shoulder to the other, the hair prickled at her neck, sending a shiver beneath her shirt. When Grayson turned, he saw her staring at the landing floor as if she were stuck ankle deep in quick sand.

Trying unsuccessfully to shake the eerie presence enveloping her, she took a quick step forward onto the bottom step, clinging to the hand Grayson held out to her.

Climbing the steps to the second story, Grayson pushed open the bathroom door at the end of the hall, gesturing her inside with an open palm. "I took the liberty of drawing you a bubble bath and laid out a couple of towels. Take your time and soak for a while. I think you've earned it today," he added, as she walked in ahead of him. Snipping the door closed behind him, he left her alone.

Sammy Jo stood with her back to the door, listening to Grayson's footsteps wilt in the distance. The bathroom was much larger than the one back home at the ranch, nearly the size if her bedroom. The original claw foot tub dominated the far wall and Sammy Jo could see her reflection in the antique gilded mirror dressing the wall above it. A kaleidoscope of prisms sprinkled the floor from the small, crystal chandelier, creating a whimsical rainbow illusion at her feet.

Beside the tub angled an oversized chair covered in luxurious royal blue velvet, two fluffy, white towels and a washcloth draping the side. Grayson's presence dominated the room. Still smelling of menthol shaving cream and woodsy musk, an arousing scent threatened Sammy Jo's carnal restraint, which already dangled dangerously by a thread.

Nearly an hour passed when Sammy Jo appeared in the kitchen doorway, after dropping her bag at the truck. Expecting to find Martheena at the stove, she found Grayson instead, placing the lid back on a saucepan, the pungent scent of rosemary spiking the evening air.

"Something smells amazing," she said, earning his attention.

When he turned to her, his expression went flat, and for an instant, he was speechless. "You look stunning," he said, with a blink.

"Thank you," Self-consciously running her palms over the sides of her dress; she smoothed the coral, form fitting fabric over her hips. "I wasn't sure what to wear,"

"Perfect…" he murmured. Her wet hair sprung into tight curls barely brushing sun kissed shoulders, her blue eyes striking in the low light. The thin-strapped dress was simple, a hint of peach gently clinging curvaceous hips. Long legs gave way to white, strappy sandals, buckled at the ankle.

Wishing she had chosen a favorite pair of Levis and tee shirt instead, Sammy Jo felt a bit embarrassed by his gawking stare. Stepping further inside the kitchen, she looked around breaking his hypnotic gaze with the obvious question. "Where's Martheena?"

"Having dinner in town with a friend, why, afraid to be alone with me?" he asked, more serious than he sounded.

"I'm not afraid of you or any other man," Sparing him a smile, she curled her lip and blew at a curl dropping in the center of her forehead.

"I believe you," With a wry glance in her direction, he winked before turning to the cabinet. Taking down two long stemmed, crystal glasses, he held one up. "Wine?" he asked.

"Please," She watched as he uncorked a bottle of Cabernet Sauvignon. Pouring each glass half full, he handed one to her. Clinking glasses with a toast, he waited for her as she took a slow sip, followed by a sip of his own.

"Can I help with something?" she asked, mentally inventorying three pots on the stove. Swirling the wine against the sides of her glass, she took a second sip, the rich berry flavor lingering at the back of her throat.

Grayson sat his glass on the counter before thumbing towards the back door. "I have filets on the grill. If you'd like to keep an eye on the Rosemary sauce, I'll check on them."

"Rosemary sauce, I'm impressed." Joining him at the stove, she cracked the lid and peeked inside of one. "Raccoon whisperer, author… and you can cook too?"

Replacing the lid, she took a small step back with her hand perched on her hip. "You're a man of many talents Mr. Wesley," she teased. Not so secretly impressed, she glanced at him from the corner of her eye and wondered what other talents remained hidden beneath his polished exterior.

"I suppose I can thank Martheena for my knack of cooking. I spent a lot of time under her feet when I was a kid," He adjusted the flame on the burner, giving the sauce a gentle shake. "She said that the kitchen is the heart of the home, but I think she was the one who kept this old place beating." His smile reflected fond memories. He picked his wine glass from the counter and turned to the door. "She taught me how to cook everything from salt pork and collard greens to sausage Jambalaya." Recognizing Sammy Jo's surprise, he tendered a wink. "I'll check on those steaks," he said, before disappearing outside.

Sammy Jo lifted the whisk from the stove, swirling it through the cream sauce. Impressed was a bit of an understatement. The truth was Grayson Wesley captivated Sammy Jo like a snake charmer and she a gullible cobra. Never had she felt this kind of enticement for a man, particularly a man she barely knew. He owned her last thought every night and awakened her with first thoughts of the morning.

The slamming screen door alerted Grayson's return a couple of minutes later, carrying two perfectly plattered Filet Mignons.

Sammy Jo put down the whisk and moved to the side. Grayson plated both steaks with Rosemary sauce, rice Au Gratin and fresh asparagus fused with pearl onions before tuning to her.

Slipping the stem of her glass between two fingers, she followed him, backing through the screen door onto the deck. If she thought his cooking skills stunned her, what waited beyond the door was nearly heart stopping. Her eyes popped wide and her mouth gaped like a catfish flopping on the bank.

White linen draped a small bistro table topped by two silver candleholders, tiny flames flickering in warm wafts of mountain air. Soft music from the big band era played from a transistor radio, lending a romantic edge to what she previously predicted to be a casual dinner.

Sitting one plate on each side of the table, Grayson reached for her chair, dragging it with a playful bow. "Mademoiselle," he tantalized, an impressive French accent trolling from his tongue.

Sammy Jo sat her wine glass on the table. Seizing a breath, she smoothed her hands over the back of her dress, folding into the chair. When Grayson leaned in closer, she could smell hints of rich musk from his cologne and feel his warm breath. After a gentle kiss that seemed teasing, he nudged her chair before moving to the other side of the table. As he pulled out his chair, his eyes never left her. Taking a seat, he dropped a linen napkin across his lap.

The sky deepened in shades of gray, the mountain air carrying the fragrance of pine kissed lilacs, harkening to a more simple time in Sammy Jo's memory. She closed her eyes and drew a sedative breath, holding it for a second as she remembered a time when the familiarity of Thatcher Hill offered solace to a young girl's dreams.

"I hope your steak is cooked to your liking," Grayson's voice brought her back from distant memories, eliciting a deliberate sigh.

Picking up her napkin, she spread it across her lap, avoiding the tempting gaze from across the table. "I'm sure it will be fine. I eat my steak anywhere between mooing and well done," she teased, spoken like a true southerner.

She sliced into the meat, piercing a piece with her fork. "It's perfect," she said, studying the pink center before slipping it between peach glossed lips.

Grayson placed his elbows on the table and joined his hands. Eyes that took on a green tint in the candlelight, peered over laced fingers. Hesitating, he waited for her reaction, captivated by her lips as she slowly chewed. Reeling in gratifying groans coming from Sammy Jo's throat, the delectable noises sounded as delicious as the Filet.

"Oh Grayson, this is amazing," Swallowing, she sliced off another piece, her grumbling stomach making her all too aware of how little she had eaten at lunch.

Satisfied, Grayson picked up his knife and fork and began cutting his meat, taking a bite. Watching the candlelight flicker in Sammy Jo's eyes, he chewed and thought what a rare treasure she was, the perfect compound of modest beauty with complexity of a multifaceted jewel.

He had dated more than his share of eligible women during years of bachelorhood, but not once had a woman taunted or intrigued him like Sammy Jo Wilcox.

Feeling the weight of his stare, Sammy Jo swallowed a piece of steak before looking up. "So tell me," she asked. Dabbing a napkin to her lips, she smoothed the linen back across her lap. "Are you famous?"

A deep chuckle slipped from his throat. Picking up his wine glass, he mulled over her question. "Well, I must not be too famous if you've never heard of me." Taking a sip, he sat the goblet down and scooped a fork of rice into his mouth. He leaned back in his chair and chewed, waiting for her response.

Spearing another sliver of steak, Sammy Jo hesitated before replying, "I don't take much time for reading," Her fork paused mid-air. "What kind of books do you write anyway?" Taking a bite, she slowly chewed and swallowed before adding, "I may decide to take up the interest," Washing down the meat with a sip of wine, her eyes drifted to the side, Grayson's intense gaze falling somewhere between tantalizing and nerve racking.

"Mostly fictional mysteries," he answered. "You know, *who done it* kind of novels," He was still relaxed back in the chair studying her. Reaching for his glass, he swirled his wine against the sides. "Enough about me, I want to hear about you."

Her eyes dropped to her plate, then returned to the other side of the table. She watched him for a beat before replying. "Not much to tell, my life probably sounds boring compared to yours," she admitted. She drew a breath and blew it out.

"I love old black and white western reruns," she grinned playfully. "My first crush was on a lawman named Matt Dillon."

"So, you have a thing for cowboys?"

"Not just any cowboy," she teased, peering beneath an ample sweep of lashes.

Grayson's intrigue was spiked. "And what else would I not guess about you?"

She shrugged. "Like I said, not much to tell," I like steak sauce on my mac and cheese," she quickly tacked on, a tasty creation she was proud of.

Grayson crinkled his nose. "Steak sauce?"

"Hey buddy, don't knock it if you haven't tried it," she said, picking at a piece of asparagus.

Folding his arms on the table, Grayson found himself leaning closer. "So, now I know that you eat mac and cheese drowned in steak sauce while watching late night western reruns, and you love digging in the dirt."

She shrugged. "I warned you, I live a pretty boring life,"

"Sounds anything but boring to me," Grayson watched her moving her food around her plate with her fork, her playful smile fading.

She rested her fork on the side of her plate and dabbed her mouth with her napkin, dropping it back to her lap. "Living with Pops and keeping him in line is a full time job," she admitted, more serious than she sounded. "Losing Grandma turned him into a lost puppy." She twisted the stem of her wine glass between her fingers staring into it, her reflection becoming sad. "It's been hard on both of us," She picked up her fork, hesitating before taking another bite.

"I'm sorry," Grayson shifted in his seat. "I know first-hand how painful that kind of loss can be,"

Sammy Jo could read emotions scrawled across his face as clearly as an opening sentence to one of his novels. Certain he could undoubtedly relate to her pain, he had felt the sting of death not once, but three times. Not only had Grayson experienced the death of his parents and grandmother, there was no was finality of the loss of his mother, no closure.

Steering the grim conversation to happier times, Grayson complimented Sammy Jo on her astounding feat of restoring Thatcher Hill's gardens to their original glory. "You've done a remarkable job with the grounds Sammy Jo," Satisfaction widened his smile. "The old place looks the same as when I was a boy,"

He had no idea how genuine his recognition was. Brush strokes of Thatcher Hill's former days painted Sammy Jo's memory like a priceless watercolor. Smiling across the table, she remained silent, but knew her vision of the estate's earlier days were accurate, down to brimming urns, bursting with crimson and ivy.

Conversation over dinner flowed from Sammy Jo's modest farm life, to Grayson's fast-paced career of journalism. Expensive wine, delicious food and even more delicious dinner companion left Sammy Jo more relaxed than she had been in two years. Scooting from her chair, she reached for Grayson's empty plate, a practiced habit she had refined since the passing of her grandmother.

His fingers circled her wrist, standing he stopped her. "Leave that. How about taking a walk with me before it gets too dark?"

The sun had long shrunk behind the ridge. The only remnant of daylight was a thin line of scarlet marking the western horizon. Crickets had begun their evening serenade, the call of a nightingale echoing through dense cover marking bordering woods.

Sammy Jo stepped around the table and laced her fingers through Grayson's and followed him down two steps, the grass already damp from mist of the evening dew. A hedge of purple lilacs bordered a forest of century old oaks and elms, opening to a trail shrouded in lengthening shadows.

"I loved playing back here when I was a kid," Grayson confessed, drawing her with him.

Sammy Jo traced his steps around a fallen log, holding tight to his hand. "It's a little creepy back here," she admitted, looping her arm through his.

"You're not scared are you?"

She did not answer right away, instead clung vice grip tight to a flexing bicep.

"This place has been in my family for more than 200 years," he said, zigzagging past a clump of veining ivy. "There's actually an old burial plot of descendants a little deeper in the woods,"

"Great!" Skidding to a stop, she tugged on his arm, troubled eyes peering up at him. "You're taking me to a cemetery?"

Grayson's mouth twitched as he smiled. Brushing a low branch to the side, he held it and waited for Sammy Jo to pass by. "Where's your sense of adventure?" he asked playfully.

"It's not my *sense* of adventure I'm worried about. Following you through the woods to visit a cemetery, I'm wondering where my *senses* are...period..." she replied blatantly, her grip clutching even tighter.

Grayson laughed outright. "You're safe with me,"

That is debatable, she thought inwardly, acutely aware of prickles racing to all the right places, compliments of the muscle bulging beneath her hand.

Fifteen minutes into their stroll, the filtering light dimmed, ghostly shadows angling like stepping-stones across moss covered ground. The air was thick and damp, smelling of soil and honeysuckle. Ahead, Sammy Jo spotted a hazy clearing surrounded by a dilapidated picket fence, sections leaning beneath weight of climbing ivy. With the gate long gone, the opening beckoned like the entrance of a haunted house.

Chapter 11

Noises of the night breathed life into the dark forest. The rhythmic hoot of an owl perched on the limb of a walnut tree pierced the air, obviously annoyed by the unwanted intrusion. Clatter of crickets grew suddenly quiet as deer hooves rustled ground cover ahead. Crickets filled the air with song again, after a doe and her fawn frolicked by, making their way to the spring fed creek, burbling a few yards away.

Hauling Sammy Jo behind, Grayson tugged her to the left of a fork, marking the narrow path. The sound of rippling water grew distant as they approached the carved clearing.

Sammy Jo's fingers curled over Grayson's arm as their destination came into clear focus. Grayson stepped over the fallen gate, random weeds sprouting knee high around it. Inside the plot of hollow ground stood two uneven rows of markers, shaded in dark green moss. Most were modest tombstones, nestled low to the ground, with the exception of two tall, eroding pillars in the center, marking the beginning of Grayson's long line of heritage.

An impressive black granite headstone with intricate carvings of two angels stood proudly near the entrance. Pink, heart shaped blooms of a bleeding heart fern clustered at the stone's base, long reaching stems draped over the side. Last hints of daylight shimmered across the stone marking Isaac Worthington's eternal resting place.

Grayson stopped at his grandfather's grave, patting an open palm on the cold stone. "My grandfather, Isaac is buried here, it took the miners nearly a week to recover his body," he said. "Although I never met him, Gram's stories of a heroic, kind hearted man made him real to me." Moving past the granite stone, he stopped in front of one of the slim, darkened pillars, brushing his finger over the rugged inscription eroded with time. "This was my great-great grandparents, Zechariah and Anna Worthington. They were the first to settle here on Thatcher Hill," Kneeling on one knee, he pulled at a clump of wavering grass. "Gram use to keep the old place up when I was a kid, planting flowers and pulling weeds. It doesn't look like much has been done in years," He let out a deliberate sigh for fading history, tossing the cluster of crabgrass to the side.

Sammy Jo brushed her fingertips across Grayson's shoulder as she stepped past him, following the trail of linking stones. Stopping at the end of the row, a small, unimpressive slab lay flush to the ground, partially concealed by overgrowth. Stooping on one knee, she tugged at a clump of bristly wild millet blades hiding the Tennessee Flagstone's surface. The coarsely chiseled name **Emanuel** and the single date of **April 13, 1955** marked the stone's surface. Beneath the name and date, simply read, **Blessed for a Moment, Love to Last Eternity.**

"Well it looks like someone has been here recently," Gathering brown, brittle remains of a decaying rose from the ground; she cradled them delicately in her palm.

Joining her, Grayson knelt and wiped an open palm over the stymied engraving. "I came here a lot with Gram when I was a kid but never really paid much attention to the markers," He eyed the stone skeptically, his curiosity stoked. "I was a typical little boy back then, more interested in snakes and bugs to be concerned with dead people,"

His expression became empty. "I don't remember Gram ever mentioning anyone named Emanuel," He shrugged and scrambled to his feet, brushing dirt from his hands onto his pant leg.

Sammy Jo stood when the chill of a cool breeze rushed past her, dancing limbs casting lengthening shadows at her feet like ghostly images. Folding her arms over her chest, she shivered.

Grayson saw something flicker in her expression, like the brief moment when the answer to a long awaited question finally makes sense. "Are you okay?" he asked after a moment.

The answer eluded her. She wasn't sure she had been okay since first pulling to a stop in front of Thatcher

Hill a week ago. The old place had plagued her dreams for years, now it tormented every minute of her conscious world.

The estate attracted her over the years like a magnetic pull, and now, standing before generations of Thatcher Hill's lost souls, she felt that same gut wrenching lure. As crazy as it sounded, even to her, she felt as though she belonged to this mountain and it to her. Feeling the heat of Grayson's eyes, she nervously licked her lips.

His hungry gaze fell to the swipe of her tongue, pulling his mouth with it. Cupping his hand at the nape of her neck, he took a deep, shaky breath before gently slanting his lips over hers.

Sammy Jo leaned into him, his body rigid beneath her. Sensations foreign to her took over. Powerless, she swallowed her protest, wrapping her arms tight around his back, digging her fingers into taught flesh. She dissolved in his arms like melting butter, her lips pressed to his. It took all she had not to moan. Her heart thrashed, her slow breath turning to pants.

In that pivotal moment, something clicked, like a key turning in a lock. There was an undeniable connection; standing at the unknown grave, something irrevocable had changed, something linking their destinies for all time.

Pulling back, Grayson glanced at her, held her eyes for a moment, and then turned back towards the grave marker. He too felt the imminent change between them, but neither spoke the words.

Traipsing back through the woods toward the house, a crescent moon hooked above them, casting an ethereal glow over the deck. Ushering the night, the Big Dipper scooped in a sea of blinking stars that seemed close enough to pluck from the sky.

Grayson tucked his hand at Sammy Jo's waist as they stepped onto the deck. Flickering candles had melted to stubs, soft music from the radio lost in the steady song of crickets. Grayson stopped at the table, blowing out the candle flame in a single breath before offering Sammy Jo another glass of wine.

"I really should be leaving. I have an early appointment first thing in the morning,"

"Isn't that one of the perks of being your own boss?" he questioned, sounding hopefully. "You can always change your appointment to later,"

"Unfortunately that's not quite how it works," she replied, with a saucy grin. "I'm meeting with a bride and groom to go over flower choices and then I have some things I need to catch up on at home."

Looking like a little boy robbed of recess; he rolled his eyes and surrendered. "Okay, then when can I see you again?"

A plastered grin chiseled crinkles into the corners of her eyes as she briefly thought about it. "How about Friday night, Karaoke at the town tavern?"

"Karaoke, I don't have to sing do I?"

She stifled a laugh at the vision flashing in her head. "Ah ha! I've finally found something the great Grayson Wesley cannot do," she teased.

"I didn't say I can't. Just that I won't," he corrected, with a wagging finger, leaving her to wonder.

Sammy Jo reached for the screen door, pulling it open. "Pick me up at 8:00," she said, stepping inside the kitchen.

Glancing up approvingly, Martheena sat at the table with a mug of warm buttermilk cupped between twisted fingers, a bright white smile beaconing from a raven complexion. "Well hello Miss Sammy Jo,"

"Good evening Martheena. Did you have a nice dinner with your friend?"

"Certainly did thank you, and how about you kids? Did you enjoy your supper?" Martheena smiled at Grayson, knowing darned well the answer to her own question. The reply plastered across his face was a clear as a mid June morning. She hadn't seen that much joy in him since he was eight years old and Gram Rosaline told him he could keep the mangy, stray mutt he affectionately named Coop.

"It was wonderful," Sammy Jo praised, turning to find Grayson standing right behind her. "Grayson is an amazing cook, which I understand I have you to thank,"

Martheena lifted the mug to her mouth, pausing before taking a drink. "Yep, the boy is a rare find alright, he'd make a good catch," she hinted coyly. After taking a quick sip, she sat the mug on the table rotating it between her hands.

Instead of commenting, Sammy Jo smiled.

Not giving Martheena a chance to add to her raving review, Grayson took Sammy Jo's hand steering her to the doorway. "Sammy Jo has an early meeting. I'm going to walk her out," he said, flitting raised brows across the room like a wagging finger. "Say goodnight Martheena,"

Martheena lifted her cup to her lips hiding a cynical grin. "Good night Miss Sammy Jo," she said above the rim.

"Good night," Sammy Jo replied over her shoulder, while being towed towards the front of the house.

Stepping onto the front porch, a cooling breeze ushered past them. Grayson glared at the rusty red pickup parked out front like a nemesis, dreading the steps separating them from the evenings end. He waited for Sammy Jo to make the first move to the top step before following.

They walked quietly to her to her truck where he cupped his hand at her neck lowering his mouth with a goodnight kiss. After stalling with hopes she would change her mind about the early evening, he pulled opened the truck door and watched her slip gracefully inside. Pushing the door closed, he waited for her to twist the key in the ignition.

Starting the engine, she dropped the truck in reverse. With her foot on the brake, she thanked him for the evening before turning around, glints of red taillights vanishing down the gravel lane. Grayson listened until the rattle of her motor dissolved into the darkness.

Martheena was still sitting at the kitchen table when Grayson wandered through the doorway. Twisting the chair across from her, he straddled it, the delight in his eyes turning solemn. Arms crossed over the back of the chair, he rested his chin on them. "Martheena, can I ask you something?" he asked.

"Sure Scamper, shoot,"

"I've been reading Gram's journal,"

Martheena's lips drew tight in anticipation of his question and he got the strange sense she suspected the subject. When she nodded, he went on. "Why didn't Gram ever remarry?"

Martheena contemplated her answer carefully. "Miss Rosaline said when Cupid's arrow pierces your heart twice; it doesn't make much sense to make yourself an easy target for him a third time,"

Grayson hesitated, drew a single breath and blew it out. "You knew about this Digger fellow?"

She eyed him skeptically from across the table wondering how much Miss Rosaline had documented in her journal. Careful not to divulge any more information than necessary, she nodded, but said nothing.

"Why didn't I ever hear about him?"

"I guess your Gram didn't figure it mattered," Downing the last swallow of buttermilk, she pushed the cup to the side.

"From what I read in her journal, he mattered to her,"

"I suppose," Martheena's posture sagged as she remembered a stormy spring night when tragedy struck Thatcher Hill, a secret neither she nor Rosaline ever spoke of again. "I reckon she didn't figure it mattered that you knew,"

Grayson stared at the floor chewing on his bottom lip. Knowing the circumstances of his Gram's death was like reading the ending to a book first. Knowing way too much to turn back the pages, he had an overwhelming need to know what led up to the epilogue.

"Perhaps," he said, simply.

Martheena scooted her chair out from the table and carried her empty mug to the sink, rinsing it. She turned the cup upside down on the drying board and stared out the window. Wind rustled through the darkened woods, whispering an even darker memory in her head. When she turned around, she folded her arms across her chest, the way she always did when she had something important she wanted him to hear. "You know Scamp; some things are better left buried,"

Fanning the flames of curiosity, her words of caution only heightened the intrigue, his attraction to the past peaking several notches. He wanted to understand Rosaline Worthington, but more importantly, he needed to understand her. Pushing up from the chair, he walked over and took Martheena by the shoulders, pressing his lips to her forehead.

With wasted breath, her words remained unheeded. Grayson's mind was set. Like red reflecting in the black glaze of charging bull's eyes, he had the truth in his sights. "Thanks Martheena," he said quietly.

Martheena had the uncanny feeling that he no more listened to her now than when he was a little boy and she scolded him for poking his fingers in the icing bowl. She watched as he bid goodnight and started for the doorway.

"Scamper,"

Grayson stopped and turned. "Yes?"

"Are you still picking up Rosaline's remains tomorrow morning?"

"First thing in the morning," he replied somberly. "The appointment with the attorney shouldn't take long."

It was a little before noon the next day when Grayson returned to Thatcher Hill. Lifting the burgundy, velvet-sleeved chest from the passenger seat, he pushed the car door closed, cradling the box in his arms. His eyes locked with Martheena's, waiting on the front porch dressed in her Sunday best. Stepping through the gate, he looked up at her, years of memories furrowing deep creases in her face.

She wore her favorite purple, pillbox hat, perched on gray peppered hair, eyes of coal peeking beneath a lacey fringe. Pushing up from the rocker, Martheena steadied herself on weak knees, glistening eyes settling on the package cradled in his arm. Her hand automatically went to the ivory broach pinned to her lapel, a gift from

Rosaline 2 Christmas' ago. Her fingers lingered as she recalled memories of the snowy winter morning.

Mounting the stairs, Grayson offered his arm to Martheena, which she took. "Are you ready?" he asked, with a reassuring smile.

"I reckon as ready as I'll ever be," Her voice was so soft that it was nearly lost to the breeze.

Grayson slowly guided their steps from the porch and through the front gate. The meadow was in his sights, the place his Grandmother had specifically requested in the letter of instructions she left with her attorney.

The day was crisp and clear with a gentle draft sweeping the hillside; hazy ribbons of white decorated a summer sky. As they made their way down the slope, the mountainside near the well came into view, bright orange Poppies peppering a wavering sea of wildflowers. Colorful butterflies flitted from one bloom to the next, their wings lifting in warm bursts of air.

Martheena's hand still clung to the crook of Grayson's arm when they stopped at the edge of streaming color. The waterfall of flowers spilled down the hillside like a map of his grandmother's life, the well marking where a life lost to her was reborn. He could sense history spread before him in whispers of the spring breeze.

Martheena let her fingers slip from the crook of Grayson's arm as he pulled the shiny walnut box from the velvet sleeve he cradled. Holding it before him, he looked at reflective sunshine shimmering from the wood surface.

When he asked if Martheena wanted to say anything, she took a step forward, her eyes filled with misty heartbreak. The tribute of her friend came easily as she spoke of the day Rosaline Worthington offered her the job of housekeeper and cook. From the moment they met, her position in Rosaline's life became clear, not as an employee but as a confidant and lifelong friend. A friendship that lasted decades, a friendship that ushered Rosaline from one life to the next.

Grayson waited for Martheena to finish before continuing with a heartfelt homage of his own. Memorialized not only as a loving grandmother, but also as a special and complex woman, Rosaline's life continued to captivate him, even in death. His heart broke with the realization she was gone forever, leaving him with distant memories that would fade with time.

As Grayson finished speaking, Martheena's soulful hum of Amazing Grace began almost instinctively, one of Rosaline's favorite hymns. The air filled with emotional song as Grayson lifted the lid from the polished wood box. Rosaline's ashes lifted in a burst of warm summer air, like a freed soul taking flight from this world. A pair of butterflies flitted from a rainbow of blooms, disappearing along with the Earthly remains of Rosaline Worthington.

Slipping the box back into the velvet sleeve, Grayson blinked back stinging tears. Reaching for Martheena's hand, he coaxed her slowly, silent heartbreak guiding their steps up the hill.

After Martheena disappeared inside, Grayson sat on the porch, the gentle squeak of the rocker guiding his mind to distant summers on Thatcher Hill. He reminisced of his love and relationship with Rosaline. Hours spent exploring the grounds, intrigue and fascination of a young boy's imagination guided his thoughts through the years.

A squall of Bobwhite quail flushed from the meadow, bursting into flight, a frantic flutter of wings drawing his attention. Grayson watched them disappear over the ridge, his eyes sinking to the well house, bordered by a display of wavering wildflowers. The same youthful intrigue that once fueled his exploration as a boy drove his mind to images of a secret life his Gram shared with a man she called Digger.

After sharing a silent lunch with Martheena, Grayson retrieved the journal from his room, returned to a warm summer breeze blowing across the porch and retreated to the summer of 1954.

The yellowed pages of Rosaline's journal painted a graphic picture of a budding romance between the lonely widow of Thatcher Hill and a young laborer named Digger. Beginning as an innocent friendship, the relationship soon blossomed into an undeniable and forbidden bond. Quiet dinners and moonlit strolls led to rare chemistry bearing no boundaries of age. Bound by the yellowing pages of life, the story of Rosaline's life evolved.

It was one such evening after dinner, followed by a nightly stroll, when Rosaline and Digger retired to the front porch. Grayson read his Gram's account, words from the past transporting him to the beginning.

After dinner, I slipped from the rocker and asked Digger to wait for me on the porch. When I told him I had a surprise for him, he rubbed a palm across dark stubbles of his jaw, brows squishing, as they often did.

I slanted him a grin and pulled open the door disappearing inside, only to return a few minutes later with a chocolate layer cake, decorated with one burning candle. Before he had a chance to ask, I explained. He had shared with me once that he had never had a birthday party. There is always a first for everything and I hope this will be the first of many celebrations together.

Digger pushed up from the rocker he was sitting in and stared into the flickering flame of the single candle. "But it's not my birthday Rosie,"

I told him that every day is a good day to celebrate life, today as well as any to begin.

When he told me that he did not know what to say, I asked him to say nothing, just close his eyes, make a wish, and blow out the candle. I watched his face animate with the reflection of a child. It breaks my heart that he has missed so much, yet makes me happy for the memory of this night.

Squeezing his eyes closed, Digger made his effortless wish, drew a breath and held it for a heartbeat before blowing the flame from the candle.

After he thanked me, I told him that no birthday party is complete without a gift. Reaching in my apron pocket, I pulled out a small box wrapped in shiny foil paper, holding it in the palm of my hand. My fingers quivered, I was as excited as he was, maybe a bit more.

Digger looked at the box and hesitated. I nudged the box closer and he took it. With trembling fingers, he slowly pulled the wrapping loose, opening the small black box. Nesting on a bed of fleecy cotton, rested a gold pocket watch. Without as much as touching the polished gold, he handed it back to me, refusing to accept such a costly gift.

I took the box from his hand and removed the watch, revealing his initials etched in fancy scroll on the backside. Dangling the timepiece before him, it gently swayed as glints of porch light glistened from the polished surface. I smiled with justification. The watch bears his initials and is of no use to me or anyone else. Taking a single step closer, I brushed the back of my fingers across his cheek and I told him that I was the one who received a gift. The watch symbolizes more than lost birthdays. It represents two paths crossed, a ribbon in time, forever weaving our destinies.

I waited for what seemed like an eternity before Digger finally took the watch from my hand. He stared at it and thanked me, admitting that he has never had anything so special.

My hand instinctively closed over his, calming his trembling fingers. Every ticking second, I will be thankful for the blessing of our time together. I tried not thinking

about what the future holds, only what the present has
given us.

Bright sunshine melted behind the western cliffs, gray clouds taking its place when Martheena appeared in the doorway, hauling Grayson's attention from the brittle pages. "Your supper's getting cold Scamper, are you going to come in and eat?" she asked, from a wedge in the screen door.

He closed the pages, staring ahead at the thin line of purple drifting from the eastern sky. Sucking in the faint smell of distant rain, a sinking feeling in his stomach dragged his mood with it. "I'm really not hungry Martheena. Would you mind sitting my plate in the fridge?"

Martheena's face drew tight, lines of worry creasing her forehead. She prayed that the secret Rosaline had taken to the grave would not come as a fateful blow to his grandmother's memory. The story she was certain left scrolled in the pages of Rosaline's diary would no doubt shed new light on the woman he knew and loved as a grandmother. Silently, Martheena let the door ease closed.

Grayson closed the pages on the journal, clipping it in his hand. Clambering from the chair, he strolled to the edge of the porch and leaned a shoulder against a freshly painted white column, his eyes wandering along a bending path to the tack room, the place a young laborer once called home.

The barn sat in a ravine, hugged by a steep incline on the eastern side. Honeysuckle crept from dense cover of timber, surrounding the structure like a vining barricade. With the leather bound pages tucked in his hand, Grayson stepped down from the porch, drawn along the pebbled trail.

Hesitating at the faded red barn, he jerked his fingers through his hair and craned his neck to the side, before pushing open the side door leading to the tack room. He stepped inside and breathed the pungent smell of dust and hay filling the dark space. The preamble of a brewing storm zipped a stray lightning bolt through outlying clouds, flashing a quick glance at the shadowy 12' x 12' corner of the barn. Reaching for the light switch next to the door, he turned it on and watched as a dim, hazy glow from a bare ceiling bulb revealed contents of the long abandoned room frozen in time.

A single cot wedged in the corner still bore a faded ticking covered mattress of down. A wooden crate sat next to it, toppled on its side. Once used as a makeshift table, it held a kerosene lantern, still filled with oil, the globe bearing a jagged crack. His gaze veered around the room to the wall of pegs holding various bridles and ropes, to a tall clapboard cabinet missing one of its doors. Aging cans and buckets lined the cabinet shelves, seemingly stitched together by dusty threads of yesteryear. The only other furnishing in the room was a ladder back chair, the hand woven seat tattered with time. Grayson's imagination flashed on images of another time, when a dark and handsome young man from Gram's past called the modest tack room home.

Walking a slow circle around the room, Grayson felt the need to swipe years of webs from the bridles, touch the rickety cabinet and sit on the dust-laden cot. As if his touch brought the past to life, he scooted back on the cot, leaned against the wall, cracked open the journal and began reading in the dim light. The horizon outside deepened to a darker shade of violet as a steady rain began dripping from the muted sky.

June 9, 1954

The day began as any other with the rooster's first call of dawn, routine chores and then breakfast of sugar cured ham, fresh eggs gathered before daylight from the roost and hot buttermilk biscuits.

It was nearing noon when Digger appeared at the back door, his hand wrapped in a blood covered feed sack. I turned from the sink at the sound of door hinges, drying my hands on a towel.

Cradled in soaked burlap, Digger's hand dripped red. His reassurance that the injury was just a scrape was anything but reassuring. The bell clanging recognition from the soaked material covering his hand quickly convinced me otherwise.

After discovering a wedge of dangling flesh, I rewrapped his hand in fresh linen and rushed him to town. Doc Higgins placed 14 stitches to close the tip of his index finger, nearly lost to the blade of a saw.

It was not until we returned to Thatcher Hill did my pounding heart return to normal rhythm. Once again, the realization of life's frailty nearly caused my chest to explode. I thought about losing Isaac and feared my future, feared that my happiness belonged to a ticking time bomb. After Digger left for the tack room, I sat alone in the kitchen and wept.

Dinner was quiet tonight. After finishing, we retreated to the front porch where nighttime settled over Thatcher Hill, winks of starlight glistening beyond the full, strawberry moon. Cool mountain air wrapped around the house, the chatter of cicadas competing with a hedge of chirping crickets.

After slow conversation of the day went quiet, Digger stood from the rocker and bid me goodnight, just as he did every night. But, tonight was different, when he reached the stairs, his hand lingered on a pillar and he stopped, turning around. As if seeing me for the first time, his gaze settled on my eyes, the corner of his mouth gently curving.

I sat in the dim glow of the porch light, quietly rocking, hands folded in my lap. I could feel strands of moon kissed copper lift in the breeze, fanning across my face. Tucking a strand behind my ear, I returned his smile.

Without saying a word, Digger ambled towards me, his steps slow and steady. He reached down to me with his good hand. I hesitated briefly, watching the tremble of his fingers, before placing my palm in his. Instinctively, he drew me from the chair. An awakening in his eyes told me that everything between us was about to change.

Inching his lips close, we kissed for the first time. My heart beat once again with a passion that I thought was all but lost, the spirit of woman reborn. When I pulled back and looked into eyes of coal, I saw the reflection of a woman in love.

Beneath the stars, soft hands of experience caressed the essence of innocence. Pure virtue of the budding man within took me back to the beginning, when my heart beat with a hunger for life, when I craved to be whole. With all boundaries erased, we became one in a place where there was no age, no defining tenets, simply two people sharing the ecstasies of an unyielding love beneath the moonlight.

Closing the pages on his grandmother's past, Grayson reflected on scribbled words of love, fervor sensed between each line. Gram's story of passion was both a blessing and a curse. Digger's love could offer her happiness she had lost to death, or earn her condemnation of an unforgiving people. In a time when unsanctioned love was considered both immoral and wrong, her newfound affection dangled before her like Eden's apple, a forbidden desire.

Sensing he was not alone, Grayson looked up at the open tack room door, fully expecting Martheena with a reminder of the late hour. Instead, he saw blackness shadowing the trail beyond. The damp, kicking wind eased the door back and forth on creaky hinges.

He blew out a breath, slid from the cot and killed the light, pulling the tack room door closed behind him as he left. Trudging toward the house, the muddied path sucked heavy soles like wet concrete. A lull in the rain left behind heavy humidity covering the path in dense fog, a weight mimicking arduous thoughts. Dark clouds filtered past an occasional glimpse of a hazy crescent moon, lending just enough light to mark his way. The warning of a second fast moving cold front sounded in distant rumbles of thunder, a prelude to turbulent weather, common during heated southern months.

Despite the late hour, Grayson was still as bright eyed as a Monday morning judge when he reached the house. Gram's diary left his brain lapping double time as he imagined the torrid affair with a young man who had healed her broken heart, a young man who offered love just beyond her reach. Dropping into a rocker, he watched distant lightening outline erupting clouds blocking the Eastern horizon. Thoughts of his Gram circled in his head, the woman he loved and admired and the woman he never knew.

It was near 2:00 A.M. when rain began steadily falling from a pitch-black sky, pinging against the metal roof. Soon the vivid images in his head faded to exhaustion, ushering him inside.

Chapter 12

Raw nerves fed by fatigue, guided Grayson upstairs to his bedroom. Propping a fan in the open window, he turned it on high, angling the damp, pine scented breeze towards the bed. After dropping his jeans and tee shirt to the floor, he flicked off the bedside lamp and dropped across the mattress, lacing his fingers behind his head. Staring at the blank ceiling, he searched for answers to mounting question in his head. The more he read of his grandmother's past, the more he hungered to know. An hour slipped by with no more answers than when he had come upstairs. The sedating hum of fan blades and steady patter of rain against the metal eventually lulled Grayson to sleep.

It seemed he had no sooner closed his eyes than they popped open, his head pounding in rhythm to thunder rolling over Thatcher Hill like a giant bowling ball. Jerked from sleepy by a wicked, howling wind, he sat up in the bed, the sound of soaked curtains snapping whirling fan blades. The room was dark with an occasional zigzagging line ripping through a black sky, flashes of white exploding over bedroom walls.

Sitting up on the side of the bed, he raked an open palm over his jaw shadowed by a day's worth of dark stubbles. Noting the digital neon numbers of his alarm clock rolling from 4:44 to 4:45, he cupped his hand to the nape of his neck, wrenching stiff muscles with a moan. It was too early to get up and the deep throbbing in his head bellowed that it was too late to try to go back to sleep.

Effects of the raging storm and restless night left him both wide-awake and frustrated. The sheets had pulled loose from the mattress and the bedspread lay crumpled on the floor, results of his recent wrestling match with an unhinged subconscious.

He leaned on folded arms and when another white flash shot through the window, an eerie awareness caught from the corner of his eye. He flipped on the lamp, his focus drawn to the crystal face of the pocket watch lying on the night table next to Gram's journal. The dim glow of the light shimmered across the shiny surface, the reflection broken by unexpected movement.

Grayson's heart skipped a beat before recoiling to his back with shell shock that sucked the air from his lungs. Another look at the timepiece and the second-hand of the watch began a slow, steady tick. With time unleashed, the minute hand meticulously moved from 4:45 to 4:46.

It can't be...but it was...

Grayson inched towards the head of the bed, pausing several seconds for his heart to steady. Looking at the watch again, he hoped that he'd been duped by his overactive imagination. After all, he had fished several bizarre stories from his head over the years, put them on paper and sold them to imaginative millions... but this was one story even his readers would not believe.

Cinching his eyes and holding his breath, he silently counted to three before opening them again.

Well that didn't work...

The damn minute hand on the pocket watch meticulously ticked from 4:46 to 4:47. With the frozen past at last free, time moved forward with a loud deafening tick.

Grayson perched on the side of the bed watching each tick of the minute hand, as if close-scrutiny would somehow change the passing of time.

It didn't...

He was still staring at the watch when dawn peeked from the mountains, a ginger haze blanketing the room. The storm had long rolled past the ridge, rumbles of distant thunder growing faint until the sound diminished completely. The only evidence left behind was nature's fresh smell of pine-laced lilac, and the occasional drip from Elm leaves sounding against the metal roof.

After a hot shower and shave, Grayson trailed the aroma of fresh ground Columbian beans downstairs for a much-needed cup. He filled the largest mug he could find, omitting the usual superfluities of cream and sugar. After the night he had, he needed the big boy stuff... strong and straight up.

Martheena sat in a chair next to the kitchen table, a bowl filled with green beans straddling her wide lap. Obviously, she had been up for hours. Proof was in the oversized pot on the stove and half-empty bushel basket of half runners she had picked up at Tuesday's farmer market. Looking up briefly with a bright smile, she reached into her bowl with twisted fingers and pulled out a bean. Snapping off the end, she broke it in half and tossed it in the near full bowl on the table.

"Well good mornin'," she greeted. "Hungry?"

Grayson shook his head, leaned against the counter and blew the steam from his cup before taking a sip. "Thanks, but I think I'm good with just coffee this morning," He sat his mug on the counter, reached for the white porcelain percolator on the stove and walked over refilling Martheena's empty cup. "Looks like you have your work cut out for you today," he noted, the coffee pot hanging mid-air. "Why do you go to all that trouble anyway? That's what grocery stores are for," He saw beady eyes of admonishment glowering at him and raised a hand in surrender. "Forget I even said that," he recanted, turning back to the stove.

His gentle smile eased Martheena's eyebrows back into place as he crossed the kitchen, replacing the pot to the burner.

Picking up his mug, he joined her at the table, reaching into the basket for a handful of beans. After stringing and breaking several pods, he perhaps answered his own question. With the calming effect of simple, southern gratification, his heart fell into a slow, calming pace.

"What do you have planned for today? Are ya' gonna' see Sammy Jo?" Martheena's voice sounded hopeful. Digging into her bowl for another bean, she watched him beneath a rim of black lashes.

"I actually thought I'd take a walk, then maybe try my luck at some writing," Reaching for another bean, he strung it before snapping it in half. "I'm running late on a book deadline. My agent has been breathing down my neck for a rough draft,"

Spending the next thirty minutes stringing and breaking beans, Grayson drained his third cup of coffee and disappeared into the woods through the back door.

Outside, the morning was crisp and clear, temperatures already capping the 70's, foretelling of a hot summer day. The sky was a brilliant blue in every direction, not a cloud in sight. The air was a bit muggy from the previous night storm, a thin layer of haze hovering at the forest edge.

Dense trees darkened the path as his stroll drew him deeper into the forest. Passing the "Y" that marked the way, Grayson found himself at the small, unknown headstone, as if his mind had been set on automatic all along.

Recalling his kiss with Sammy Jo the night before and the strange presence that he knew they both sensed... his imagination exploded with the powerful force of dynamite. His writer's block crumbled to dust, inspiration settling in his mind with a plot twist for his novel that would have left Sherlock Holmes scratching his head. For the first time in weeks, the dialogue for Chapter 13 trickled into place.

At a hastened clip, Grayson sprinted back to the house, ducking beneath low hanging branches, hurdling decaying remains of a fallen log. Skipping the bottom two steps of the back deck, he rushed into the kitchen, stopping for a heartbeat to catch his breath. With a wide grin, he scurried past Martheena standing at the sink, mumbling something over his shoulder about getting it out of his head before he lost it.

Twisting the cap on a filled Mason jar, Martheena shook her head, daring not to imagine what had lit a fire under the boy's tail. Obviously, he had no time to explain. With a solid smile, she watched him disappear around the corner his feet pounding every other step.

Not only did Grayson's newfound revelation aim him in a new direction for his novel, it had restored his loss of enthusiasm and eagerness to write. Journalism had always been what gave him his sense of adventure and inspiration. Each time he began typing, his words drew him deep into another life, a new world. With his fingers on the keyboard, he became master of his existence, creator of his own demise.

As of late, his world was spinning out of control and so was his writing. With creativity extinguished, the ending of his latest book snuffed like a flame in the wind. At the end of chapter twelve, he placed a period, which transformed into a massive barrier, a story without an ending. He may as well have written, *THE END*, all in bold italics, because the story in his head skidded to a halt. That was before he studied the inscription of the small, modest grave marker, igniting a spark of imagination into a blaze of motivation.

Chapter 13

Shoving the bedroom door open at the top of the stairs, Grayson reached for his Italian, leather computer case tucked in the corner, throwing the strap across his left shoulder. His mind was spinning possible plot scenarios for his novel like a Vegas roulette wheel, waiting for the final winner to fall into place.

At the bottom of the stairs, Martheena's deep baritone of a Loretta Lynn classic mingled with the clatter of Mason jars, dropping into the canning pot. Stopping by the kitchen for a cold drink, Grayson dropped the weight of the computer bag from his arm onto a kitchen chair.

"I'm headed down to the tack room to do a little writing," he said, tugging open the refrigerator door.

Martheena slanted him a glance from across the room. "The tack room?"

He pulled out a bottle of root beer and unscrewed the cap. Bringing the bottle to his lips, he hesitated before taking a drink. "Yea, I thought it would be cooler down there, maybe the change in scenery will stimulate the old brain." Watching her from the corner of his eye, he took a swig from the amber colored bottle.

Martheena shrugged. "Don't matter none to me where ya' write your stories," Lifting another blue, glass jar by the lid, she lowered it with a set of long tongs into the simmering water. "Saved enough of these for a pot of beans and ham hocks, I suppose you will be up later to eat…" Her motherly glare made the question seem more like a demand.

"Yes mam, when have you ever known of me to miss a dinner of ham and green beans,"

"Good, I guess that's settled then," Martheena wiped her hands on her apron before busying herself with slicing fresh peaches, drying on the cutting board.

Grayson smiled, and snatched his computer case from the chair, tossing the strap over his shoulder. "If you need anything, you know where you can find me,"

Twisting the knob on the tack room door, Grayson nudged it open, wandering inside. A gray mouse scurried over the toe of his shoe and he wasn't sure who was startled more, him or the mouse. With an ambiguous grin, he flipped the switch of the single bulb, casting a dim, ruddy glow over the space he had visited the night before. Scoping the room for additional light but finding none, he dropped his case on the dust-laden cot and made his way through the creaky slat door that adjoined the tack room to the open barn.

It had been years since he had been in there, yet not much had changed. Hazy light filtered through four eastern windows, shedding illuminated silhouettes over a dirt floor. Although it had been decades since livestock occupied that corner of the barn, it still reeked of hay and manure.

The hood of Grandpa Isaac's John Deere peeked beneath a gray, tattered canvas, green paint dulled by dust and time. He remembered climbing in the seat as a boy, pretending it could take him places only a young lad could imagine. With a smile, he wondered if maybe that was the beginning of an overactive imagination that made him three time winner of Pulitzer Prize for Fiction, and two time victor of the Nobel Prize in Literature.

Try as he might, he could not resist the urge to yank the canvas from the hood, a plume of dust erupting into stale air. A cough followed by two sneezes forced him to the back corner of the barn where he discovered a horse stall, stocked with a lucky find of cast off furnishing from the house.

Dragging the gate open, he rummaged through a crate and located an early circa, tarnished brass lamp, the bulb still screwed in the socket. Almost magically, wedged in the corner, a small roll top desk caught his attention from the corner of his eye. Wriggling between the wood box and wall, he wiped his hand over the dust-laden piece, vaguely recalling it in Grams parlor many years ago.

After freeing the crate from the stall, he dragged the desk from its resting place, across the dirt floor, jerking it the last few feet, through the tack room door. Angling it beneath the window, he stepped back with hands on his hips and nodded a satisfied smile. Not exactly luxury accommodations of his New Hampshire loft, more like a command center of inspiration. Finally, he slid the tattered ladder back chair into place, the perfect fit.

The computer felt good in his hands, like an extension of his body. He rolled back the desktop and sat it down, powering the laptop on. Easing his weight carefully onto the chair, he waited nervously for the crack of wood. It had no doubt been years since anyone had sat on it.

As the computer screen flashed on, Grayson limbered his fingers, logged in and scooted the chair closer to the desk, wiping clammy palms on his jeans. His nerves were banjo string tight, one-half turn from snapping. It felt a bit like his first time, a little naïve and exciting all at the same time.

A painstaking ten seconds passed, the computer desktop flashing, icons dropping into place one by one. The processor had been in longer hibernation than a mid-winter Alaskan grizzly, taking its time to load. Cupping his hand at the back of his neck, Grayson stretched tight muscles and took a deep breath, with an intentional slow exhale.

Clicking the mouse twice, he opened the notorious manuscript file, the daunting, blank page of Chapter 13 staring up at him. There it was… the ominous chapter where failure began. Weeks had passed, an impenetrable wall blocking his story. He chewed at his bottom lip, his eyes boring a hole into the bold, black caption.

Maybe there is reasonable logic why superstitious engineers omit level 13 from building plans and people both dread and fear Friday the 13th. He grumbled below his breath with a second thought, admitting that maybe those are also the very reasons why people end up in little padded rooms; he shook the thought from his head. It was just a number…he tried convincing himself.

Plunging head first into words swimming in his brain, nimble fingers began typing, slowly at first, then kicking up speed. A cemented writer's block began crumbling, one word at a time.

Opening a locked door on his imagination, inspiration fell out like proverbial skeletons from a closet. By the time Chapter 13 ended, the mid-day sun had moved directly overhead, the afternoon temperature spiking 80 degrees. The cool, shaded air of the tack room dissipated, leaving behind the stifling heat of a hot box. Hot, thirsty and satisfied with his cunning plot twist; Grayson closed the manuscript file and headed up the dirt trail leading to the main house.

He was barely though the front gate when the salty aroma of ham and beans melded into the sweet scent of fresh baked peach cobbler.

Mounting the porch steps two at a time Grayson swung open the screen door and turned into the kitchen.

Martheena leaned into a whirling fan wedged in the window above the sink, ebony skin glistening with damp achievement. Tight rows of freshly canned green beans lined the cupboard, a still warm cobbler cooling on the window ledge, fruits of an afternoon's labor.

She turned and was happy to see him, even happier when he pulled open the refrigerator pulling out a cold drink with the announcement he was driving to Highland for a surprise visit to Sammy Jo. Her feelings toward the farm fed beauty of Highland were no secret. In many ways, Sammy Jo reminded Martheena of a young Rosaline, all the gifts of a prize pickin' in one package... spry, independent and a beauty to boot.

Grime powdered the hood of Grayson's black BMW as he turned onto the dirt road of Wilcox Farm. Plumes of gray dust rolled from the under carriage like smoke signals. Obviously, the torrential rainfall dumped on Thatcher Hill the night before bypassed Highland all together, leaving the fine powdery surface of summer intact.

In the rippling creek ahead, Grayson spotted Stewart, darting back and forth, bouncing paws competing in a game of catch the frog. He smiled when overzealous Labrador temperament landed the dog smack dab in the middle of the water, shaking droplets from wet fur in afterthought. Downshifting into the shadows of the covered bridge, the car idled, emerging from the other side, Stewart quickly gaining on the bumper with a hasty bark.

Almost immediately, Grayson spotted Sammy Jo near the barn, standing knee high in Fescue. She wore classic cut-off jeans and an oversized tee, western boots capping shapely calves. Looping a noose over Sadie's head, she was obviously oblivious to the car rolling slowly down the lane. Bypassing the house, Grayson pulled to a stop near the pasture, poking a hand out the window as Sammy Jo glanced up, a surprised smile at the alerting bark.

Jerking at the rope, Sadie clopped lazily behind Sammy Jo, occasionally loitering for a quick nip of swaying blades. Grayson was already out of the car, leaning against the closed door with one ankle crossing the other, arms folded over his chest when she tugged Sadie through the gate.

"This is certainly a nice surprise," she said. Easing on tiptoes, she pecked his lips with a teasing kiss, Sadie's head nudging past her.

"Saturday is a long way off," he said, panning his fingers over Sadie's velvety muzzle.

Sammy Jo watched sunlight glimmer in hazel eyes and for a second imagined there was more to his unexpected visit.

"How did your appointment go this morning?" he asked, avoiding the purpose of his visit.

"Roses and daisies," Sammy Jo declared decisively, patting the velvet of Sadie's nose with an open palm. "My favorite wedding bouquet,"

"Are brides usually that easy?" he asked.

"Who said the decision was easy?" With a quirky smile, she gave two quick tugs to the rope, urging Sadie around the side of the barn where a bucket of soapy water awaited. Grayson followed.

Without hesitation, Sammy Jo twisted on the hose spicket, giving the animal a good soaking before slipping her hand into the leather strap of a brush. Dunking the brush in a bubble-filled bucket, the grateful mare gave a quick snap of her tail, sending a shower of water droplets through the air. No need for prompting, Sadie moved closer and waited for the much-anticipated stroke of suds across her wet coat, glistening in the sunshine.

Sammy Jo angled the brush from Sadie's back down her ribs and got the distinct impression something more than bridal bouquets was on Grayson's mind, yet he still said nothing. Instead, he straddled a bale of hay watching the hypnotizing slip of the sudsy brush over Sadie's back. It was not until Sammy Jo reached for the hose and began rinsing the lather from Sadie did he speak.

"Sammy Jo, there's something I want to talk to you about,"

There it was...the mysterious more...

"Sure, what is it?" she asked over her shoulder, finishing the rinse of Sadie's sudsy mane.

"Do you believe in life after death?" he asked bluntly.

"You mean heaven and hell?"

Grayson shirked. "I guess, more to the point, do you think loved ones can reach us after they're gone?" he rattled like a drunken sailor. Delusional mystery plots fermenting in his head were finally taking a toll on his sane thinking.

Sammy Jo dropped the hose, water splashing across the toe of her boot. Expecting there was more he wanted to talk about, she sure did not see that one coming.

"Never really thought about it, why?" She grimaced. Turning her back to him, she cranked the spicket closed. Thinking about the secret she was keeping, her mind jolted to the eerie past of Thatcher Hill.

And she was afraid he would think *she* was crazy...

"I didn't sleep much last night," he confessed. "Maybe its Gram's journal...maybe it's the grave we found. Hell, maybe I'm losing it," he added, his voice sounding a mile away.

Joining him on the hay bale, Grayson scooted over and made room for her. Sammy Jo continued watching him through narrowed eyes, waiting for an explanation.

"A storm woke me just before dawn this morning." He plucked a piece of straw from the bale, poking it between his teeth. Chewing nervously at the wedged blade, he continued. "I picked up the pocket watch from the bedside table and..." He looked away for a moment and when his eyes returned, something had changed. His expression stirred into a mixture of confusion and fear. He heaved a breath and blew it out. "The watch began running Sammy Jo..." he spat.

She shrugged and dug deep in her long list of rational explanations, trying to make sense of his revelation. "I guess that could happen. Maybe it was taking it out of the damp cellar," she thought about it for a moment and added, "I guess it's not impossible that it would dry out and just start running again,"

"In perfect time Sammy Jo," A dark brow hooked above his eye. "The watch began running in perfect time," he repeated. He drew the words out slowly, their impact as swift and hard as a dropping sledgehammer. He nearly choked on the confession, realizing how crazy it sounded. Instantly, he regretted telling her, but it was too late, the feral feline was out of the bag.

Scrambling to her feet, Sammy Jo stared down at him, her skin taking on a grayish pallor. She realized her attempt at logic was a complete and total failure. Silence following his confession left her wearing a confused expression. She worried that maybe discovery of his Gram's journal, along with the mystery grave, was causing his mind to slip a little.

Well…maybe, a lot…

The lines in her face were brittle. Like the lightest movement may cause her expression to shatter. Pondering his revelation, she hooked her thumbs through her belt loops, not sure what to say.

No longer was she worried he was losing his mind, she was looking *crazy* square dead in the eye…

Quietly, she digested his admission, her brain simmering like a pot of winter soup. Surely, there had to be an explanation and she was not sure a ghost was the logical choice.

"The damn watch just started running," he echoed, unsure if he was trying to convince her, or himself.

Sammy Jo's eyes questioned his before she walked back to Sadie, a long sigh punctuating her thoughts. Try as she may, she could not summon a rational response.

"You must think I'm a nut case," Following her, Grayson placed his hand on her shoulder from behind.

No comment...

He dropped his hand, turned and ran a palm down Sadie's flaxen mane, waiting in the silence. When Sammy Jo did not reply, he spun around and dragged heavy feet towards his car. That had to be the most tactful rejection he had ever received from a woman.

"Wait, where are you going?" she called out from behind him.

Grayson stopped and turned, throwing both hands in the air. Flicking his eyes to the sky long enough to find the words, he looked back at her. "I know this all sounds crazy Sammy Jo, it sounds crazy to me,"

She nodded slowly not knowing what to say. It did sound crazy, but just like her childhood dreams of Thatcher Hill, there had to be a logical explanation... *at least she hoped there was, or maybe they both need long-term therapy.*

Dipping her head towards the barn door, she snatched up Sadie's rope in her hand and gave it a swift tug with a quick step forward. "Bolt needs his bath next," she said.

Chapter 14

Sammy Jo led Sadie to her stall, flipping the gate latch before calling to Bolt. As if Sammy Jo's intentions were obvious, the Stallion made quick strides towards the swinging gate, anxiously nuzzling his nose into the noose she dangled. He followed her lead to the open barn door, his tail contentedly swishing in anticipation.

Grayson trailed Sammy Jo from the barn into the sunshine, but said nothing. After they rounded the side of the building, he returned to his seat on the bale of hay, dangling clasped hands between his legs. His head drooped, staring at the damp soil beneath his feet

"You're not getting off that easy," Aiming the water hose in his direction, Sammy Jo pulled the trigger and giggled. Grayson popped up from the hay bale like a Jack in the Box, shrieking a squeal that sounded more like a pig with its tail caught in the door.

"Damn Sammy Jo! You could've just said you wanted help," With a shudder that worked its way from the ground up, he yanked the icy, well water drenched tee shirt over his head, flinging it to the ground.

Sammy Jo was still laughing when he sprinted toward her, sunshine glistening from a rippling chest. Snatching the hose from her hand, he flashed a dubious grin that rested somewhere between mischievous and wicked.

"Don't you dare," she warned, throwing both hands up with a quick step back. Her laugh faded, replaced with the dramatic pout of a lower lip.

"Or what?" Inching dangerously close, icy water droplets splattered on her boot.

"That water's freezing," she said, wiggling behind Bolt for cover.

"You don't say," The corner of his lip curled playfully, as he contemplated the idea of a wet tee shirt.

Her eyes trickled across Grayson's bare chest, and then down bulging, goose bump covered biceps. The warmth igniting her insides made her wonder if a good soaking was not exactly what the doctor ordered.

"Is it too late to ask for help?" she whined, doleful eyes peeking over cover of Bolt's back.

Mentioning nothing more of the mysteriously running watch, Thatcher Hill or ghostly visits, they spent the next two hours bathing Bolt, and shoveling steaming, manure piles from the horse stalls. Sammy Jo teased the city slicker about his inexperience in *poop scooping*, but secretly noted there could not be a farm hand within 100 miles that could rival the deep tanned, brawny physique anchoring her attention with ironclad fixation. She found it a relief when Grayson finally slipped his sun-dried tee shirt over his head, hiding fleshy temptation from sight.

It was nearing suppertime when Grayson left Wilcox Farm, headed back to Burlington. He watched in the rear view mirror as Sammy Jo sat on the front porch step, a cold glass of sweet tea pressed to her sweat-dampened forehead. She had to be the most beautiful creature he had ever laid eyes on, barring none. Yet the look on her face when he told her about the running watch haunted him. He suspected total disappointment in her reflection, learning the man she believed him to be was a sham, nothing short of a fruitcake.

Sammy Jo let a long held breath seep from her lungs, watching Grayson's car disappear down the long gravel lane. As hard as she tried, his revelation about the running watch made about as much sense as her recurring dreams of Thatcher Hill. Both were impossible, yet both achingly real. She took a long drink from her glass, sitting it down alongside Grayson's empty glass on the step. Her mind pinged on images of the vast estate perched high on a hill.

Two quick honks of a horn yanked her attention from thoughts of Grayson and Thatcher Hill, to Pop's navy blue Ford pickup bounding up the lane, dust billowing behind. Surprised by his early arrival, she jumped to her feet, stepping down to meet him as he emerged from the other side of the covered bridge, pulling to a stop in front of the house.

Arm propped out the open window, he twisted the key in the engine, pipe dangling precariously from the corner of his mouth. "I passed fancy pants on the way in. What business did he have here?"

Sammy Jo smiled, patting Jim on the arm. "Well hello to you too Pops," she said, before swinging open the truck door. "How was your trip?"

Jim slid from the seat, planting both feet on the ground, before wrenching his stiff back. Pulling the pipe from his mouth, he pressed his lips to Sammy Jo's forehead. "Okay, I guess," he replied, turning toward the bed of his truck.

Hooking her arm through his, she followed her grandfather as he took a step forward. "I thought you weren't due back until Saturday,"

"Finished up early," Poking the pipe between his teeth, he reached in the bed of the truck with his free hand and pulled out the green canvas bag from his army days, tossing it over his shoulder. "Well, you still haven't said, what did ole' fancy pants want?"

"Stopped by to say hi," she answered, evasively. Tugging at her grandfather's arm, she steered him toward the house. "Hungry?"

Jim knew trying to drag information from his granddaughter when she did not want to talk, was like threading a bull through a needle, so instead of pressing further, he nodded and trailed her inside.

The next two days were gruelingly long for both Sammy Jo and Grayson, speaking briefly on the phone once. Grayson called to confirm that he would pick her up at the ranch on Saturday at 6:00, a brief conversation that lasted only a couple of minutes.

Friday Grayson washed and spit shined his car to the point his reflection was sharp enough to talk back. He was leaving nothing to chance when it came to impressing the southern beauty from Highland. A quick trip to town netted him a new pair of western boots with custom, silver toe tips and a plaid western shirt. Foregoing the Stetson, bull hide cowboy hat suggested by the sales clerk, he figured the whole John Wayne look might be a tad over the top.

Up early, before 6:00 A.M. on Saturday morning, Grayson stayed busy all afternoon. He finished edits on Chapter 14 of his novel, as well as a telephone conference with his publicist, mulling over release dates and book signing engagements. It was near 4:00 when he finished his call, dropping his cell phone in his shirt pocket. Pulling the tack room door closed behind him, he went up to the house to shower and change before for his first official outing with Sammy Jo.

Sammy Jo's Saturday afternoon was not nearly as lucrative as Grayson's. She too was up early, far before sunrise, went to the shop and tried her hand at some bookkeeping, which quickly proved a bad idea. After failing to balance her bank account, she broke two vases and slammed her finger in a desk drawer. Shattering the coffee decanter was the last straw. She decided it was time to go home and tear into the grueling task of finding something to wear for her date.

Just as suspected, her disappointing wardrobe choices quickly outnumbered the gains in her checkbook. Sailing over her shoulder went a white, lacey blouse, much too prissy, then the rodeo tee, a last minute purchase from TSC with a bag of chicken feed last week, much too casual. One shirt after another added to the quickly growing pile on the floor. Snatching a turquoise green sundress from the very back of her closet, she hesitated before tossing it, cupping the waist against her instead.

Bingo...

Accessorizing with a braided leather belt, mid-calf boots and sterling hoop earrings, she gave one final look in the full-length mirror, pleased with her choice. Not too fussy, her selection added just enough femininity to captivate the opposite sex, Grayson Wesley, her intended target.

Sammy Jo was sitting on the porch swing, hands folded in her lap, staring down the long lane when she at last caught sight of Grayson's BMW. Glistening like a polished stone in the setting sun, the speeding car jolted from one side of the path to the other.

Stepping to the edge of the porch, she met Grayson as he pulled to a stop out front, the low rumble of the engine growing silent. Her bare shoulder leaned on the post, her eyes wandering to the unopened car door in anticipation.

Grayson pushed the door open and poked out one cowboy boot clad foot, followed by a second. Slipping from the seat he let the door click closed behind him. Like a freshman on his first date, the words wedged sideways in his throat when his eyes locked on Sammy Jo.

She stepped down from the last step and smiled, tucking a loose curl behind her ear, caught in a burst of air sweeping down from the hills. Slowly approaching his car, her small smile circled into a playful grin.

Dressed more like a cowpoke than a city slicker, her mind began dancing with curiosity of facades hidden beneath the suave exterior of her new friend.

"You look like a real cowboy," she teased, her eyebrows perched above daunting blue eyes, reflecting from a turquoise dress. She stopped in front of him and brushed her fingers across the red and black plaid fabric of his western shirt, before straightening the open collar with a final, approving pat. Her gaze landed on the hollow of his throat then down to the sweep of thick, dark masculinity peeking from the V of open pearl snaps.

Grayson swallowed hard and blew out a breath, nearly choking. "And you…" His stuttering elicited a smile from Sammy Jo. He swallowed and tried again. "You're a real vison Sammy Jo,"

With a teasing curtsy, she dragged her eyes from his broad chest, resisting the urge to touch, and thanked him. Intertwining her fingers through his, she towed him toward the house. "I need to say goodbye to Pops before we leave,"

If anything could cause the knot in Grayson's stomach to cinch any tighter, it was the mere mention of James Wilcox. It took a lot to intimidate Grayson, but the man waiting inside was as threatening as an overzealous prosecutor was at his first murder trial. Standing in front of Jim Wilcox was like standing at the guillotine, waiting on the guilty verdict.

Stepping to the porch Grayson quickly forgot all about James Wilcox. His gaze trailed turquoise fabric, ending on the gentle sway of Sammy Jo hips as she climbed the porch steps ahead of him. Her hand slipped from his as she reached for the screen door, pulling it open with a squeak. Grayson stood awkwardly behind, guiltily snatching his eyes to the side when she turned and asked over her shoulder, "You coming?"

With a skeptical nod, Grayson followed her inside. Jim was dozing in the worn leather, fireside recliner, opening his eyes at the sound of the hinges. His blank stare automatically shifted to Grayson, making him want to throw himself on the mercy of the court and plead guilty. Guilty of what he had no idea...but nonetheless, he was certain he must be guilty of something. Accusing bullets shot from Jim's eyes like buckshot.

"We're leaving now Pops,"

Leaning down to kiss her grandfather's cheek, Grayson watched hard lines soften, and realized it was nothing personal that Jim had against him. It was the all-encompassing love he had for his granddaughter that was so threatening to James Wilcox.

"We may be late Pops, don't wait up," Sammy Jo winked at her grandfather before turning back to the door.

"Good night sir," Grayson turned to follow Sammy Jo but halted and turned. Dipping his head at Jim he added, "Don't worry Mr. Wilcox, she's in good hands, I'll bring her home safe and sound," For the first time Grayson recognized a brief glimmer of something besides repulsion in the man's coal black eyes.

Sammy Jo and Grayson parked near Wilcox Floral and Gifts and strolled hand in hand along the streets of Highland, neither rushing nor lagging. Seemingly, in no hurry, they stopped to peer in the display window of the five and dime before moving on, enjoying the evening.

The sun began its slow descent into the western horizon, brush strokes of purple and gray slicing dusk. A gentle breeze ushered early evening air down from the mountains. Summer temperatures cooled slightly, giving Grayson the excuse to slip an arm around Sammy Jo's waist, pulling her closer. With matching strides, they made their way to the edge of town where a pair of geese honked overhead, pulling Sammy Jo's attention to the dimming skyline.

Her eyes followed the pair, disappearing behind a cap of blue pines, their calls growing faint. "Did you know that geese pair for life?"

"You don't say," Grayson watched her intent gaze, imagining the thoughts in her head, the soft, romantic side she kept hidden beneath a strong, well-defined exterior.

At the last traffic light in town, they did not bother waiting for the signal to change before crossing the empty lanes to the other side. Drawn to loud music, blaring through the tavern's propped door, their pace slowed.

Vehicles lined the street in front of the bristly, brick building, mostly 4x4's on steroids, with Remington dressed gun racks suspended from the rear windows. Neon lights announcing local's favorite drafts flashed from the pub window, their muted red glow reflecting from brown canvas shading the walk.

Grayson stepped onto the curb hesitating, thankful they decided to park his car at Sammy Jo's shop and walk to the tavern, taking advantage of the nice evening. He could only imagine how his flashy BMW would look parked between two of the beastly trucks, like sushi sandwiched between southern griddlecakes.

As if sensing Grayson's trepidation, Sammy Jo bumped his shoulder with her own as they walked, long lashes rolling up playfully. "It's not as bad as you think. Just a bunch of hicks out to have a little fun," she winked, earning her a hint of a smile.

Stepping inside, the packed pub made Grayson wonder where everyone came from. Obviously, a popular spot for free spirited partygoers, he would have bet his life savings that most of them were from surrounding towns, or at the very least, two-thirds. Highland's population was too small to attract such a crowd, even on Saturday night.

Glancing around the packed room, he felt as out of place as a cat in a canary cage. A tight row of heel clicking, toe taping line dancers stretched across the polished heart pine floor, moving in rhythm to an old classic from the man in black. Several couples squashed the bar, a gale of laughter erupting from a corner pool game. Sammy Jo hooked her arm through Grayson's, hauling him towards the crowded bar.

Less than a half dozen steps inside the door, a cowpoke looking like close kin to Big Foot, with a bristly beard to match, eased from the shadows. Towering more than a few inches above Grayson's 6' 3", the man stared down with not as much as a hint of a smile cracking a stone sober expression. The brute sized Grayson up and down, making him feel more like a bloody slab of meat under a hungry grizzly's inspection.

"Who's your friend Sam?" Big foot's country twang was as pure southern as Sammy Jo's, but his tone was deep and gruff.

"Hey there Harley…this is Grayson Wesley. He's visiting from New Hampshire. Grayson, Harley Wiesenborn." Sammy Jo motioned with her hand and nodded, as if she were introducing a town dignitary.

"Harley Wiesenborn…as in ex…" Harley growled through clenched teeth, with an emphasis on ex. His vile attitude spewed like green goo. Poking out his right hand, Grayson swore he saw his left eye twitch.

Skeptically accepting the grip, Grayson wondered for an instance if he would pull back a bloody nub. The expression plastered to the ogre's face was about as discreet as a bull in a Texas teashop, and so was his rock-solid grip.

Grayson made a mental note. "Ex...maybe...but definitely not by choice..."

After a mechanical handshake that felt awkwardly close to threatening, Harley dropped Grayson's hand. With a quick nod, the goon turned and disappeared into the crowd without as much as another word.

Sammy Jo leaned in and cupped her hand at her mouth, raising her voice above the blaring beat of drums. She wore a quirky smile that seemed to hide secret amusement. "Don't mind him. He's harmless,"

Watching size 14 boots pound the wood floor, Grayson was not so sure.

"Let's get something to drink," she said, worming through the crowd with Grayson's hand in tow. Stopping at the bar, Sammy Jo wiggled between two couples swiveling atop stools, signaling the bartender, which from the attentive smile; Grayson speculated was another admirer from a long list.

After Grayson agreed to join her in whatever she was having, Sammy Jo ordered two Bud Lights in bottles. Grayson paid, adding a healthy tip, before tucking his wallet in is back pocket, following the swish of Sammy Jo's turquoise dress to an empty corner table.

Pulling out her chair, he waited for her to sit before wedging himself between the table and wall with a clear view of the jam-packed room. A hefty pull from the longneck bottle, he waited for it to slide down before following with a second swig.

Automatically scanning the crowd, Grayson felt the bore of Harley's glare. Sure enough, Goliath's head peered over a cluster standing near the dance floor, his eyes set on Grayson like a locked and loaded missile on countdown. With a narrowing stare, his chin lifted, the way a master marksman locks on his sights.

Puffing out his chest with all the ruffled feathers of a barnyard rooster ready for a cockfight, Grayson's knuckles turned white around the neck of amber glass held tight in his hand. Returning fire, Grayson held his bottle up with an imaginary toast and dodged daggers firing from brazen eyes with square on accuracy. With the bottle pressed tight to his lips, Grayson took a slow, satisfying swig, a sour smirk hidden beneath.

Eat your heart out Big Foot...

Sammy Jo glanced across the dance floor in time to see the crude gesture waving from the middle of Harley's right hand. Inching her chair closer, she leaned into the table. For an instant, her voice was lost to the loud tune of Brooks and Dunn's *Boot Scootin' Boogie*. "Don't mind him; he's just a little defensive. We dated on and off during high school but it didn't work out. He feels more like a brother to me," she added, tilting her bottle for a drink.

Her ill attempted explanation flopped face down on the table between them. Unconvinced, Grayson's brow bowed with his candid reply. "That may be how you feel darlin', but where I come from, if a man looked at his sister the way he's looking at you, he'd be arrested and buried in the jail's concrete foundation."

Harley disappeared into the crowd from time to time but seemed to pop up every few minutes, like an annoying infestation of spring pigweed. An insolent stare punctuated reminders to Grayson that he was on guard.

A couple of beers later, Grayson swigged the last drink from his bottle and slid it across the table. Shocking Sammy Jo with the biggest surprise of the evening, he leaped to his feet on cue as a Hank Williams original pumped through the speakers.

Dragging Sammy Jo from the chair, Grayson pulled her to the center of the dance floor. White, flickering bulbs crisscrossing the ceiling, sliced a rowdy crowd already gliding effortlessly to the Electric Slide. Taking a spot front and center, he laid down dance moves that would make any southern mama proud.

Sammy Jo's clumsy feet stumbled out of step more than once, her focus fixed on the surprising transformation of her partner, instead of her dance moves. Noticing she was not the only female in the place to take notice, all eyes glued to Grayson's tight jean clad booty shifting in steady beat to the music. It was obvious that every woman in the place, single or not, would be proud to slip a little of that eye candy on their arm and usher him right out the back door.

The chorus faded, Sammy Jo's head blowing up as big as a puffer fish when Grayson leaned in kissing her on the lips, giving all the salivating women in the bar a reason to wipe the drool from their mouths.

Unfortunately, the women were not the only ones with drooling mouths. Warming a bar stool across the room, Harley foamed at the mouth like a rabid dog. By now, he had polished off a twelve pack and was working on nursing a bottle of Jim Beam. Swaying on the stool, he was obviously drunker than *Hooter Brown*. Straddling a fence of appropriate behavior and not giving a damn, he was dangerously close to falling off. Sammy Jo was relieved when Betty Ann, an old high school acquaintance who had always had an eye for Harley, offered to take him home.

Sammy Jo figured Harley had drunk enough to pickle his liver and was happy to see him stagger across the room on Betty Ann's arm. Whatever the reason he was leaving, she was happy that he headed for the door without incident, leaving Grayson's nose squarely intact. Each step Harley took, required deliberate concentration on his part, as he stumbled over cinder block feet, his eyes focused on the door.

When the DJ announced open mike and the first poor rendition of *Achy Breaky Heart* ripped loose, Sammy Jo swigged down her last drink of beer and suggested they leave.

Grayson was out of his chair and on his feet before she could finish her sentence. He had not taken his eyes off her all night and all he could think about was the sweet taste of coral glossed lips. Staring at her across the table in a crowded bar was about as frustrating as holding his favorite candy bar wrapped in barbed wire.

Tucking his hand at her waist, they wormed their way through clusters of people. Some giggling at the off-key squelch of Miley Cyrus want to be's, and others too drunk to notice.

The night air was cool beyond the stuffy single room tavern, a dome of stars suspended above the mountain. Moving further down the block, the blare of loud music eventually faded into cool, dew kissed breeze.

Grayson wrapped his fingers around Sammy Jo's hand, silently strolling Highland. They first wandered down one side before crossing at the corner and then up the other side of a town long gone quiet. Most of the town's population had turned in with the chickens, the remainder wearing the polyurethane off shiny wood floors of Mel's tavern.

Pausing at a bench in front of Highland's one room library, Sammy Jo smoothed the hem of her dress and sat down, patting the seat next to her. Grayson took advantage of the opportunity to get close, wedging himself in the tight space. Arm draped loosely over her shoulder, he could feel her slow, steady breath against him.

Chapter 15

A good ten minutes ticked by, neither talking, although Grayson got the distinct impression Sammy Jo had something picking at her mind. Once she opened her mouth to speak but quickly slapped it shut, fidgeting with her hoop earring instead.

"Is something wrong Sammy Jo?" Grayson pulled her hand to him, drawing imaginary circles against the back with his thumb. His mind replayed the hurt on Harley's face when he entered the bar with Sammy Jo on his arm, and for a moment, worried if she was being honest about her feelings for the overgrown beast of a man.

Grayson feared that maybe his showing up in Highland was perfect timing and he was nothing more than a convenient pawn in a game of cat and mouse between Sammy Jo and her high school sweetheart. Her sudden change in mood made him wonder if her true interest lay in a country mouse disguised as a rugged, mountain man.

When she looked up, a teardrop brimmed her lower lash, which she quickly swept away.

"What's wrong sweetheart?" Grayson's thumb swiped a second eluding tear, brushing it from her cheek.

She shifted awkwardly on the bench, crossing one leg over the other before switching back. Her eyes flitted nervously over cracks in the sidewalk at her feet.

"Sammy Jo?"

Sapphire eyes reflecting moonlight slowly lifted with a long-suffering look. "Grayson, I've not been totally honest with you,"

There was the sucker punch Grayson had been waiting on all evening. He had dodged Harley's fist for the last few hours, the unsuspecting knockout blow coming from his 120-pound date. A crumbling ego slammed like a severed elevator. He could not believe it, duped to trust that Sammy Jo cared for him, only to learn he had been beat out by an overgrown, bearded barbarian.

"You know when you told me about the watch?"

Now he was more than a little confused...what the hell did the watch have to do with Harley Wiesenborn?

"Yes,"

"Well..." she swallowed, her focus falling back to the dominating sidewalk crack. "You are not the crazy one. I am..."

The words brought Grayson to his feet. Plowing his fingers through his hair, he faced her, waiting silently for an explanation.

In hopes that she would not sound as insane as she felt, Sammy Jo paused. There was no easy way to tell him the truth. No matter how it came out, she was going to sound like she had more than a few nuts in her Wheaties.

"When I came to Thatcher Hill...well...that actually was not my first time there," Spitting out the confession, her nose crinkled, the tainted words leaving a bad taste in her mouth.

Shuffling back a step, a crease furrowed Grayson's forehead. "But, you said you didn't know the place," Suddenly, he wondered which could be worse, Harley Wiesenborn's gargantuan fist or a lie she was hiding. At least with Harley, he had a fighting chance.

"I didn't think I did," Slowly scooting to the edge of the bench, she frowned, and then stood. She liked Grayson and feared what she had to share would drown any chances of a relationship, but she had to be honest with him. The longer she waited, the harder the truth would fall.

Gripping both of his hands, her eyes glazed in tears, moonlight reflected from glistening pools. "When I came to Thatcher Hill that morning to give you an estimate, I didn't know where I was going, but when I pulled up," Sweltering tears fell, slowly at first, then in a steady stream, chasing one another in hot streaks down her cheeks. "Grayson, I don't remember ever being there, but I've dreamed of your grandmother's manor since I was a little girl."

With that, Grayson dropped her hands and plopped down on the bench. Exhaling loudly, he raked a shaky hand through his hair, nearly poking himself in the eye. He was right; Harley's fist would be easier to swallow.

*Maybe that was what attracted him to her...she
was as crazy as he was...*

Sammy Jo squeezed in the seat next to him and
lifted her chin defiantly. The secret was out and there was
no stuffing it back. She willed the pitiable tears to stop
and swallowed a sob. If ever there was a time to be strong,
it was now. She had one chance to convince Grayson that
she was not as nutty as a squirrel's winter stash. She
opened her mouth and her history with Thatcher Hill
slowly unraveled.

"The dreams started when I was just a little girl,
maybe 7 or 8 years old. I don't remember a time when
Thatcher Hill was not a part of my life," She twisted closer,
folding her hands in her lap. "I described it to my
grandmother once, hoping that I had visited the place as a
child. At least then it would make sense, but grandma said
the house did not sound familiar,"

"Then why? How?" he asked, trying to make sense
of the impossible. He was getting pretty darned good at
trying to understand impractical these days, his life
seemed to be a matted mess of impracticality.

She shrugged, thinking back to earlier days when
the manor offered peace and tranquility. "I don't know. In
the beginning, your grandmother's estate was a beautiful
place in my head. I actually looked forward to nightly
visits," Her smile was genuine. "It was majestic, like the
white mansion on Gone with the Wind," Her gaze filtered
past him as she pictured the memory. "The urns out front
overflowed with bright red geraniums and ivy. The sun was

so warm and real I could feel it on my skin," Suddenly her smile faded, rosy cheeks replaced by ashen gray.

Grayson sat quietly, watching the life drain from her face along with the happy memory.

When her eyes returned to him, they had lost their luster, replaced by a cold, steely hue. "But the dreams changed. In time the house took on…" Her words trailed as she tried to imagine how to explain the tragic loss of her beloved house on the hill, how the dreams took the cynical twist of a late night horror film. "It became a place of sadness and loss. I feared a secret hidden inside. I don't know how but I sensed something horrible had happened behind the upstairs window, something horrendous that changed the course of time."

Grayson put his arm around her shoulder, drawing her to him. He could feel the quaking she tried so desperately to conceal.

"The beauty was gone, Grayson" she said, her voice nearly lost to the warm breeze. "My manor house became nothing more than a dark, black hole in the night,"

"That's it? You don't know what made the image in your head change?"

She gulped for courage of the one last revelation she knew she had to share. Grayson would either try to accept her crazy confession, or get up and run for the hills like a man with good sense. She desperately hoped it was not the latter.

"In the beginning, the dreams were consistent, unchanging. After my grandmother died a couple of years ago, they transformed, as if the house was trying to reveal a hidden secret." Sammy Jo pinched her eyes closed, images of her last nightmare still splashed across her memory in living color.

"I never made it through the front door of Thatcher Hill until a couple of weeks ago, after you came into my shop." She opened her eyes and could feel her heart pound her ribs, the way it had the night her dream shed light on the truth.

"I stepped inside the front door for the first time, drawn to a darkened stairwell like a magnet. I ached to understand what had happened at the top of those stairs. I needed to know." She tilted her head back and welcomed a cool burst of air lifting damp hair from her neck. "I heard a deafening thud on the steps, a thumping that grew louder. When all was quiet, a porcelain doll lay shattered at my feet." Rapid blinking did not erase the frightening image from her head. "If I live to be a hundred years old Grayson, I'll never forget that glassy, lifeless stare." She let the breath seep from her lungs, relieved that the truth was finally out. She needed to tell someone before she exploded. Sammy Jo prayed that Grayson would be the one person who would understand and not judge her. "That's the last time I dreamed of Thatcher Hill. The dreams stopped as suddenly as they began all those years ago,"

With Grayson's arm draped over the back of the bench, they sat silently. Several minutes ticked by, minutes that seemed like an hour. Finally, Sammy Jo mustered the courage to ask, "You think I'm crazy, don't you?"

Grayson understood better than he wished. He leaned forward looking her squarely in the eye. "Did you think I was crazy when I told you that the watch started running in perfect time?" When she did not answer right away, he plopped back against the seat and laughed out right. "Never mind, on second thought, don't answer that," Crossing one ankle over the other, he laced fingers behind his neck. Winks of light blinking through filtering clouds drew his attention to the night sky.

A good sign she thought, checking him out from the corner of her eye. At least she was not looking at his backside sprinting down the street.

The ride back to Wilcox Farm was quiet, each wrapped tightly in thought. Wind, along with the hum of the engine, blew through the open windows of the BMW, drowning out country music that Sammy Jo had tuned on the radio for background noise. Neither knew what to say, so they said nothing.

Pulling down the lane of Wilcox Farm, Sammy Jo was not surprised to find Pops sitting on the front porch, gliding away the minutes. When the headlights flashed across the front of the house, he pushed up from the swing and disappeared inside, the wooden screen door slapping shut behind him.

"He still doesn't trust me much, does he?" Grayson propped his elbow out the window after cutting the engine.

"Pops doesn't trust anyone where I'm concerned," she admitted. "But I guess there could be worse things," She reached for the door handle, pushing it open.

"Yea, like role call at the state prison," When Sammy Jo looked at him without cracking a smile, Grayson quickly regretted the humorless remark. He swung open his car door and stepped out, avoiding wedging his foot further down his throat. Meeting her at the other side, he pushed the passenger door closed and tucked his hand at her waist. "Sorry, I guess that wasn't so funny after all,"

Sammy Jo pinched her lips closed, a slight smirk suggesting that maybe she did find a scrap of humor in his witty interpretation of her grandfather's extensive security measures.

They made their way wordlessly onto the porch. After glancing through the screen door to make sure that James was not peering down the barrel of a shotgun, Grayson pulled Sammy Jo to him with a long goodnight kiss, a kiss that he could only wish would lead to more. Reluctantly bidding her goodnight, he started to step away, but asked the expected question before reaching the steps, "When can I see you again?"

"Tomorrow Pops and I go to church service and then a picnic social afterwards. Maybe next week," Seeing the disappointment etched into his face she added, "Besides, it's about the chase. A real lady wouldn't let you catch her so fast."

Chapter 16

Grayson drove along the dark stretch of winding back roads, his thoughts scrambling, from Harley Weisenborn to Sammy Jo's revelation of childhood dreams. He had always thought of himself as rational but was beginning to doubt his own sanity, first the pocket watch and now Sammy Jo's bombshell about dreams of Thatcher Hill and her imagined hidden secret. Recalling her chilling confession, all rationality sailed through the open car window, along with the cool rush of mountain air that left shivering goose bumps in its wake.

Less than a mile from home, Grayson's speed increased down a steep grade in the road, his thoughts wandering aimlessly. As he leaned into the deceptive curve, tires squealed tight to black pavement. Slamming his foot on the brake pedal, headlights flashed on a wall of evergreens, fish tailing from one side of the road to the other, before skidding to a stop on the coarse shoulder. Gravel pinged metal, the flash of a white tail buck vanishing in the thicket just beyond the hood. Limbs clattered the underbrush as the rump of a deer disappeared into the dark ravine.

With his foot tight to the brake pedal, Grayson gripped the leather steering wheel hard enough to leave an imprint. Squeezing his eyes shut, he pressed his forehead to his hand, blowing out a terse breath. Sounds of the fleeing deer faded into rustling brush, the slow idle of the car engine the only remaining sound.

If anything could cause the moment to be anymore surreal, it was the quick burst of chilling wind through the open car window. His back stiffened when he heard the faint echo of what he believed to be a voice, not so much a word as a sound, a human sound.

Yanking the car in neutral and jerking the emergency brake, Grayson left the motor running and edged the door open. The interior light cast a ruddy glow over gravel and dirt. He scanned the shoulder and then the empty roadway in search of the sound. Surely, no one would be out on foot this time of night, at least no one of sound mind.

Sliding from the seat, he moved quietly to the rear of the car, his eyes darting to a rocky cliff bordering the other side of the road, and then back again. Dragging his fingers across the trunk of the car, he moved slowly to the edge of the roadway. The steep, undisturbed embankment below revealed nothing, yet he was unable to shake the strange sensation he was not alone. The wind had stopped and the voice gone, that is, of course if there had been a voice in the first place.

Perhaps one too many beers, spine-chilling talk of a pocket watch that began running after lost decades, and strange dreams, had thrown Grayson's imagination into a stiff tailspin. Listening intently, the only thing he heard was the trill exchange of distant coyotes. Hoping it was nothing but the wind he heard in the first place, the icy chill raking his spine suggested otherwise.

Climbing back in the driver seat, Grayson slammed the car door. He released the emergency brake, gripped the shifter and eased into first gear, accelerating onto the roadway. Tires chirped to second, the prickling sensation vanishing in the solid darkness behind him.

A click of the right turn signal indicated the blackened gravel lane snaking up the mountain to Thatcher Hill. He downshifted, gathering speed up the steep slope, headlights flashing across the rutted path.

Perched high on the hill at the top of the lane, the house was dark, all but a single lamp in the foyer and the porch light Martheena left burning. Grayson pulled to the gate and eyed the manor through the windshield with a new sense of awareness. The manor suddenly felt two-dimensional, the house he loved while growing up at the front of his mind, and the one lurking in the back that was hiding a dark secret. With mounting questions that would surely lead to a sleepless night, he got out and climbed the steps to the porch before sagging into one of the rockers.

A near full moon cast a gray blanket over the grounds, muted chirp of crickets beckoning from the tack room below. The shack attached to the barn seemed to summons Grayson from the darken holler, a muted light inside absorbed by hazy glass windowpanes.

Following his instincts, Grayson left the shelter of the porch and traipsed down the trail, stopping short of the tack room door. The slow, click of footsteps seeped from under the door, like a steady pace against worn wood boards. When he stepped closer and put his hand on the knob, the sound ceased.

With a slow twist, he shoved open the door, the porcelain knob bouncing hard from the wall. Only the tattered threshold separated him from the footsteps inside. Fists balled at his side, his eyes flashed across stretching shadows cast by the glow of a single desk lamp. Hairs on his neck prickled to an empty room.

Once inside, Grayson wandered back and forth at a steady click next to the bed, stopping once to listen. The room was empty and the adjoining barn quiet. Adding another entry to the ever-growing list of weird happenings, he switched off the desk lamp and pulled the tack room door closed behind him, hesitating for one last listen before stepping onto the trail.

He sauntered up the trail and climbed the porch steps with his hands shoved in both pockets. Dropping into a rocker at the main house, Grayson watched the tack room below, and waited. The night had become eerily quiet, even the crickets drew silent in the thick brush. After thirty minutes of babbling self-therapy, he chalked his nightly spooks off to nothing more than exhaustion and an over imagination before retiring to bed.

The church pews of Highland, Grace Baptist packed shoulder to shoulder on Sunday morning, the monthly picnic social attracting regularly attending parishioners as well as guests from neighboring towns. Sammy Jo briefly wished she would have invited Grayson, but quickly dismissed the thought. Since her grandmother's death, Sunday morning worship followed by lunch at Franny's diner was solely reserved for her and Pops. If there were another reason to resent Grayson, Jim would find it on his own, Sammy Jo did not need to make the hunt any easier for him.

A paper plate cradled in her hands, Sammy Jo carried fried chicken, potato salad and baked beans to Jim, who had found an empty chair under the shade of a maple, watching a couple of youngsters tossing a soft ball.

"You don't have to wait on me," Jim uttered, glimpsing up at the paper plate balanced in both hands. "You eat that and I'll get me something in a bit," He glanced from the heap of food, back to one of the boys tumbling across the ground in a stretching effort to catch the ball.

"I didn't fix it," Sammy Jo grinned, sitting the brimming plate in his lap. "Sister Shrugs did," A wide smile filled in answers to all the questions between.

Widow Shrugs had her eye on Pops for the last year, commenting at least once every Sunday how much she missed having a man to dote on. Pops however did not have time for such shenanigans, and as much as told her so, on more than one occasion. Sammy Jo still found it amusing to watch the pudgy elder with tinged blue hair and rouge stained cheeks flirt with her grandfather, and even more amusing to watch him squirm beneath her probing eye.

Turning to walk away Sammy Jo could not resist adding a little pat to his sore spot, "Oh Pops, Sister Shrugs said she cut a special piece of that fair winning cherry pie just for you," With a wink, she spun and headed back to the serving line, sidestepping the suspected snippy retort.

Jim was gnawing on a chicken leg when Sammy Jo returned, dragging a chair next to him. Without giving her a chance to start in on Sister Shrugs, he delved into her love life instead. "I'm surprised you took a day off from Mr. Fancy Pants for the Lord today,"

She pushed a fork through baked beans before casting an accusing eye. "Grayson is really a pretty nice guy. If you'd give him chance, you'd see,"

"Just doesn't seem your type, that's all," he shrugged.

"And just what exactly is my type Pops? Please enlighten me."

Jim cleaned the last shred of meat from the chicken bone while he thought about an answer.

"That's what I thought," she said, stretching for a water bottle at her feet. Uncapping the plastic bottle, she took a slow drink. "You're going to have to make up your mind," she added, twisting the lid back into place. "You don't want me sitting around the house fussing over you all the time, but I find someone to go out with and you pick him apart worse than you did that chicken leg," She dropped the bottle to the ground and threw her hands in the air.

Jim knew he was slacking a bit on Christian principles. Pastor Daniel's Sunday morning sermon on Matthew 7, *"Judge not lest ye be judged,"* was still ringing loudly in his ears.

"It's just that I want what's best for you, that's all," He dropped his head and his bottom lip pouted like a scorned child.

Sammy Jo sat her plate on the ground and stood, straightening the pleat in her navy blue skirt with her hands. Leaning in, she kissed Jim on the cheek and took a step back with a smile. "Well how about you give me a chance to figure out what's best for me on my own."

Jim's eyes gleamed with pride as he watched her walk away with a stern reminder that she was not exactly the little girl once needing his protection. The truth was, maybe he should feel a little sorry for the poor schmuck who won her heart. She certainly was not going to be an easy filly to tame.

Sunday morning, Grayson sat in the tack house staring at the blank computer screen in steely silence. Tumbling a pencil through four fingers and then back again, he tapped first the eraser and then the sharp lead against the wood surface of the desk. He had taken a cup of coffee down with him nearly an hour ago, which had long grown cold, not typing the first word on his manuscript. All he could think about was the sound he heard along the roadway the night before, and the steady pace of footsteps behind the tack room door. The memory sent shudders up both arms, prickling the hairs on his neck.

"The wind," he mumbled aloud. "It had to be the damned wind along the roadside," Mentally convincing himself it was nothing more than the scurry of mouse he heard on the tack room floor, the unnerving events trailed one another through his head like a mad dog chasing its tail.

Dropping the pencil, he slammed the computer screen closed and snatched the cup of cold coffee from the desk. He was not getting any work done today and was kidding himself if he thought different.

When he got up to the house, Martheena was just coming through the kitchen door from church, pulling the bobby pins from her favorite, purple, pillbox hat. Grayson offered to pour her a cup of coffee before refilling his own.

"No thanks," she replied. "Corned beef and cabbage is the diner's Sunday special, thought maybe I could talk you into taking an old lady into town for lunch." Dropping her hat on the table next to her black, patent leather purse, she tugged white gloves from each finger of her right hand and waited for him to answer.

Dumping the cold coffee down the drain, Grayson sat the cup on the counter asking for a few minutes to shave and change into something a bit more suitable for a lunch date with his favorite girl.

Dropping a ring of keys in Grayson's hand a few minutes later, Martheena pushed open the back screen door, insisting over her shoulder that he drive her car to lunch. She claimed that she felt safer in her 1980, gold metallic Buick, than the dinky, model excuse of a real car parked out front.

The short drive to town consisted of small talk, bouncing from the slow writing progress of Grayson's novel to Martheena's excitement about her Garden Club's upcoming bake sale. Pulling into the one empty space left in front of the diner, Grayson followed Martheena inside. Leading down a narrow aisle, separating a wall of occupied booths from a red, swivel seat lined counter, she stopped at the back corner booth. Wedging in the seat across from Grayson, she spread a paper napkin over her paisley, lavender skirt, patting it in place.

A waitress dressed in blue jeans and tee shirt that could not be far from high school graduation, sashayed up to the booth. After running her hand languidly down a long, blonde ponytail, she pulled a pencil from behind her ear flipping open a pad she took from her apron pocket. Tapping the pencil on her nametag bearing the name Lucy, she asked for their drink order. Her eyes settled on Grayson, slowly dragging over him like running her finger down a five star restaurant menu.

"Sweet tea with lemon," Martheena answered with a grin, watching Grayson squirm beneath curious, teenage hormones.

"The same for me please," Reaching for the menu tucked behind a napkin holder, Grayson glanced up, catching the surprise wink of wispy lashes before the waitress turned and walked away with an inexperienced, exaggerated swagger.

Without bothering with a menu, Martheena ordered the corned beef and cabbage when Lucy returned with their drinks, Grayson opting for the beef hot shot that he remembered from his youth, ordering extra gravy on his potatoes. Waiting for Lucy to leave, he leaned on folded arms and watched Martheena across the table squeezing a lemon in her glass, then stirring a spoon through crushed ice. He knew her well and figured there was more on her mind than bake sale cookies or his writing headway.

"You didn't say. How was your date with Sammy Jo last night?" Tapping the spoon on the side of the glass, she dropped it on the table taking a long, intentional drink, leveling curiosity over the rim.

"It was nice," he answered, dangling a tidbit with a wry smile. "We went to the tavern, did a little dancing, then took a walk through town," Fishing a lemon wedge from his glass he squeezed it, dropping it in the tea. His thoughts fast-forwarded from the tavern to the bench in town. The memory of Sammy Jo's revelation flashed like strobe lights in his mind, bleaching the color from his face.

"Something wrong Scamper?" Martheena could read him as well today as she could twenty years ago, the proof lifting a brow over observant brown eyes.

Grayson poked at the ice in his glass with a finger, expecting she would ask sooner or later. "It's complicated Martheena,"

"Complicated or you don't want to talk about it?"

"I guess both," he admitted, wiping his finger down water droplets easing down the side of his glass. Lifting the tea to his lips, he took a slow drink. Looking past Martheena, he knew there were some things better left unsaid.

Nothing more mentioned of his date with Sammy Jo, they talked instead about plans of selling the house and Martheena's intended move to Atlanta. Sadness crept into the conversation and for a split second Grayson wondered if selling Thatcher Hill was the right choice.

Chapter 17

Returning to Thatcher Hill after lunch, Grayson parked the car at the rear of the house, slowly ushering Martheena on the crook of his arm, up the deck steps to the kitchen. Just as the screen door slammed shut behind them, rain began sprinkling from a single cloud that had stalled over the mountain. Slivers of sunshine slanted through spotty, gray clouds, so the spring rain, Grayson knew, would be brief.

Quickly dismissing thoughts of working on his manuscript, which had been less than productive earlier, he instead retrieved Gram's journal from his bedroom, carrying it with him to the front porch. By the time he stepped outside, the brief shower had subsided, nothing remaining but the smell of rain and annoying mist that made the air thick and sticky.

Kicking off his classic leather boat shoes, he folded into one of the rockers, tucked a tanned, bare foot under him and cracked the leather binder to the page where he last left off, his eyes automatically finding the last paragraph.

A scamper of a squirrels darting up the bark of the Elm, drew Grayson's attention from the yellowed pages, before ending on the tack room in the holler. He sensed sadness for the man memorialized in his grandmother's writing, wondering what tragedies marked their path, a future held captive by forbidden love.

With his foot pushing against the floorboards, the gentle rock drew him back to the open page, Gram's words and his imagination transporting him through passage of time to the summer of 1954.

August 1, 1954

My life once again feels full, offering hope and a reason to face each new day. The love I have for Digger gives me a purpose to heal, to bring my little girl home again. I seem to grow stronger each day, hope for tomorrow replacing fear of today.

I got a letter from Bell yesterday. She said Cora is doing well. She has made new friends and although she asks about me daily, has adjusted well to Indiana farm life. I believe everything happens for a reason. Perhaps Digger came into my life as a means to hold me together, until I can bring my daughter home again.

I know the emotions I hold for Digger should feel wrong, the love I share with this younger man, but it doesn't. If what I feel is so wrong, then why does life feel so right? We make each other happy and is that not what life is supposed to be about? Then I think of what people would say, how they would talk, how they would judge me if only they knew.

I slept in the tack room for the first time last night. I fell asleep in Digger's arms, waking early morning to the sound of truck tires kicking gravel up the lane. Panic raced through my veins when I realized it was Andrew. Hiding in the barn, I waited as Digger made the excuse of my early run into town. I suspect Andrew knows, although he would be the last to judge me. He has witnessed my struggles firsthand; maybe some small part of him hopes I can find happiness again.

August 3, 1954

Waking just before dawn, the room was spinning like an out of control top. Flushed and clammy, perhaps I carry a slight fever. Scrambling eggs for Digger, I could not bring myself to take even a bite. The smell alone made my stomach churn. A summer virus is plaguing town and unfortunately, I fear I have contracted a bad case of it. If I am not better by the weekend, I will visit the doctor for a tonic.

August 8, 1954

The virus is no better, perhaps a bit worse today. I vomited this morning and again tonight. The only thing I can seem to keep down is dry cornbread. I keep my distance from Digger. He has picked up a job at the mill in town and is trying to get the house roofed before winter. The last thing we need right now is for him to get sick.

August 9, 1954

I cannot believe I am sitting here, writing these words. I think I have suspected all along, but perhaps if I did not acknowledge it, it would not be true.

I do not have a virus at all; my time did not come this month. I am with child…

The mere thought of food nauseates me. Sitting at the kitchen table this evening, I pushed a fork through dumplings, picking at a small bite of chicken, washing it down with a sip of buttermilk. Digger noticed and asked if I was still not feeling well, reaching across the table to touch my hand.

Guilt ridden, I instinctively pulled my hand away snatching a napkin from the table. I dabbed at the corner of my mouth and shook my head avoiding eye contact. I fear he would see the truth in my eyes. Digger cannot know of the news, at least not yet.

There is much to consider, tarnishing the memory of my beloved husband, my firstborn Cora, my reputation with the townspeople, and as important as any, Digger's position in all of this. I am a prideful woman and refuse to shackle a man with a future dealt against him like a stacked deck. If there is ever a time to show my strength, it is now. Not only does my future depend on it, Digger's and our unborn child's future depends on it as well.

The journal thudded to the porch like a black rock, Grayson's eyes fixed on brittle pages of time staring up at him. He wasn't sure what hurt more, learning about his grandmother's pregnancy, or the fact that she kept the secret hidden from her family her entire life.

The scandalous truth slugged him in the gut, driving him to his feet. He kicked the diary across the porch, watching it skid to a stop beneath a chair. Dragging heavy feet to the edge of the porch, he leaned against a white column and glowered at the tack room like an evil nemesis. Standing apart from the barn, the slanted roofed addition represented a lie, the sham of a woman he believed his grandmother to be. He went still; words from his grandmother's diary ringing painfully loud in his head.

Grayson stomped from the porch and down the dampened path, the tack room locked in his sights. His heart pounded harder with each step he took, anger simmering in his veins. By the time he reached the door, boiling rage had replaced anger. Not bothering with turning the knob, he thrust a bare foot against the wood like a maddened ninja. Pine splintered, the recoiling door slamming the wall. Murky shadows opened before him like an empty tomb.

Grayson stood in the doorway imagining the deceit, the lies. The cryptic space was dim, light filtering through hazy windows and across the ticking covered mattress. Two quick strides landed him next to the bed. Gripping the dust-laden mattress in both fists, he heaved it against the wall. Powdery particles erupted in the air like molten ash. Spinning he struck the desk lamp with his arm before kicking the ladder back chair into splinters. He snarled though clenched teeth, dumping the desk to the floor in an adrenaline-fueled rage.

Beet red flushed his face, the veins in his neck pulsating in rhythm to a thrashing heart. Anger exploded in his ears, random rants targeting a past life.

Dropping to the floor, Grayson pulled his broken computer to him, easing the shattered screen closed. Ticking minutes eventually slowed the heaving in his chest to an even tempo, the pounding of his heart falling steady.

He was not sure how long he sat there on the tack room floor chasing his grandmother's words around in his head. It must have been hours because the sun had already began its slow descent when he walked outside.

Earlier humidity had lifted, replaced by a gentle, cooling breeze. Just beyond the jagged ridge of pines behind the house, dusty colors of an arched double rainbow dissolved into a gray skyline, a mythical bridge to heaven.

Shoving both hands in his jean pockets, Grayson trudged to the house, stopping short of the porch steps. Staring at the open diary that had all but buckled his knees only hours earlier, a tangled web of emotions muddled his thoughts, all of which led to physical pain in his chest.

Suddenly regretting ever finding the journal, it cost him the ultimate price, death of life, as he knew it. What he believed to be a close relationship with his Gram was nothing more than a fluke, erected on a stack of lies. The back of his neck started to sweat and his heart kicked him in the back just as it did when he first read those haunting words *I'm with child*.

Putting one foot in front of the other, he slowly climbed the porch steps. He stopped at the diary and instead of picking it up, kicked it out of the way, as if it were a venomous viper ready to strike.

Dim, blue light from the television playing in the parlor fell across the entryway floor just beyond the screen door. Martheena was still up and he wasn't sure if he wanted to see her or not. After all, had she not equally betrayed him, knowing the truth about his grandmother and letting him continue believing in a charade? Her silence was the same deceit as the inked pages in the diary.

Pulling open the door, he heard Martheena's voice call out to him.

Stepping inside, Grayson stopped in the parlor doorway. He crammed both hands in his pockets clenching tight fists beneath the fabric, in a futile attempt to restrain resentment gnawing at his insides like a cancer.

Martheena poked her knitting needles into a ball of purple yarn, dropping it and the scarf she was working on into the canvas bag at her feet. Immediately, she knew Rosaline's buried secret was free. Proof shadowed Grayson's face in ashen gray. Cold, accusations peered at her from the doorway; dilated pupils of his eyes like empty burrows.

Pointing the remote at the television, Martheena clicked it off, patting the sofa seat next to her. "Come sit Scamper, I think it's time we have a talk."

Instead, Grayson walked to the opposite side of the room and plopped down in the leather recliner angled next to the stone fireplace. "So now you want to talk?" His remark crackled sarcasm, fingers of one hand drumming the arm of the chair.

"I take it you know," Martheena fidgeted nervously with a loose button on her faded, yellow housecoat.

Grayson's eyes shifted from the steady tick of the antique Regulator wall clock, to growing night beyond the window, then back to Martheena with a cold glare.

He had always believed naively in his grandmother, that she was a loving mother and grandmother, honest and sincere in everything she did. In a beat, words scribbled decades ago erased those beliefs, rewriting her entire life as nothing more than a pile of lies. Rosaline gave her only daughter away, as if she were nothing more than a piece of used furniture, then hid the birth of a second child from her family. Watching Martheena shift on the sofa like a guilty defendant caught in an incriminating lie, reminded him of the secret she too kept. She was no better than Rosaline.

"Yes, I know about the pregnancy," he confirmed callously. Dark brows stitched together, seconds ceremoniously ticking with each sway of the clock pendulum. Neither spoke. Tight muscles threading down Grayson's neck froze his shoulders in place. He slanted a glare across the room and sliced the silence. "What happened to the baby? Did she give it away too?"

His sharp tongue pierced Martheena's heart like a sword, tearing open memories of old wounds. Remembering her longtime friend's heart wrenching pain from the past, Martheena's reaction quickly turned to anger. The crook of one finger wagged the air, her words swift. "Don't you ever disrespect your grandmother that way again Grayson Wesley," she shouted.

She was quick on her feet, faster than Grayson had ever seen her move. For a second he wondered if she was going to cross the room and give him a good wallop upside the head with the fist she held balled at her side. From where he sat, her scrunched face made her look more like an angry boxer ready for round one, than the old woman she was. Not once in his entire life, did he ever remember her calling him anything but Scamper and the tone she was using sounded just as foreign.

"You have no right judging Rosaline!" she snapped. "Your grandmother was a good woman, would never hurt a soul. She always put everyone else ahead of her own needs, your grandfather, your mother… *you*," The assertion of Martheena's last word cut to his soul, a haunting pale draining the color from Grayson's face. Sucking in a shaky breath she eased back onto the sofa, her knees suddenly becoming weak, her chest tightening around a broken heart.

"The baby Martheena, what happened to the baby?" Grayson's low voice drifted into the steady tick of the clock.

Reaching into her knitting bag, Martheena pulled out the ball of yarn, twisting a strand around the needle as if time had snapped back minutes. When she looked up and started talking, it sounded like a rehearsed conversation; one she'd practiced many times in her head since he first discovered the journal in the cellar.

"Your Gram hired me about halfway through her pregnancy. The sickness never left her, she was sick all the time. The last months she became very frail," Tugging the yarn tight, Martheena coiled another loop of yarn around the needle. "The little fellow came over a month early." Her eyes froze to the needles she gripped in her hand. "And there were complications with the birth. I've delivered many a baby, but it happened so fast, there was nothing I could do, there was nothing anyone could do." She dropped the needles nimbly in her lap and drew a ragged breath. "He took only but a couple of breaths, died right there in his mama's arms," she added on a whisper, hot tears pooling in her eyes.

Grayson winced, scrubbing both hands over his face. Everything clicked into place, the baby swaddling from the cellar chest, the simple stone in the family plot. "Did my mother know?"

Marthena shook her head.

"And Digger, what happened to him?"

"I think you need to hear that from your grandmother," Dropping her knitting on the sofa, Martheena wrestled to her feet. "Good night," she said, shuffling towards the door. Stopping short, she turned with a tear glistening on an ebony cheek. "She loved your grandfather Scamper. That did not mean she didn't deserve to love again..."

After sounds of shuffling slippers slowly mounted the stairs and faded behind the closed bedroom door, Grayson went onto the porch, retrieving the journal from beneath one of the rockers. He knew he had no choice but learn the ending to his grandmother's story, his first regret being, there was nothing stronger than a bottle of 2010, Luce Toscana wine in the house. From the twisting in his gut, he figured a fifth of Crown Royal was more in order for the long night he feared awaited him.

Chapter 18

Monday morning Grayson's eyes opened to irritating sunlight clawing the bedroom walls, the bedside clock announcing the ungodly hour of 8:00 A.M. His head pounded worse than if he would've been lucky enough to find a hidden bottle of Crown Royal in the downstairs pantry, finishing it to the last, well deserving drop.

Usually he was up by now, dressed and on his third cup of coffee, but last night was anything but usual. The last time he noted the neon hour on his bedside clock, it was 4:00 A.M. and he was just finishing an entry where Digger surprised his grandmother by planting a garden of orange Poppies near the well. She still had not revealed her pregnancy to Digger, leaving Grayson to wonder what happened, why they never married. Perhaps the scallywag learned of her pregnancy, leaving her to deal with humiliating repercussions on her own. The painful thought made his aching head pound even harder.

Shoving the open diary from his chest, he swung both feet over the side of the mattress and sat up, still dressed in the same blue jeans and crumpled tee shirt from the night before.

Raking an open palm from dark stubbles to his stiff neck, he craned his head, slow steps automatically guiding him to the window. Curtains fanned in the early morning breeze, the yellow sun suspended just above the highest ridge of pines. Tall orange poppies waved from the meadow of wildflowers near the well as he imagined his grandmother's surprise symbol of love planted decades ago.

Remembering his quick judgement from the night before and the reaction it received, he made a mental note to try to be a bit more understanding, at least where Martheena was concerned. She loved his grandmother like family and the last thing he wanted was to cause more pain. Unwavering loyalty and unconditional love was two things he loved most about Martheena, her response to his insolent anger an exemplar of both.

After a hot shower, Grayson dressed making the dreaded trek downstairs to plead his rehearsed apology; knowing darned well Martheena would not be quick to forgive his hasty judgement or harsh words. She was a loving and loyal companion to his Gram, always had been, always would be...

Thirty minutes later, Grayson appeared in the kitchen doorway. Clean clothes and the fresh shave did little to hide remains of a gruelingly long night. Dark circles rung his eyes, his complexion haggard and sallow.

Finding Martheena in the kitchen as he did every morning, this morning hickory scented bacon did not spatter and pop from an iron skillet on the stove, nor did she bother turning with a wide toothy grin. She sat at the table and too looked like she had not slept. Her withered posture slumped from memory of losing her best friend for the second time. Raven eyes froze to the coffee cup clutched between twisted fingers, but she said nothing.

Silently moving to the stove, Grayson filled a mug from the percolator and sprinkled in a spoon of sugar. Leaning his weight on both hands, he gripped the sink and stared out at a framed, blue sky, the sun bright, not a cloud in sight. No need prolonging the inevitable, he purged a breath and lifted his cup. When turned around, he found Martheena still staring blankly into her cup.

"Do you need a refill," he offered with the mug hovering at his lips. Still not bothering to look up, she shook her head and slid the half-empty cup to the side.

Without taking a drink, Grayson crossed the room and sat his mug on the table. Standing behind Martheena, he rested an open palm on her shoulder and could feel the knotted tension beneath his hand. Following a consoling squeeze, he apologized for his outburst and lack of respect for the woman they both loved.

Dropping onto the chair next to her, he reached for her hand and leaned in closer. His faint voice quivered. "You have to understand Martheena, reading the pages of that diary; I've met a side of my grandmother I never knew existed. It's hard for me to swallow," He sagged deeper in the chair and frowned. The familiar knot from when he first learned the news of his grandmother's pregnancy cinched his stomach tight again.

"She's always been Gram to me...not a beautiful young woman in a steamy love relationship with a..." Second thinking his first choice word, he continued, *farmhand.*

Martheena patted the top of his hand with her free one. Her customary sense of reassurance surfaced just in time, like a life preserver to a drowning heart. "I know how hard this is for you Scamper. It was hard for me to watch Miss Rosaline go through the loss and pain," Clasping his hand, she raised her chin and added defensively, "She was human, she made mistakes,"

Grayson straightened. "So you agree that her relationship with this Digger guy was a mistake," He sounded hopeful, as if he needed validation of the ill feelings ravaging his gut.

Martheena blinked back tears, slowly twisting her head. "No, I didn't say that. I said she made mistakes." She looked past him, to the window above the sink. Her mind flashed to that dark, fateful night so many years ago, and the secret buried in the woods. She now considered the consequences she and Rosaline never discussed.

"Maybe it would've been better had she told your mom about Digger and the baby. Maybe that would've helped Cora understand your grandmother better, that her mother's life decisions were not as black and white as she believed,"

Martheena struggled from the chair and shuffled to the kitchen sink, staring out at two hummingbirds flitting from one potted geranium bloom to the next. Her fingers curled tight over the sides of the sink.

"She suffered a lot, your Gram." Martheena's voice was weak and Grayson could barely hear the words, but the pain was overbearing. "Maybe it was not her intention to keep secrets. She just wanted to spare you and your mom the same pain she had suffered."

When she turned, Grayson's eyes softened with an inner glimmer that made Martheena hope he had at least found peace with what he had learned. He did not have to understand Rosaline's past. He just needed to accept it, a crucial acceptance, or she feared his relationship with Rosaline would be lost to a painful history.

"I'm trying to understand Martheena, really I am." Grayson raised his eyes to the ceiling, squeezing them shut.

"That's all I ask Scamper, just try, for your Gram's memory and for your sake. Don't let this eat away at what you and Miss Rosaline shared,"

Forty-five minutes later Grayson found himself coasting down the steep lane of Thatcher Hill, headed to Highland. The morning was crisp and clear, hazy slivers of sunshine angling strokes of light across shaded gravel. Slowing the car nearly to a stop at the bottom of the hill, he waited for the nonchalant waddle of a pudgy groundhog to cross to the other side before he glanced both ways, pulling onto the main road.

Leaving the cooler air of dense tree-covered shade behind, he accelerated, the sunny morning air warmed by a few degrees blowing through the open window. Dropping his sunglasses from his head to his nose, he approached the first tight curve in the road, his mind glinting to memories of the night before, the flash of a deer, the near crash, but more importantly, the sound and presence he swore lured him from the car.

His mind lapped from thoughts of the echo along the roadway, to imagined footsteps in the tack room, skidding to a halt on the gut wrenching words, *"I'm with child,"* Sounding more like the makings of a twisted novel than real life, unfortunately, the crush of his heavy heart knew better.

Feeling like he was teetering dangerously close to the edge, he had to vent to someone. He needed to put the pieces together, to understand what was happening. His sanity hung in the balance and Sammy Jo was the only person he felt comfortable telling. Anyone else may think he had already fallen headfirst insane.

He had already unleashed the first skeleton from his closet when he told Sammy Jo about the running pocket watch; why not add to the growing pile of bones with his latest tales of spooky sounds in the night and phantom footsteps.

An hour later Grayson turned the radio down and braked at the first of three traffic lights in Highland. Considering not a single car passed through the intersection as he waited for the light to change, he impatiently drummed the steering wheel with his fingers and questioned the need for traffic signals at all in the tiny burg.

When the light turned green, he accelerated and slowly picked up speed, returning a hospitable wave from a man dressed in bibbed coveralls entering the corner bank.

Easing his foot from the gas pedal, he approached Franny's Diner, his heart sinking when he did not spy Sammy Jo's rusty, red pickup parked out front. Instead, a yellow, Volkswagen beetle proudly displaying plates, BUMBL B, angled in the space at the front door of Wilcox Gifts.

With the driver door open, Lettie Mae bent inside, retrieving a book bag from the passenger seat. Slamming the door closed, she slung the bag over her right shoulder, peering across the roof. Catching sight of the black, BMW idling down the street, she pitched her hand in the air with a dimpling smile.

Pulling to a stop, Grayson leaned toward the open passenger window, shoving his sunglasses on top of his head. "Morning Lettie,"

"Mornin'," she said, taking a step toward the car. Shifting her book bag from one shoulder to the other, she leaned folded arms on the door and asked the obvious, "Looking for Sammy Jo?"

"Yea, is she coming in this afternoon?"

"Maybe later, I'm not sure. She said she had some running to do…you may still catch her out at the farm though,"

"Thanks," he said, with a smile. "I'll try her there."

Lettie Mae patted the door and stepped back as he lifted the clutch from the floor. Pulling away, he shifted into second gear, glancing at Lettie in the rear view mirror, her hand in the air.

Watching the car grow smaller, Lettie Mae stood at the curb wondering how the girl with the least romantic ambition, hooked the most promising bachelor to pass through Highland...ever. All she needed to do was give him a little yank and reel him in.

"Sammy Jo never was much for fishin'..." Lettie Mae mumbled aloud. Turning towards the door, a haphazard grin slashed her face.

Sailing through the last green light in town, Grayson accelerated, Highland melting into the landscape behind. In the eight minutes it took him to reach Pine Hollow Road, his mind drifted, playing two scenarios in his head. In one, he would tell Sammy Jo about the muffled sound and footsteps, where she would proceed to pat him on the arm with convincing reassurance that he was not as crazy as he sounded. In the other, less desirable one, he would reveal his unstable mental state, where as she would shout orders to vacate her property, accompanied by a threat of calling the police, or worse yet, a staff of men in little white coats.

With his mind focused on everything but the road ahead, Grayson did not give notice to the darkening skyline, or fresh mountain air replaced by the stench of scorched pine. It was not until he neared the turn onto Pine Hollow Road did his eyes lock on thick, coal-black, smoke billowing above the Eastern ridge.

Slamming the gas pedal to the floor, the car skidded sideways around the corner, fishtailing down the first lane on the right. The gnawing, empty pit in his stomach suddenly spilled terror. A quick glance confirmed his worst fears. The ominous cloud was emanating from Wilcox Farms. Halfway down the lane he spotted the barn in the distance, orange flames rolling from century old planks, clawing at the metal roof like long reaching talons.

The front end of the car bounced from a rut, nearly tossing him from his seat, swerving from one side of the lane to the other as he fumbled his cell phone, wedged in the pocket of his shirt. His shoulder slammed the door, his eyes simultaneously flicking from the graveled road, to the screen on the phone in his hand. Surprised he actually hit the right numbers on his first attempt; he heard a calm, female voice on the other end.

When the 911 operator answered, he blurted a panicked demand. "Pine Hollow Road, Wilcox Farm, a barn fire, send the fire department!" Not waiting for a reply from the operator, he pitched the phone onto the seat beside him, jerked the wheel hard right with both hands, then back to the left, shooting through the covered bridge like a rocket.

His heart skipped a beat when he emerged from the other side and did not see Sammy Jo's dented pickup parked in front of the house, but nearly stopped beating all together when he noticed Jim's Ford parked next to the barn.

Stomping the clutch, Grayson crammed the shifter in second gear pinning the accelerator to the floor, spitting a rooster tail of gravel and dirt into the air. Within feet of the barn, he slammed the brakes, the car sliding sideways, the snarl of crackling wood drowning the sound of the revved engine.

He was out of the car yanking his tee shirt over his head before the car finished rolling to a stop. With wadded, thin fabric cupped to his face, he darted towards the open doorway. Heat radiated from black smoke like a blast furnace, hissing flames engulfing scorched wood inside.

"Mr. Wilcox! Mr. Wilcox, are you in there?" His shouts became lost in in a wall of billowing, black smoke.

Rolling plumes filtered from the heat, stinging Grayson's eyes. Despite the cloth over his face, he coughed at the suffocating vapors stealing his breath. Tripping a few steps back from the inferno, he listened for a response, but heard nothing but snapping flames.

With a second attempt, Grayson took a step forward bellowing louder than he ever thought possible. This time he heard a response melding with the loud crack of wood, not a voice, rather a muffled whimper.

Dashing to the side of the barn, Grayson turned on the water spicket, dousing his head and clothes in water, before drenching a feed sack he found tossed over a nearby bale of hay. Carrying it with him, he ducked through the front of the barn, the wet feed sack draped over his shoulders, a soaked tee shirt cupped to his face. Dodging a downpour of glowing red embers, he snaked around fallen debris and smoldering bales.

The smoke was dense, hindering his chances of ever finding Jim Wilcox, if indeed he was even in the barn. Disoriented in the blackened haze, Grayson zigzagged across the floor, stumbled and fell, crawling towards the whimpering he once again heard permeating the roar of flames.

It was near Bolt's stall he felt Jim's lifeless body, a coat of fur wrapped around his head like a safety blanket.

"Good boy Stewart..." Grayson muttered through the cloth he held tight to his face. Clambering to his knees, he dropped the wet tee shirt to the ground, hooking both hands under Jim's arms. Dragging him towards the quickest escape, the horse stall seemed the swiftest way out.

Weakened from the intense heat and smoke inhalation, Stewart belly crawled behind, collapsing just outside the doublewide door opening to the wilted pasture.

Grayson hauled Jim's body a safe distance from the burning barn, flipping him onto his back. Pressing two fingers to his neck, he felt no pulse, fearing the worst.

Arguing with his parents that he would never use the CPR class they insisted he take at the youth center when he was a kid, every detailed instruction came back, down to the creepy memory of his mouth over that of a scarlet haired, plastic dummy.

The count of thirty chest compressions, followed by pinching Jim's nose and breathing into his mouth twice, he repeated the process. Again, he knelt over Jim's lifeless body. One hand on top of the other, he plunged steadily in the center of his chest with trembling weight of his body. This time he sensed a presence standing over him, the same inexplicable presence from the cemetery, and again from the roadside the night before.

What seemed like eternity, actually only took about three minutes before Jim thrashed and began coughing, gasping intermittingly for air while swinging both arms like a prized fighter. Grayson dodged a flying fist before automatically glancing over his shoulder, but as suspected, no one was there.

A shaky exhale and Grayson collapsed back on his heels. With a bowed head, he sat silently waiting for the relief to sink in. All the *what ifs* raced in his head; what if he had decided not to come to see Sammy Jo, what if she had been at the shop, stopping him from coming to the farm, what if he were too late and Jim died. The last thought shook him for Sammy Jo's sake.

Jim struggled, pushing up on one elbow. Narrowing a confused gaze to Grayson, he then glared at Stewart's still body coiled in a furry heap near the barn. When he looked back to Grayson, another cough choked the dreaded question.

The stir of saving Jim's life ebbed when Grayson's eyes followed Jim's to the barn and realization set. He would have to give Sammy Jo mournful news after all. Grayson had spared Jim's life, but not without casualty.

Stewart too played a role in keeping Sammy Jo's grandfather alive until help arrived, a role that obviously cost him his life.

The shrill of alerting sirens blared in the distance, growing louder as firetrucks approached Wilcox Farm. Two long honks from the engine horn announced their arrival, followed by an ambulance twisting down the lane.

Grayson stood, dragging heavy footsteps towards intensifying heat. His eyes settled on Stewart's limp body lying in withered grass just beyond the horse stall. After the dog's selfless, heroic actions, the least he could do was spare him from perishing in the blaze.

By now, long reaching flames shot from the open stall, lapping at the wavering roof. Not only did spewing flames jeopardize Grayson's safety, it also threatened total collapse of the 150-year-old structure.

Reaching the dog, Grayson knelt on one knee. He quickly slipped one arm under Stewart's limp neck, the other under his belly. He started to raise the singed remains when the tail lifted and slapped the dirt, not once, but twice. Grayson recoiled with a shockwave that shoved him onto his rear end. Stewart lifted his head, blinking brown eyes, before his head drifted back to the ground.

A menacing creak drew Grayson's focus to the roof, a surge of adrenaline fueling quick action. Scooping Stewart in his arms, Grayson staggered to his feet and back three steps just as blazing wood overhead gave way, an eruption of fire and embers exploding into a gray, smoke filled sky.

Chapter 19

Glass sliding doors of the emergency room separated, a strong smell of antiseptic and ammonia infusing the summer air. From the doorway, Grayson noted blush colored chairs lining a wall of windows, as well as two tight rows through the middle of the room, mostly empty.

A small group of waiting family clustered near the main entrance, talking quietly among themselves in hushed tones. Grayson excused himself, inching past the group to approach the reception area. A nurse sat behind the counter, her head bent a she concentrated on the computer screen. It was only after Grayson gave a mock cough did she look up.

"May I help you," The woman looked up, her eyes sticking to a strapping bare chest smudged in black soot. Her jaw relaxed, leaving her mouth slightly agape.

"Yes mam, they brought a friend of mine in by ambulance, Jim Wilcox," Not exactly a legitimate description of their volatile relationship, but if the woman behind the counter knew how Mr. Wilcox' really felt about him, Grayson figured he would not only be denied information, but would probably be thrown into the parking lot by his ears.

Bright red spread from the woman's cheeks, burning her ears when she realized she was staring. Automatically jerking her eyes back to the computer screen, she gave two swift clicks of the mouse.

"Yes, he just arrived and is being examined." Awkwardly looking up from the screen, she surveyed him once again before hesitantly asking, "Would you like for me to find you something to put on?" The offer was more to discourage the distraction of her roving eyes than for Grayson's sake.

Grayson wiped the back of his hand across his forehead before smearing black, grimy soot on his jeans. "Yea, that would be great," he answered, not bothering with an explanation.

She left her desk returning a couple of minutes later with a light blue hospital gown, handing it over the counter. "Sorry, this was all I could find." They shared a smile before he took the gown from her hand. "It may be a few minutes," she added. "If you'd like to have a seat," Gesturing to a table in the corner, she offered him complimentary coffee.

Frazzled nerves fueled Grayson's monotonous pace back and forth across the small waiting room floor.

Wringing his hands in tense silence, he glanced at the wall clock, the third time in ten minutes.

He had called Sammy Jo's shop getting no answer, as well as phoning her cell, which went straight to voice mail. The message he left was brief and to the point. Hoping to avert panic, he reassured her that her grandfather was okay before undermining his attempt with the added snippet that he was in Oakland Memorial.

Another fifteen minutes passed before the receptionist behind the counter summonsed Grayson, leading him through a set of swinging doors and down the hall, stopping at the fifth room on the right. A dusty rose-colored curtain drawn around the bed blocked Grayson's view, the steady beat of a heart monitor the only sound from the other side. After the nurse turned and walked away, Grayson stood silently stalling.

"Well, are you going to come in or not?" Salted with sarcasm, Jim's voice was a bit shaky.

Drawing the flimsy curtain to the side, Grayson poked his head inside, watching Jim shift in the bed, jockeying for a more comfortable position. Two plastic tubes in each nostril, he tugged them loose, obviously annoyed by their presence.

"You should probably leave those there," Throwing caution to the wind, Grayson wandered to the bed, positioning the tubes back in place. "You took in quite a bit of smoke,"

Jim's gaze filtered down Grayson's hospital gown, gaping in the front, partially concealing black traces of the fire. Shifting his focus to the window, Jim nearly choked on the huge scoop of humility stuck in his throat, events of the past hour looping in his head. Had it not been for Grayson's timing and courage, Sammy Jo would have been planning another funeral, and they both knew it.

"You saved my life," Jim's impudent tone sounded both grateful and ashamed. He looked back to Grayson and gripped the side rails, struggling to pull up in the bed. "Not that I probably deserved it." His voice was raw.

Grayson hooked a hand under Jim's arm, drawing him upright in bed before handing him a Styrofoam cup of water from the table. "You certainly did not deserve to die."

Jim stifled a laugh at the curtailed statement, wondering if there were more Grayson was tempted to add. Accepting the cup, he wedged the straw in his mouth sucking a slow sip. When he handed the trembling cup back to Grayson, his mouth bowed slyly. "Scorch my evil ass a bit, just not die…"

They both laughed at Jim's ill attempt at humor.

"Anyway, thanks," he said, his tone switching to a more serious tenor. "I'd hate to think of what my dying in there would've done to Sam,"

Grayson walked to the window, poking his hands in his pockets, staring out at the lot. They both knew all too well the answer to that statement.

"I don't think she could take losing you," Grayson said, watching Sammy Jo scramble from her truck, slamming the door closed behind her. Dashing in the direction of the emergency room, her pace escalated to a jog.

Precisely two and a half minutes later, Sammy Jo burst into the room, tennis shoes skidding to a halt at the foot of her grandfather's bed. Sucking in a sharp breath, she blew it out, looking visibly relieved when she saw him sitting upright. A glistening of unshed tears glazed blue eyes.

"Oh my God, you really are alright," Clinging to the end of the bed, Sammy Jo steadied trembling legs. "I was afraid you were..." Hot tears stung her eyes and she could not bring herself to say the ugly word.

"I'm fine," Jim interrupted, "I'm too mean to die."

"That's not funny Pops," She rushed to his side, welling tears made her barely able to focus. She fumbled with the bedsheets through a watery haze. Peppering him with questions, she fawned and fussed over him like a mother hen, adjusting the head of the bed, tucking covers snuggly at his feet, only for him to pull them loose again.

"What happened?" Standing at the foot of the bed, Sammy Jo's gaze shifted from her grandfather to Grayson's soot smudged face, and then back to Jim in search of an explanation. "And what's he doing here?" she asked, an accusing finger shooting through the air. "Why didn't you call me yourself Pops?"

Jim put his hand up to silence her babbling. "If you'll take a breath, I'll tell you," Motioning to the chair beside the bed he ordered her to sit, which she obeyed.

Brushing the hair from her face, she folded her hands in her lap and drew a shaky breath. "Ok, I'm listening,"

"There was a fire," he started. "In the barn... I'm not sure what started it."

"Oh God," She choked a whisper, her shoulders sagging.

"Bolt and Sadie are fine. I got to them in time, turned them out in the pasture. I should've left well enough alone, but I thought I could at least save ole' Red." Fondly mentioning the nickname of his 1948 Farmall tractor, he wilted deeper into the mattress.

"Pops, you didn't!" she scoffed, her back shooting rigid.

"He did," Grayson, answered blatantly for him. Tugging at the flaps of the hospital gown, he shot an accusing eye at Jim. "Probably not the smartest thing he's ever done," he added scornfully.

"Do you mind?" Jim scowled across the room, beneath dented brows. "This is my story."

"This is our story," Grayson corrected. "But go ahead," he added, flitting fingers of one hand through the air.

Jim turned back to Sammy Jo. "Not sure what happened, I think a roof rafter or something fell, knocked me right upside the noggin. It was lights out."

"And where do you come in?" Sammy Jo asked starkly, turning to Grayson. Her eyes flitted across the baggy cotton gown capping his knees. "Were you hurt too?"

Leaning palms on the air conditioning unit, ankles crossed, Grayson filled in the blanks. "No, I'm not hurt. I sort of lost my shirt." A cheeky grin curved his lips when he noticed her checking the gown out further, training her eyes on the dark, masculine patch coiled in the center of his chest. Not bothering to pull the persistent opening closed, he continued. "I stopped by the shop to see you. Lettie Mae told me that you might still be at the farm, so I stopped out," he said, matter of fact. "That's it."

The blatant words were as sobering as a bucket of ice water dumped on her head. "That's it? That's all you have to say?" She bolted to her feet and began pacing back and forth, her feet stomping louder with each step.

"I saw smoke from the corner of Pine Hollow," Casually walking to Jim's bedside, Grayson leaned both hands on the bed rails. "The barn was pretty much engulfed by the time I got there." His mind flashed back to the fire, his gut wrenching at the thought of how close Jim came to meeting his maker.

"It was a good thing Stewart was hanging around. He's the real hero." Grayson looked from Jim to Sammy Jo's quick pace across the floor, her hands ringing incessantly. "That damned dog stayed with your grandfather until I got to him,"

"Stewart?" Instantly, her pace skidded to a stop, her breath halting at the same time.

Grayson nodded. "He's fine," he said, cutting off her obvious next question. "A few singed hairs are the worst of his injuries." Looking back to Jim he added, "I found him shielding Mr. Wilcox from the flames. It could've been much worse."

Sammy Jo blew out her breath, unaware she had been holding it.

Jim's eyes rolled to Grayson. "I think we can drop the Mr. Wilcox now," he mused.

"Go ahead," Sammy Jo ignored her grandfather's words, impatiently gesturing for more with her hand.

"I dragged Mr. ...I got Jim outside," Grayson corrected, feeling a little awkward with the informality. Sauntering back to the window, he stared into the parking lot before twisting back. He knew if Sammy Jo was upset now, what he had to tell her next was going to send her bouncing off the ceiling. "He was not breathing at first, so I performed CPR."

"CPR, oh my God..." Sammy Jo shrieked, dropping her face in her hands with a shiver. "I cannot believe this," When she looked back up, a glinting spark replaced the teas in her eyes, the explosion Grayson feared, not far off. "You should have known better Pops," Stomping a foot, she spun to the bed and swatted at the air, "You should have known better!" Suddenly realizing her voice had rose to near shouting, she lowered the volume, but only enough to stop the nurses from calling security. "You could have been killed Pops!"

Marching back and forth next to his bed, she stopped and stared up at the ceiling tiles, before casting an accusing eye at her grandfather.

"Could have been," Jim emphasized with a slow string of words. Stunting her rants, he tried his best to minimize the situation. Fidgeting with the oxygen tube in his nose with one hand, he wagged one finger in the air with the other. Sammy Jo glared at his finger, staving off the impulsive urge to break it off and hand it to him.

"How can you act so nonchalant about this Pops?" This is serious!" she barked.

"It *could've* been serious Sam, it's not. I'm fine," He dipped his chin, repeating reassurance in much the same tone he did when she was a little girl, "I'm fine,"

She growled through clenched teeth, plopping in the chair next to his bed.

"Don't you get too comfortable there little missy," Glaring down his nose, one dark brow floated into Jim's silver splashed hairline. "You need to get on back out to the farm and tend to things."

"Not on your life," she snapped, scooting to the edge of the chair. "I'm not leaving you."

Like an attorney pleading her case, she presented him with every logical reason to stay, and he countered with every possible excuse to leave.

"You need to get home and round the horses up before nightfall. Call Jeb Porter and see if he can make room for Sadie and Bolt in his barn while we figure something out," When she didn't answer he shifted his gaze to Grayson still leaning against the air conditioner, arms folded across his chest like an innocent bystander. "Think you could try and talk some sense into that thick head of hers?"

At Sammy Jo's wilted look, Grayson intervened. "You know, your grandfather is right, there's a lot that needs tending back at the farm," Wandering to Jim's bed, he gripped the side rails and looked down with a saucy grin. "Besides, there are plenty of pretty nurses to watch after your grandfather."

Poor nurses...

Sammy Jo gnawed on her lower lip, struggling for a viable excuse not to leave her grandfather.

"You'll be much more help to me at home," Jim slipped his hand between the rail reaching for her hand. "I promise I'll be fine Sam. They said I can probably go home tomorrow."

Taking his hand, her eyes circled up to meet Grayson's, the hazel green hinting a gray tone in the fluorescent light. He nodded reassurance.

"Ok, but I'm going to call and check on you every hour. If there is any change in your condition, I'm coming back."

After kissing her grandfather goodbye... twice... she headed for the door only to stop short. Turning she asked one last time about staying. Jim scowled a reply, which she wholly expected.

Grayson slipped his arm around Sammy Jo's waist after leaving the room, leading her down the hall and through the waiting room. Several more waiting patients had filtered into the room, two children playing a game of tag around a row of chairs. Sammy Jo stopped short as a little boy scurried past with a giggle, before continuing through the doors and into the parking lot dotted with cars.

The sun was beyond peak, making its slow descent towards the pine skyline, a cooling breeze cautioned decline of daylight. Pulling open her truck door, Grayson waited for her to climb inside, clicking it closed behind her, his hand lingering.

Gripping the steering wheel with both hands, Sammy Jo dropped her forehead against it, at last letting a flow of stubborn, restrained tears break free.

Grayson reached inside steadying her quaking shoulder. "Your grandfather is tougher than shoe leather." He heard her sniffle with no reply. "He's strong. He'll be fine."

Her head snapped up as if he had poked a sore spot. "And so was my grandmother, she was strong too, right to the second her heart stopped beating, and she collapsed while picking apples in the produce department," She wiped the back of her hand across her eyes. "She was strong too, but she still died,"

Grayson pulled the truck door open dragging her from the seat and into his arms. He held her silently until the shuddering stopped and the tears subsided.

Taking a step back, Sammy Jo tugged at the hem of her shirt, composing herself. "I'm sorry,"

"For what?"

"For acting like a weak, blubbering fool,"

"You are not a blubbering fool and you most definitely are not weak. You may not have me figured out yet Ms. Wilcox, but it didn't take me long to realize the kind of woman you are."

Looking into Grayson's eyes, she admitted inwardly for the first time how fond she had grown of him. They had known each other for such a short time, yet he made her feel safe, confident. Her gaze skimmed her grandfather's hospital window just past Grayson's shoulder. Now, she could add grateful to that growing list. He made her feel grateful...very, very grateful.

Chapter 20

Braking to a stop at the last traffic light in Highland, the vague stench of scorched wood became undeniable, forewarning the nightmarish scene looming only miles down the road. The reeking odor twisted Sammy Jo's stomach with thoughts of how painfully close she came to losing the one person in life who made life normal.

Glancing in the rear view mirror, her eyes connected with Grayson's, making her stomach ring even tighter. His soot-smudged cheeks reminded her of his role in the near fatal tragedy, how she could very well have been planning a funeral, instead of arranging boarding quarters for the horses. The traffic light turned green and she accelerated past the diner and gift shop with a closed sign hanging in the window, leaving the silhouette of town behind.

At the last bend in the road, Sammy Jo slowed and twisted the wheel onto Pine Hollow Road. The reek of smoke lingered in a gray haze hanging low over the mountain. Black bands coiled from Wilcox Farm, infusing the once blue sky in murky desolation. Sammy Jo heard a painful groan escape her lips.

Word of tragedy travels fast in small towns. Trucks of neighboring farms and friends, eager to do their part, dotted the gravel lane, a longstanding southern tradition during times of hardship. Sammy Jo turned down the lane, angling between several vehicles before emerging on the other side of the covered bridge.

Lettie Mae stood at the bottom of the stairs, next to her beetle, her eyes swollen and red. She met Sammy Jo at the truck as it pulled to a stop.

"Oh my God Sammy Jo, I am so sorry," Not waiting for Sammy Jo to turn off the engine, Lettie Mae jerked open the cab door. Fresh tears began to drop. "I came as soon as I heard... your Grandpa? Will he be ok?" she rattled, without a breath.

Sammy Jo slid down from the truck seat and watched Grayson pull to stop on the other side. He stepped out and pushed the door closed before their eyes met over the hood of her truck. She sensed the emotions they shared, ranging from grief to grateful. "Thanks to Grayson,"

Lettie wrapped her arms around Sammy Jo's neck, resting her chin on her shoulder. "A couple of women from the lady's church group brought food and cold drinks for the firemen. I hope it was ok, I used the key on the back porch to open the house for them."

"Thank you Lettie." Sammy Jo peered over Lettie Mae's shoulder to the mound of smoldering embers near the pasture, ruins of where the barn once stood. Snowy ashes rained down from a smoke filled sky, blanketing the ground in powdery white. A single firetruck remained, dousing glistening cinders with a fine spray of water. Alternating red and white lights oscillated from the truck, reflecting from a ceiling of suspended smoke. The smell of smoke and sound of stubborn hissing flames was a memory forever branded on Sammy Jo's brain.

Grayson made his way around the back of the truck stepping up next to Sammy Jo. He smiled when the squeak of the screen door pulled their gaze to a scruffy black lab wiggling through the opening, easing down the steps on blistered paws. Dropping to her knees with open arms, Sammy Jo wept tears of thanks, the dog nudging against her.

Sister Shrugs followed from the doorway shuffling to the edge of the porch. Clinging to a post for support, the other hand rested across her thumping chest. Her fair complexion had faded one shade lighter to ghostly. "Your Grandfather Sammy Jo, is Jim alright?" Breath stifled, she waited in painful anticipation of the feared news.

Sammy Jo smiled tenderly at the ailing widow, "I was told personally by Pops that he is too mean to die."

Sister Shrugs gripped her chest even tighter and backed to a rocker just as her knees buckled beneath her. "Thank you dear Jesus." she thanked in a shaky whisper, sinking deep into the chair.

Sammy Jo stepped around Stewart and rushed up the steps, dropping onto one knee. She clasped the widow's hand in her own. "He is going to be just fine Sister Shrugs." Patting the back of the widow's quivering hand, she added, "He will probably need some fussing over in the days ahead though. I may need your help."

Tenderness crinkled the corners of relieved eyes. Sister Shrugs mind fast-forwarded, conjuring menus for the days ahead, including her chicken and hand rolled dumplings, another blue ribbon winner.

It was then that the growl of oversized mud tires ground to a stop in front of the house. In all the chaos, Sammy Jo had not taken notice of Thaddeus Porter's faded green pickup parked near the pasture, loading Sadie and Bolt into the long horse trailer fastened to the hitch.

Jeb Porter's farm was one of the largest in Highland, mirroring Wilcox Farm's Southern border. Sammy Jo and Jeb's son, Thaddeus, had grown up together, sharing early milestones, including learning to ride a bike and her first kiss, shared just after her thirteenth birthday. The kiss, long tucked away in Sammy Jo's memory, summed to more of an awkward peck than an actual kiss. Thaddeus on the other hand, carried it close to his heart, like a treasured nugget of adolescence.

Thaddeus dropped down from the seat, a cross between backwoods rugged with a dash of charm, right down to the slip of straw wedged between perfectly aligned, white teeth. Beginning to think there was something in the southern water; Grayson could not help noticing that the hills sure seemed to grow their boys on the extra-large side.

Thaddeus towered easily at six foot, four inches if he stood a foot. Every brawny inch of tanned muscle bulged beneath tight sleeves of a plaid button down shirt.

Wavy blonde hair curled at his shirt collar and blue eyes matching the color of sky, gleamed when he looked at Sammy Jo.

Sammy Jo started from the porch, leaping from the bottom step, her mood noticeably elevating several degrees. "Hey Thad," she called out. Rushing to him, she encircled both arms around his neck.

Grayson stood next Lettie Mae with both hands shoved in his pockets, watching like a riveted spectator as the two embraced.

Lettie Mae could almost hear the wheels spinning out of control in Grayson's head and leaned toward him, bumping his shoulder with hers. "A neighbor, just an old friend," she whispered, trying unsuccessfully to tame the green-eyed monster perched on his shoulder.

Not accustomed to this unfamiliar emotion, Grayson cringed, jealousy giving a two fisted squeeze to his pounding heart. "There seems to be a lot of old friends floating around these parts." Grayson flinched, his mind shooting to good old Harley and his heated reaction when Sammy Jo entered the tavern on his arm. But, unlike Harley, whose hair stood on end at the mere sight of Grayson, Thaddeus barely even noticed his presence. Watching the *old friend* cradle Sammy Jo in his arms, Grayson wondered how she had managed to remain single, when she apparently had a male following as long as the Mason Dixon line.

"How's your Pops, is he alright?" Thaddeus asked, not at all eager to let her go.

Sammy Jo gave him a pat on the back and took a step back, tugging his attention with her. "He'll be fine," she answered. "They're keeping him overnight for observation." As she turned to face Grayson, Thad noticed him for the first time. "Thad, I'd like for you to meet a friend of mine, Grayson Wesley. Grayson, this is Thad Porter, our neighbor." Sammy Jo looped her arm through Thad's, pulling him toward the house.

The word *friend* suddenly sounded brutally depraved, as he realized that his feelings for Sammy Jo had far outgrown the chummy definition. As if offered an appetizer of slimy Earthworms, Grayson reluctantly moved one foot forward, his right hand dangling mid-air, only inches from Thaddeus' hand.

"Good to meet you," Grayson heard the words randomly leave his mouth but confirmed what the little green monster sitting on his shoulder was whispering in his ear...*liar*. He was as about as happy to meet Thaddeus Porter as he would have been to shake hands with Jack the Ripper in a dark alley.

Thaddeus turned down a cold drink offered by Sammy Jo, promising to stop by the next day for a rain check. Thumbing over his right shoulder, he reminded her that he still had to get Sadie and Bolt settled in their new sleeping quarters.

"Pops and I really appreciate you and your Pa doing this for us." Sammy Jo followed Thaddeus to his truck and waited as he grabbed the steering wheel, effortlessly hoisting himself into the seat of his boosted Chevy diesel. Slamming the door, he propped his arm out the open window and gave her a wink. "Anything to help out Sam,"

Grayson hoped Lettie did not notice the growl that had escaped through clenched teeth. It came as automatic as a belch after a swig of bad whiskey.

Sammy Jo took few steps back with her hand in the air and waited for Thaddeus to disappear through the covered bridge before joining Grayson and Lettie already making their way onto the porch.

It was long past sunset when everyone had left, with the exception of Grayson. A lone fire truck was the last of the rescue crew to leave. Sammy Jo watched as the lights from the engine turned onto the main road, flickering from sight. Rocking gently in the porch rocker, she looked toward the night sky, blinking stars barely visible through smoky, gray bands drifting from the barn ruins.

Sammy Jo cut into the silence and asked Grayson to walk with her to the heap of smoldering remains, her voice soft and reverent, as if she were speaking of the dead. Grayson reached for her hand, gently guiding her from the porch and down the short distance, neither talking as they walked.

Air near the barn was hot and stagnant, an occasional rustle of scorched, brittle leaves from a nearby Oak, and the sad coo of a distant owl, the only audible sounds. Sammy Jo dropped Grayson's hand, crossing her arms over her chest. Surveying the mound of sullied rafters, she caught sight of her grandfather's early model Farmall. Charred remains took the place of bright red paint lost to the inferno.

"He not only loved that old tractor, he respected it," she declared. "Refused to sell, said she helped make him who he was."

Grayson slipped his arm around her waist and let her talk.

"I cannot believe all that has happened today." She tried unsuccessfully to swallow a sob as a lone tear eluded her eye. "I left my Pops this morning just like any other, and to think..." Her words trailed and she could not bring herself to admit what may have been her last morning with her grandfather. Instead, she added, "I guess we never know what life hold for us."

Sammy Jo's arm circled Grayson's waist, leading him silently through the pasture gate and partway up the hillside. Plopping down in wavering grass, she wrapped her arms around bended knees, her eyes falling to a perfect view of the incinerated debris below.

Grayson sat down next to her, remembering the account from the journal, the shocking revelation that had brought him out to the farm in the first place. Just like Sammy Jo, life had handed him his own fist full of suffering. She nearly lost her grandfather to death; words from beyond the grave had stolen a piece of his grandmother from him.

They watched spirals of smoke thread into the night sky like wavering ribbons, free embers glistening in the mountain breeze. After a short time, Sammy Jo laid back in the cool grass, staring into the sable sky. An infinity of stars blinked through puffs of gray smoke.

Grayson lay down beside her, lacing his fingers over his chest. After she reached for his hand, pulling it to her with a squeeze, his heart beat clam and steady. It was the first time in two days he felt at peace. The mere touch of her hand righted a world of mental chaos.

Rolling onto his stomach, he leaned on his elbows, gazing down at her. Mellow moonlight reflected in her eyes, copper hair spread across soft, green grass. The lure of her beauty was more than he could resist. Forgetting about everything but the temptation lying only inches away, he leaned closer. Feeling her warm breath against his face, he tangled his hands in a mane of silken copper and pressed his lips to hers. His kiss was soft and gentle, yet meaningful. Spotting gentle kisses along her face, he stopped at her hair, breathing in the familiar scent, allowing his body to melt against her.

He moved to her lips and kissed her again, softly at first. Sammy Jo made no effort to stop him. Instead, she wove her fingers into his hair pulling him tight, her lips gently parting. Grayson's passion, fueled by her response, grew stronger. His breath quickened, his heart thrashing his ribs. Fingers tangled in copper ringlets, he moved over her, pinning her to the ground.

Sammy Jo hungered for his touch, his kiss. She clung to his neck and moaned. Her hands drew down his body, caressing taught cotton of a borrowed tee shirt stretched over his back. She could feel the ripple of strength beneath her fingers, the flex of tight muscles.

Abruptly pulling away, Grayson flipped onto his back and stared at the moon drifting in and out of sight. Sammy Jo rolled onto her stomach propping her head in the palm of one hand. The slow sigh she released was sheer frustration. Bewildered, she looked into troubled eyes and recognized doubt.

"What's wrong?" Sammy Jo pushed up from the ground, crossing her legs Indian style. She pressed her palm to his heaving chest and could feel his wildly beating heart beneath her hand. "Didn't you like it?"

Grayson snorted a breath and tucked both hands beneath his head, watching a cloud block the moon. "Like it? What is there not to like?" His eyes moved to Sammy Jo, trying to make sense of the hasty maneuver himself. For a split second, he too questioned his sanity. A man would have to be stark crazy to turn away from such beauty.

"You are the most stunning woman I have ever seen Sammy Jo and my feelings for you should be obvious. That's why I have to stop," After a brief hesitation, that he wasn't sure was to convince him that he was dead wrong, he added, "While I still can."

"I don't understand." She pulled her hand from his chest and her eyes dropped to the side.

Grayson sat up and sighed, brushing his quivering thumb across her moist lips. The truth was he did not understand either. For a reason he could not fully comprehend, he believed their paths were meant to cross, their destinies intertwined. Just as surely as he knew they were destined to be together, he knew the timing was not right.

Chapter 21

After crediting a restless night to a concoction of emotions ranging from anger to frustration, Grayson laid in bed, his mind bouncing from Rosaline's pregnancy revelation, to the feel of Sammy Jo's body beneath him in the meadow the night before. It had taken every ounce of self-control he possessed to stop his advances, when every thread of his being wanted to make her his own. Squeezing his eyes closed, he imagined what might have been, had he not insisted being so noble. A long painful moment passed as he mulled the thought in his head, a thought that made every manly fiber of his being ache.

Bolting upright in bed at the rap of knuckles on the bedroom door, Grayson glanced at the illuminated dial of his clock radio angled on the nightstand. Well past 10:00 A.M., he swung both feet over the side of the bed and stood grabbing for his jeans, tossed across the arm of the chair. He forced in one leg, hopping on one foot to keep his balance. "Yes?" he called, wriggling in the other leg before jerking up the zipper.

Martheena's voice penetrated the heavy wood door. "Are you going to sleep all day Scamper?" she asked. "You have an appointment with that realtor in about an hour," she reminded.

With all that had transpired in the last days, Grayson totally forgot about the appointment with Harry Theobald to tour the grounds. Today he would place a real estate sign in front of his grandmother's estate, the reminder only adding to the digressing chaos in his head. With a disparaging shrug, he buried his fingers in dark mangled hair before reaching for his shirt, dropping it over his head. It was too late to cancel the early morning appointment. The best-case scenario was a quick shower and even quicker cup of coffee before the realtor arrived.

"I'll be right down Martheena." Listening to the sound of slipper wrapped feet shuffling to the stairway, he gathered a change of clothes and trudged down the hallway, slamming the bathroom door behind him.

Grayson was just finishing his first cup of coffee on the front porch when he heard the engine of the gray sedan making its slow, vigilant ascent up the winding gravel lane. Not bothering to stand, he waited for the car to pull to a stop at the picket gate, the motor cutting silent. It was only after Mr. Theobald opened the car door, dragging a brief case with him, did Grayson sit down his cup and walk to the porch edge.

"Good morning, Mr. Wesley I presume," The pudgy, balding man exclaimed cheerfully before slamming the car door and pushing his way through the gate, his black leather case tucked prudently under his arm.

Grayson was not sure if it was the annoying high pitch of the pint-sized man's voice that irritated him, or the dreaded purpose of his visit. Whatever the reason, Grayson cringed with a forced smile meeting him at the top step with an extended hand. "Good morning and please call me Grayson,"

After an eager handshake and repeated request for Grayson to address him simply as Harry, the realtor buffed an open palm over a shiny, balding head and followed to one the rockers lining the front porch. Plopping down, he hastily opened the brief case sprawled across his lap and pulled out a neat stack of documents.

"Nice place you have here," Harry adjusted wire-rimmed glasses perched on the bridge of his nose, his gaze skimming the vibrant meadow of wildflowers and poppies. Scanning the breeze swept acreage, his sights ended on the curving path leading to the barn below. "So sorry about your grandmother's death," he added in afterthought.

Grayson reached for his cup from the side table, tipping the last swig of coffee. "Yeah, me too," he mumbled. "Would you like a cup of coffee before we get started?" he asked politely, but hoping the irritating man would say no. He could not get this meeting over fast enough.

"No thanks," The realtor's reply came quick, wasting no time on getting down to business. "We can do a fast walk through if you'd like before signing a few papers." Thumbing through the paper clipped stack, he checked the order of documents.

"This is all a matter of formality anyway." Fanning a hand in the air, he dropped the papers back in the brief case and sat it at his feet. "I doubt the place will ever hit the Realtor Listings anyway." He rattled like an auctioneer perched on a soapbox, his smile widening as he wiped clammy palms on his trouser legs.

Grayson swore he saw the refection of greedy dollar signs glinting in his olive colored eyes.

"Hope you don't mind, but I gave the address of your grandmother's home to a couple from Nashville the other day. They are looking for a property to relocate and expand on their business. I told them to drive up and see if this is something that may fit their needs."

"And..." Grayson tapped one foot against the floorboards waiting for further explanation. When Theobald nudged his glasses up on his nose and stood silently walking to the edge of the porch, Grayson followed behind.

"Well, are they interested or not?" Grayson's patience with the little man was wearing transparent thin.

"Oh yes..." he squeaked happily, shoving both hands in neatly pressed trouser pockets. "They love the property," After a slight pause he added, "Although there is some updating they would like to do." When Theobald spun around, he did not realize how close Grayson stood, his nose nearly bumping into a broad chest. Pulling one hand from his pocket, he poked a finger over Grayson's shoulder and pointed to the large plate glass windows on either side of the front door.

"The little lady pictures bay windows along the front of the house and of course she wants to change the paint colors. You know women, they want to put their own spin on things," he chuckled, sardonically.

Plans the potential buyer had for Thatcher Hill battered Grayson's conscience, the final blow coming when the realtor revealed plans for construction of a new barn.

Spinning around, Theobald dipped his head to the century old barn standing in the hollow. "The couple owns a construction business with a lot of heavy equipment. The first thing on their agenda is to tear down the old barn and replace it with something a bit more modern and efficient."

Grayson's face crumpled as though he took a fist to the gut. His focus followed the trail leading from the house, ending on faded red planks covered by a green tin roof. Imagining the old red barn in ruins and replaced by a shiny metal structure was equivalent to his childhood imploding.

His eyes drifted to the ship lapped overhang leading to the tack room. A physical squeeze in his chest nearly choked the breath from his lungs. His grandmother's life had taken a significant twist within the walls of that room, a secret she had carried and protected her entire life. Suddenly the pains of an unexpected pregnancy turned into a crushing need to protect his grandmother's hidden past.

Before Theobald could mentally destruct any more of Thatcher Hill, Grayson clenched him by the shoulders and spun him towards the rocker where his brief case lay on the floor. "I think I've changed my mind about selling," he quickly spat. "I'll call if I have a change of heart."

"But…" With a finger prodding the air, confused Harry Theobald dug for every sensible reason to refute Grayson's change of heart. "The real estate market is up right now…and I have a buyer who will pay top dollar…and…"

Grayson snatched the brief case from the floor shoving it in Theobald's pudgy middle. "I said I will call if I change my mind," Short of throwing him off the property, Grayson clenched Theobald's shoulder, shoving him to the steps, helping him down the first two. "I appreciate you coming out this morning," he added mechanically.

Harry stepped a safe distance onto the grass before turning. "I think you are making a big mistake here Grayson, you…" He started to say more but Grayson cut him off mid-sentence with a glare that bordered threatening.

"Okay…" Harry stomped toward his car, tripping on a loose shoestring. With his briefcase wedged under his arm, he jerked open the car door and shot a nasty look in Grayson's direction, second thinking any additional comment. Instead, he pitched his case across the seat and climbed in, starting the engine. Slamming the car in reverse, he turned around and shot down the narrow gravel lane, not nearly as slow or vigilant as his ascent.

Grayson dropped into the rocker and smiled triumphantly as he watched the dust settle. Now that felt right…

After pouring a second cup of coffee and returning to the front porch, Grayson heard the rattle of an engine growing close. Before he caught sight of Sammy Jo, the unmistakable clunk of her red pickup preceded her, drawing up the corners of his mouth. A dreaded day was getting better by the minute.

The rusty Chevy skidded to a halt at the gate. Sammy Jo cut the engine, swung open the cab door and jumped down from the seat, a broad smile plastered to her face.

"Someone seems to be having a good day," Grayson projected, sitting his cup on the side table. Inching to the edge of the porch, he leaned a shoulder against the column, noting the bounce in her step and rosy blush on her cheeks.

"They're releasing Pops from the hospital this afternoon." she replied cheerfully, shoving the gate open ahead of her. "I had a few minutes before time to pick him up, so I thought I'd stop by."

"I'm glad you did." He waited for her to mount the stairs, offering her his hand at the last one.

Leaving the top step, Sammy Jo placed her palm in his, with unhurried ease, rose on her tiptoes, and stunned him with a kiss.

"What was that for?" he asked, his eyes settling on full lips.

"Do I need a reason?" Her eyes followed her palm smoothing over his chest. She remembered the aching desire from the night before, a memory that had plagued a long, restless night.

Grayson locked his hands at the small of her back, tugging her against him. "No mam," His voice turned husky, the glint in his eyes a dead giveaway to the heated testosterone pumping through his veins like an overzealous teenager. He savored her softness and moaned, his mouth twisting over hers with a kiss so powerful that it stole her breath. Picking up where the night before had ended, his gut tightened and so did every strand of his manly being.

When at last Sammy Jo pulled back, she sucked in a quick breath, looking up into his flushed face. Swiping her thumb over his bottom lip, she smiled with a small sense of victory.

"I have thought of very little else since you left me frustrated last night Mr. Wesley," she chided playfully. "I wasn't quite finished,"

Grayson released a jagged breath and grinned. "Are you finished now?" With a wink, his appraising look spoke volumes.

"For now," she mocked, with a roguish grin that made him wonder what mischief was playing out in her head. Finding a spot in one of the porch rockers, she flicked off one flip-flop, pulled her foot up, tucking it beneath her.

"It looks like it's going to be a beautiful day," Squeezing her eyes shut, she drew a deep breath of warm, mountain air and blew it out.

Grayson sat on the floor facing her. Wedging his back to one of the white pillars, he pulled up one leg, weaving fingers of both hands around his bent knee.

When she opened her eyes, she found him staring at her. She squinted, trying to gauge what he was thinking, but he was unreadable.

Grayson's attention fell first to the well house before transferring it to the barn, now in partial shade from the rising sun. "I had an appointment this morning with a realtor about listing Gram's estate," he confessed. "I'm surprised you didn't pass him coming up the lane."

The smile in Sammy Jo's eyes faded and her face went lily white. She impulsively kicked her other foot free of the flip-flop, pushing up from the rocker in slow motion. Wandering to the other side of the porch, she folded her arms across her stomach and stood silently, her eyes fixed like super glue on the red barn below. She had known Grayson only a few short weeks, yet he rattled her composure unlike anyone she had ever known. Now he was leaving.

Grayson quietly crept up, slipping his arms around her waist from behind. Her body tensed beneath his touch and for a moment, he expected her to pull away. Instead, she stood silent and unmoving, her back stone rigid.

Grayson pulled his hands from her waist and spun her to him. Steely eyes raked the distant skyline, avoiding him. Her chin lifted in a proud, indignant angle, refusing to admit the delusional fantasy that had been building in her head over the past weeks. Expectations of anything other than a fleeting friendship are the kind of fantasies that only happen in fairy tales, not the mountains of Tennessee.

Foolish and vulnerable, her wounded ego oozed regret for throwing herself at him like a girl with a schoolyard crush. She should have known better than let her emotions run wild. Grayson was not the taming type. They both knew from day one that their relationship was temporary. He hired her to do a job. Her job was finished and so was any obligation they had to one another. He would leave Burlington and return to his city life of public engagements, book signings and fancy women.

Framing her face with both hands, Grayson's thumbs stroked the silky smoothness of her cheek as he smiled down at her. He had known from the first time he laid eyes on Sammy Jo the kind of woman she was. She was opinionated and stubborn with ironclad will, and the icing on the cake, she was the most beautiful woman he had ever laid eyes on. Sammy Jo Wilcox was the kind of woman he wanted to get to know better, the first woman he pictured himself spending the rest of his life loving.

Grayson hooked his finger beneath her trembling chin, tugging her attention to him. As their gaze met, Sammy Jo recognized the reflection of passion in his eyes as her own. The lure of his lips only inches away was as tempting as dangling candy at a toddler's nose. When Grayson pulled her against him, she felt some of the fight leave her, aching to feel his arms around her one last time.

Slanting demanding lips over hers, Grayson held her against him. His touch unhurried and intentional, he kissed her. Her nails dug into taught muscles rippling down his back. She searched for the strength to stop but failed. Weaving her fingers into his hair, she clung tightly to ecstasy weakening her knees, memorizing his touch.

The passionate kiss took the wind from Sammy Jo's sails, leaving her painstakingly still. Moving from swollen lips, Grayson brushed a soft kiss across her temple, his warm breath adding to her desire. She opened her mouth to tell him that she understood he had to leave, but the lie stuck in her throat. The only thing she truly understood was that she felt whole in his arms and the last thing she wanted was to say goodbye.

Grayson took a step back, and turned. Shoving both hands in his pant pockets with a broken sigh, his thoughts scattered like marbles on the walk. Once again, his gaze fixed on the barn below.

"Sammy Jo, you know that I came to Burlington to settle Gram's estate and sell the house. The plan was to return to New Hampshire afterward, I have a life there."

"I know," she answered starkly. His words grated already raw nerves. Biting at her lower lip, she winced in preparation for the dreaded farewell speech.

"But that was before I met you," he said softly.

Sammy Jo's body went numb, fearing she was hearing things. Had he not just told her that he met with a realtor about listing the estate, and what about his plans of returning to New Hampshire? Puzzled, a thin sheen of perspiration dampened her forehead as she anxiously waited for an explanation.

He pivoted, stepping closer, the deep lines in his forehead softening. "This trip has not exactly turned out as planned." He confessed, glancing past her, to the meadow, memories wavering in pops of bright orange color. Reminded of the secret recorded in the pages of his grandmother's journal, and the twist his life had taken over the past few weeks, he realized selling Thatcher Hill was no longer an option. He brushed the back of his fingers over her flushed cheek. Several painstaking seconds passed before he continued. "I don't know where our relationship will go from here Sammy Jo, but one thing is clear, it cannot end like this." He paused before adding, "I've decided not to sell Thatcher Hill." The corner of his mouth twitched before slicing into a broad grin. The glint in his eyes and quiver of his voice revealed relief of his confession.

Sammy Jo' spine stiffened, growling between clenched teeth. Impulsively poking her index finger in his chest, she forced him two steps back. Terse air gushed from her lungs and she inhaled the first deep breath in five minutes. "Do you think you could've drawn that out any longer?" She barked, not sure, if she wanted to hug him or slug him. Not waiting for him to answer, she rushed into his arms flinging both arms around his neck, peppering his face with wild kisses.

Chapter 22

Grayson listened to the rumble of Sammy Jo's motor fade into the tree line and waited for the dust to dissipate before he left the porch and trudged around the side of the house. Instinctively, he ducked between two lilac bushes and followed the dirt path into a thicket of dense trees. As if mechanically drawn through damp overgrowth, he ended at the clearing in the woods, standing solemnly before the small, modest grave.

He stared down at the slab of rock, his mind reverting to Gram's staggering admission and his illuminating conversation with Martheena. No longer a mystery, the tombstone engraving became painfully clear. He now understood the significance of the carved words and the consequence his grandmother paid for them.

Withered and desiccated rose petals strewn at the base of the stone, faded remains were proof that his grandmother grieved in solitude for a lost child, bereavement she carried to her death. As if reading the inscription for the very first time, his eyes drew over the words; **Emanuel, April 13, 1955, Blessed for a Moment, Love to Last Eternity.**

A soft whistle drew his attention from the humble monument, to a small, fawn colored lark prancing anxiously on a branch above him. Startled by a sudden gust of cool air ushering from the dense woods, the bird took flight, flapping wings disappearing into a hedge of darkness.

The ushering chill sent a tremor of awareness rippling from raised hair on Grayson's neck, ending in tingling fingers bunched in his pant pockets. He had experienced the peculiar presence before, first from the darkened roadside near thatcher Hill, and again at Wilcox Farms as he attempted to resuscitate Sammy Jo's grandfather. This time he did not bother turning to explore the ghostly source. Perhaps now he understood.

Trailing back to the house, Grayson retrieved the journal from beneath one of the rockers, its resting place since yesterday's tirade. Despite the pain from learning of his grandmother's pregnancy, Grayson had to know the rest of the story. The truth of why Digger left could be no worse than the incriminating rendering he had painted in his head.

Tucking the diary to his chest, he carried it with him; his eyes pinned on the tack room door. Stopping short of the entrance, he released a ragged breath and nudged the broken door with his foot.

With a step past the threshold, he surveyed destruction of his outburst, shambles mimicking his emotions. Splintered wood and broken glass strewn over dusty planks, soft light filtered through a single glass window.

A slow, steady pace back and forth over squeaky boards fueled Grayson's courage to drop to the floor near the window and flip the journal open to the bleak entry of August 9, 1954. Needing verification of the pain still aching in his chest, he reread Gram's elucidating words and revealed pregnancy.

Retracing the entry, he heard Martheena's voice echo in his head, "She loved your grandfather Scamper; that did not mean she did not deserve to love again."

Finishing with the account of his grandmother's admission, Grayson realized it was nearly a week before she continued with documentation of her relationship with Digger. Their torrid affair had reached an impasse, a crossroad in which Rosaline must make a painful choice. She must sacrifice her happiness or sacrifice Digger's future. Just as each sunrise leads to sunset, the ending of a moment in time was in sight.

August 14, 1954

Life has become a blur. I can focus on nothing but the life growing inside of me. I must make a decision, each choice heartbreaking. My thoughts circles to the only logical possibility. I cannot go on with this charade and have decided it best to set Digger free. He need not know about the baby. He is young with a future. I cannot put the responsibility of fatherhood on him at his young age. I know if I tell him about the baby, he will feel obligated to do the noble thing and stay. I cannot, I will not, live my life with a man shackled to me out of obligation.

Rosaline's following words rendered graphic details of the painful termination, the sacrificial annihilation of her happiness.

August 15, 1954

Supper tonight was painfully awkward and quiet. I believe Digger sensed something was dreadfully wrong, barely touching his food. After helping clear dishes from the table, he placed the last plate in the sink and did not seem surprised when I told him that we needed to talk. As if leading an animal to slaughter, he followed me to the porch but refused to sit after I asked him to join me.

The summer air was hot and soupy, the sun melting like a giant fireball behind the mountain. Golden embers of fading daylight glistened in the treetops. The evening was perfect, if not for the dirty deed wedged in my throat, words that would surely break Digger's heart.

I painted on the facsimile of a smile and patted the arm of the rocker, pleading for him to sit. Practiced words rattled in my head. There was no easy way to end our relationship.

Reluctantly, Digger dropped onto the edge of the chair with weighted apprehension, his body stiff. Refusing to look at me, the waning sun disappeared behind the ridge, glints of light reflecting from eyes of polished coal.

Despite every effort to remain composed, my voice cracked, my chin quivered. I told Digger that he was dear to me, our shared time special. After a deep, pained breath, I pinched my eyes closed searching for courage but found little. When I opened them again, Digger was staring at me, eyes once filled with youthful vitality, now dull and lifeless. I could not bring myself to face the pain, so I turned away.

With my eyes fixed on folded hands in my lap, I squeezed the painful ending from a shattered heart. Barely able to breathe, I murmured the words. Digger was young with his whole life ahead of him, a partial truth.

Sharp, burning words slashed Digger's heart, blood draining from his face. When he repeated the words to me, his tone was thick with indignant offense. I looked up at him and saw destruction suffered at my hands.

If I live to be one hundred years old, I will never forget the pain in his voice or resentment carved into his face. I reached to touch his hand, but he jerked away. Flinty eyes glared at me as the betrayal sank in. Bolting from the chair, Digger trudged away and turned his back. Uncomfortable silence followed.

I traced his steps to the edge of the porch and touched his shoulder. He winced. Pain of the final words would hurt me as badly as Digger hearing them, but I had to finish what I had started. It was then that I told him that I was lonely. Our relationship was one of companionship, nothing more. Each deceitful lie brought the pain of a knife twisting in my gut. I asked him to leave Thatcher Hill with as much conviction as I could muster.

Digger slammed a fist into the white porch column, leaving a smear of bright red blood from bruised knuckles. With a quick step back, my shoulders jolted. Never had I seen such rage in the tender, young man I had come to love. It was heartrending to think that my love and protectiveness had wounded him, leaving behind an angered callous heart.

The evening air filled with sarcastic laughter after I apologized. "Sorry? You are sorry?" he snarled. Spinning toward me, his lip curled like a mad dog. "What do you have to be sorry for? I'm the fool," His bitter words challenged.

I bit back tears and could taste blood from my bottom lip, clenched between my teeth. My head whispered that this was the right thing to do. My breaking heart shouted that it was not. Instinctively, I pressed my hand to the secret hidden in my belly, in search of courage. My chin lifted boldly and I swallowed the yearning of selfish aspirations. This was my time for strength.

My final word to Digger was goodbye. Wishing I could kiss him one last time, I turned and went inside, pushing the door closed behind me before I lost my nerve to tear glazed eyes.

I watched from cover of the curtain as Digger stepped down from the porch, pausing at the bottom step. I wondered if he would turn around and make one last plea, secretly wishing he would. Instead, he staggered down the path to the tack room with a wounded heart.

Pain smeared across Digger's face tormented the night. Nodding off once or twice, I gave up and rose just before dawn, slipping into my robe. I had to say something to ease Digger's pain. I at least owed him that much.

Not sure, what I could say to help him understand without telling him the truth, I knew I had to try. I followed the shadowy path to the tack room with every intention to right the wrong I had done.

I rapped on the door, and waited for stirring from the other side, but there was only silence. After knocking a second time, I called out to him, my stomach sinking with the stillness. The knob twisted in my hand, the squeak of hinges impeding on the quiet beyond.

Milky moonlight bathed the ticking covered bed, blankets still tucked neatly in place. Two steps inside the shadow filled room, my tear filled eyes trailed to a glint of moonlight, gleaming from the pillow.

Draped over faded fabric was the pocket watch I had given Digger. Once a symbol of love, the timepiece now lay as a despondent reminder that time is nothing more than borrowed moments, possessed by fate.

I cradled the gold piece in my hand. Petrified in time, the hands of the watch froze at 4:44. Rubbing my finger across initials engraved on the back, I lovingly whispered Digger's true given name. Clutching the watch in my fist, the first of many tears trickled down my cheek.

As Gram's last words ricocheted in Grayson's head, he flinched, a stabbing agony piercing his chest. Easing the journal closed, he brushed trembling fingers over the faded leather, a sudden coldness gripping his insides. The three words of Digger's given name echoed in his ears. Slowly, as if hypnotized, he dropped the diary; clambering from the floor with his thoughts fixed in place.

The watch had stopped at exactly 4:44, the precise time it began running the night of the storm. The chain of events leading to August 15, 1954, 4:44 A.M., charted his grandmother's life like a map. Her entire future became a casualty of circumstance, as did his.

Like a rat trapped in a maze, he was not sure which way to run. His first instinct was to pack up and high tail it back to New Hampshire, no explanation, no goodbye. After rationality chased the shock from his head, he realized he had only one option. He had to repair history, for Gram's sake, for Digger's sake.

Chapter 23

Grayson staggered around the house for three days like a wounded bear, grumbling each time Martheena mentioned Sammy Jo's name. It was too late to try to convince his heart that he did not love that woman; he had already fallen over that cliff headfirst, although ever having a relationship with his perfect woman seemed about as likely as rewriting the past.

As hard as he tried, he could not imagine how it could ever work out between them. The admission he had read gnawed at him, the impossible situation clear. Obstacles in their relationship kept piling up, the last revelation from his Gram's journal topping it off with a rotten cherry.

Slumped at the kitchen table Friday morning, Grayson buried his fingers in dark mangled hair, tugging at the headache pounding his brain like Chinese war drums.

Twisting the water faucet, Martheena filled the percolator from the sink, rotating the lid in place. "I don't understand what happened between you two Scamper," she said, turning off the running tap. "But you need to give the little gal a call. It's as obvious as the frown on your face that you miss her."

Grayson grunted, scooting back in his chair. "Listen Martheena, I don't mean to be rude, but the last thing I want to talk about right now is Sammy Jo," he snipped.

The little country vixen was all he had thought about for the past three days and nights, earning him nothing more than a scrambled brain and headache. Spending any more time on the subject seemed a squander of time. There was only one possible conclusion to his relationship with her. The sooner he put an end to the fiasco and get on with his life, the better.

Catching a whiff of sarcasm in his voice, Martheena sat the coffee pot on the stove and adjusted the flame on the burner. Turning to him, both fists dug into rounded hips, black eyes flashed caution from the other side of the room. "You either talk about her, or you're gonna' explode boy,"

There was a kernel of truth in what she said. Sleep had been impossible and the truth was eating him alive from the inside out. He could not go on pretending that he did not know the truth. Embedded words from the diary echoed in his brain, with every thought of Sammy Jo.

Martheena shuffled across the room patting his shoulder with a sense of calmness. "I know you can figure this out. You have your Gram's blood coursing through you."

Not exactly encouraging words, Martheena had no idea the legitimacy of her statement. His Gram's blood coursing through his veins was the core of his problem, the single wedge blocking a future with Sammy Jo.

"When did you last talk to her anyway?" Martheen asked, dragging the opposite chair from the table. Easing her weight onto the squeaky frame, she folded her arms across the table, waiting impatiently for a reply.

It was apparent that Martheena was not going to let him off easy. He would either have to tell her the truth, which he vaguely considered for all of two seconds, or make something up. Opting for the latter, he felt a spurt of guilt, but it quickly dissipated when he considered the ramifications of honesty. He could not make sense of any of what he had learned from Gram's diary, how could he expect Martheena to understand?

"The last time we spoke was Tuesday. She stopped by on her way to pick her grandfather up from the hospital." He could tell from the blank look and grimace on Martheena's face that the little bit of information he offered was not nearly enough.

"I figured I'd give her some time to play catch up. She has a lot on her plate right now, with the fire and all." Cupping his hand to a stiff neck, he craned it to the side, bones snipping in place. That statement sounded bleak and unconvincing, even to him.

Martheena struggled from the chair, waddling to the other side of the table. Clapping Grayson's back, she made the one single statement to make him cringe with guilt. "Ever figure that maybe the little gal could use a little support right now?" Leaving the kitchen without another word, she left him to ponder what Sammy Jo must be feeling, the words front and center, *abandoned* and *alone*.

Despite his best efforts to dismiss the guilt, it wrestled harder with every mental argument he conjured. One thing he had learned about Sammy Jo, she was proud and independent. Help was not something she was accustomed to asking for, although he knew her situation was overwhelming. Nursing her Pops back to health and dealing with insurance companies and contractors was a full menu, even for Sammy Jo.

Strong coffee bean aroma perked, signaling a fresh brewed pot. Grayson crossed the kitchen and pulled down a mug filling it. A trip to Wilcox Farms, he concluded, was in everyone's best interest, and he feared he was going to need much more than a pot of strong coffee to see the dreaded venture through.

After a long, hot swig, he carried the cup up to his room sitting it on the bureau. Staring at the top drawer like an archenemy, he sucked in a breath and blew it out before yanking it open. Lying on top was the pocket watch, the beginning and feared end of his relationship with Sammy Jo. Snatching the watch from the bureau drawer, he gave it one last glance before thrusting it in his pant pocket.

It was early afternoon before Grayson finally approached Wilcox Farm. Stalling, he spent the last three hours maneuvering tight curves and steep grades of the

Tennessee Mountains, although he could not recall one scenic detail along the way. Frantic, his attention trained on how he would break the astonishing news, rehearsing a dozen different possibilities. Unfortunately, they all sounded like rantings of a crazy man.

Turning into the drive Grayson spotted Jim sitting alone on the porch swing, Stewart curled at his feet. Sammy Jo's truck was nowhere in sight. Grayson was not sure if he was disappointed that she was not home, or relieved for her sake that she was not.

Rolling to a stop, he cut the engine and watched Stewart stand and stretch lazily before sauntering down the stairs, his tail whipping in rhythm with each step.

Jim slowed the swing, threw a hand in the air and smiled. Grayson had to admit that the old fellow had fared well. For the first time, he recognized remnants of a handsome, youthful man, hidden beneath years of age. Time stamped wrinkles in eyes of polished coal, still filled with vibrancy of a man nearly half his age. Thick, black hair threaded with strands of silver added to the distinguished character that had grown more grandeur in passing years.

Jim waited for the slow sway of the porch swing to stop completely, before standing and making his way to the railing. "Afternoon," he said leaning on both hands, watching Grayson stoop to give Stewart a good rub behind the ears. "Looking for that granddaughter of mine?"

Grayson stood, the mere mention of Sammy Jo causing his heart to pound. Unsure of how she would react to his news, he was certain of one thing; it would not be favorable on his part.

"No Jim, actually I came by to talk with you." Shoving his hand in his pocket, he clutched the gold watch and drew a long, shaky breath.

"Me?" Jim asked blankly.

Grayson nodded with a step forward, his thumb stroking the watch like a good luck charm buried in his pant pocket. "Sammy Jo's not here?" A darting gaze landed on the screen door, then back to Jim.

"She ran over to the Porter spread to break the news that they're going to have barns guests for a bit longer. I think those damned insurance people are growing their own wood for the barn lumber. It looks like we may be looking at the end of summer, if not fall, before they begin rebuilding."

Distracted by the annoying tug in his gut, Grayson became lost in the thread of conversation. Gram's journal entry left him pondering this very moment since closing the pages.

"Why? I thought you said you were here to see me?" Jim moved to the top step, pulling Grayson's attention with him.

"Yea, I am" Ambling toward the porch, Grayson had the sudden urge to turn and dart back to his car without as much as a goodbye. This was going to be harder than he had imagined. Stopping at the bottom step, Grayson stared up, imagining how this day would forever change Jim's life.

Chapter 24

Grayson tailed Jim back to the porch swing, taking the seat next to him. It made no sense to break the news slowly. You can swing a hammer any way you want, but in the end, the crushing conclusion is the same. No, swift and direct was the most merciful approach.

Grayson watched Stewart wound into a ball at their feet before sucking in a jittery gulp and blowing it out. "There's something we need to talk about Jim,"

Before Grayson had a chance to finish, Sammy Jo's truck came barreling down the lane, a cloud of dust churning the air behind. Several rapid honks of the horn signaled her arrival, her hand waving out the open window.

"Well, speaking of the little devil," Leaning forward on folded arms, Jim stopped the sway of the swing with his foot and watched Sammy Jo skid to a stop, gravel pinging the undercarriage. The engine sputtered a few times before clunking silent. Flinging open the cab door, she dropped western boots to the ground and slammed it shut, dashing to the porch before the dust had a chance to settle in the lane.

Grayson's mind went blank, his thoughts scattering like stars in a June sky. Eyes dribbled down a white sleeveless tee, to short cutoff jeans, giving way to long legs. With one last look at her, he would rather bite off his tongue than spit out the dreaded words perched on the tip of it. No doubt, learning of her grandfather's hidden past would be as painful to her as it was to Grayson when he first read of his Gram's veiled history.

Sammy Jo vaulted up the steps and was leaning over him before he had a chance to say hello. A snappy kiss to the lips, she took a step back with both hands settled on her hips and beamed. "And just what do I owe this pleasure?" she asked, without preamble.

"Actually, he's here to see me." Jim supplied.

Sammy Jo leveled a suspicious eye at Grayson before plopping in a wicker chair opposite them. "Talk about bursting a lady's bubble," she teased. Folding one leg over the other, a western boot pumped the air in steady rhythm. "And here I thought you'd missed me."

"*Oh, you have no idea,*" he pouted inwardly. Grayson's face went pallid, strained lips pulled tight. Wishing he could fast forward past the pain he was about to inflict; he stood and cleared his throat. Cold blood pulsated in his neck and he stuffed trembling hands in his pant pocket, the touch of menacing gold beneath his fingers.

Sammy Jo and her grandfather exchanged puzzled glances, each with their own speculation about what brought Grayson to Wilcox Farms. Jim suspected that perhaps the city slicker had got up enough nerve to express interest in his granddaughter, but from Grayson's strange demeanor, Sammy Jo feared he had changed his mind about her and decided to sell Thatcher Hill after all, high tailing it back to New Hampshire.

Wrong on both accounts, Grayson swallowed hard. His gaze first shot to Jim then skid to a halt on Sammy Jo's icy blue eyes, rapidly blinking. Turning away, he could not bring himself to look at her, his pain mirroring hers.

With a slow, steady pace across the porch, Grayson fumbled with the watch in his pocket. Pausing at the steps, he considered one last time rather or not he was making the right decision. With the timepiece clasped tightly in his hand, he knew there was only one decision he could make. Painful as it may be, it was the right choice.

"There is something you both need to hear and there is no easy way of saying it." He turned around, his shoulders drawing tight, his spine ram rod stiff. A ghostly white washed over his face as he tugged the watch free from his pocket. With two slow-moving steps, he stopped in front of Jim, trembling fingers dangling the wavering sway of a chain.

"I believe this belongs to you,"

Jim went deathly still, the rattling words in his head muddled and unclear. Sammy Jo watched the same dreadful pale stain her grandfather's face that she witnessed the day her grandmother died. Loss and heartbreak carved deep crevices into his handsome features; his pupils became dark, empty holes.

In slow motion, Jim's right hand caressed faded ink of a thorn-snared rose on his left arm, memory of a lost love. His reply came in not more than a raspy whisper. "Rosie..." His chest ached, the pain of many years ago raw again. For several silent seconds he did not move, simply stared trancelike at the gentle swing of the watch.

"Gram left a journal," Grayson finally gathered the courage to glance at Sammy Jo. Her chin quivered, an empty stare fixed on the watch held by his fingers.

After the shock settled, Jim reached up, touching the timepiece with his finger, as if to convince himself it was not a dream. Opening his palm, Grayson dropped the gift of many decades ago in his hand. Gently, Jim rubbed an index finger, bearing the scarred memory of a sawblade, over scrolled initials, JEW.

"Rosie was your grandmother?" Jim asked, as if needing to hear the words for them to be true.

Grayson replied with a nod. "There's more," With all the strength he could muster, Grayson revealed the secret his grandmother took to her grave, the baby she mourned until her dying breath. "She gave birth to a son Jim, your son," After a slight hesitation he added sorrowfully, "He died moments after he was born."

Grayson's eyes finally connected with Sammy Jo. Memories of the grave they discovered together passed between them and the strange closeness he sensed that night.

With that, Sammy Jo's stomach clenched, breakfast dangerously close to spewing at her feet. She turned pasty white as tears threatened to spill from her lower lash. She too remembered the modest grave that she and Grayson had discovered and the bits of faded rose petals scattered at the base. Even more importantly, she remembered the icy chill that made her shiver. Her arms instinctively encircled her waist and she squeezed.

Without so much as a word, Sammy Jo stood and wiped the tears from her face with the back of her hand, while waiting for trembling knees to steady. Taking a slow, unsteady step forward, she stopped in front of Grayson but refused to make eye contact. She stared ahead at the door instead.

Grayson wished he could read her thoughts, but he couldn't. Her eyes were glassy, her expression empty. With her hand on the screen door handle, she pulled it open, pausing briefly before disappearing inside.

Grayson watched Sammy Jo until she was out of sight before dropping next to Jim on the swing. They sat in uncomfortable silence, neither knowing what to say.

Scrambled memories filled Jim's head, a past that never made sense, a past he must now piece together. He pushed his foot against the floorboards, the swing drifting slowly.

Several minutes lapsed before Jim found the strength to speak. "I never understood what happened between Rosie and me. She was my first you know?" His eyes glued to the watch he held in his hand and he could almost see the reflection of her bright smile in the shiny gold surface.

Grayson nodded, feeling a twinge of guilt for knowing first hand, the intimacy Jim shared with his Gram.

"She loved you," Grayson said, knowing all too well of the heavy ball and chain his grandmother dragged through life. "She's loved you all of these years, never giving her heart to another."

"I never understood what changed between us. Everything seemed perfect in a young man's eyes...then she asked me to go." The past came back; images of the night Rosaline asked him to leave Thatcher Hill and the anguish that turned a piece of his heart to petrified stone. A lingering grimace drew his face tight.

"Gram learned of her pregnancy and did not want you burdened with a child."

Jim winced, painful words stabbing him in the heart. With the watch clutched tightly in his fist, he sprung from the swing and stomped abruptly to the porch railing, as if he were trudging barefoot across shattered shards. "Is that how Rosie felt, that our baby was a burden?" Staring across the stream winding beneath the covered bridge, white knuckles clenched the porch rail.

Grayson joined him at the railing. "No Jim, never, Gram loved you with all her heart." He squeezed Jim's shoulder and could feel knotted muscles beneath his hand flinch. "And she loved the baby she carried; it was your future she was thinking of. You were young and she did not want you to feel obligated to a family. Gram wanted you to chase your dreams."

"Obligated, chase my dreams?" Jim's tone flooded with disdain as he recalled his first hard lesson in love and the terminally wounded soul it left behind. His fingers gripped the railing tighter, his knuckles becoming paler with each torrid detail. "She was my dream. Rosie was all I wanted."

Grayson cupped a hand to the nape of his neck, craning taut muscles. "The point is, she loved you and wanted what was best for you," Before Jim had a chance to launch a grenade, Grayson quickly corrected, "Or at least what she thought was best for you."

"You played that fiddle well son, never missed a beat," Jim said tartly, his shoulders slumping. He stepped to the side and down the steps, Grayson following. After they walked several feet, Jim opened his mouth to speak but quickly snapped it closed. It took a second try before he could get the words out. "I've carried that night with me like a battle scar," he admitted. "Resented what gave it to me, but proud I survived it. Now to learn after all these years that she did love me..." His voice trailed the bittersweet thought.

Matching strides, they walked in ankle high grass toward the barn rubble, stench of scorched wood still heavy in the air. Jim twisted his head. "I still can't believe all of this."

Grayson wrinkled his nose, his brows locked tight. He remembered his Gram's candid account of an affair with a man she affectionately nicknamed Digger and cringed. "You can't believe it? How do you think I felt when I read that after my grandfather died, good ole' Gram had an affair with a man nearly 10 years her junior?"

Jim stopped and poked the watch in his pocket for safekeeping. "Because your grandfather died did not mean Rosie should spend the rest of her life alone son. She was a beautiful woman with a lot to offer a man." He shrugged one shoulder defensively and walked on. "I could not believe when she asked me to leave. I knew our relationship began partly because of her loneliness, but I always believed there had to be more to it. No woman could fake the kind of devotion I felt from her."

Grayson quickly caught up. Taking Jim by the arm, he tugged him to a stop. "She came to the tack room that night to see you Jim. Gram wanted to make things right, but you were already gone."

Carefully weighing Grayson's account, Jim raked an open palm down his jaw. Raven eyes softened. Maybe things turned out just the way Rosie had intended. Deep lines tugging at his mouth diminished into a gentle smile. Treasured thoughts of Rosie and the months he spent on Thatcher Hill sent the warmth of that summer to his chest. Reflections of a time long ago filled his head, a summer when a boy became a man.

Rosie would always own the special corner of his heart reserved for first time love. She taught him the meaning of devotion, never taking love for granted. In the end, she selflessly set him free to fall in love and marry his Emma, to grow old with a woman he cherished. He had experienced more love in his lifetime than any one man deserved.

In the silence, Grayson watched a flock of starlings take flight from a tree in the pasture, following them past the house until they disappeared beyond tall pines tipping the ridge. His distant stare returned to the house, settling on the empty porch beyond. He thought about Sammy Jo and the pain his news had brought her and winced. He shared her pain, for not only the past and heartache their grandparents suffered at fate's hands, but the future as well. He feared history would loop back, stealing away the one woman he had ever loved.

Digging the watch from his pocket, Jim's eyes settled on the passing of time and sighed. "She called me Digger you know," he said with a gentle smile. Grayson nodded. "Rosie taught me a lot about life," he said. "But the most important lesson I've learned, time does not stand still, it waits for no man to ponder the future." His fingers curled over the crystal face with a squeeze before following Grayson's gaze to the house and empty porch.

"She'll come around." Jim said matter of fact. "If there is one thing I know about my Sam, she's a smart one." Bumping a shoulder into Grayson, Jim caught him off guard, nearly knocking him off his feet. "She gets that from her grandmother's Irish side of the family," he added curtly, his nose tipping the air.

Stumbling to the side, Grayson recovered his balance. "I hope you're right," he said, gnawing on his lower lip with a slow step forward. "That feisty little red head has plagued my every thought since I found her dangling from that shelf in her stockroom. The thought of losing her takes away any insight of a future. My life would never be the same."

"Give her a little time." Jim leaned toward Grayson as they walked, his voice lowering as if he had a secret to share. "It isn't you that she's angry with anyway. It's me."

"I don't think she's angry at you Jim." Grayson hooked his thumbs in his back pockets as they walked, remembering the confusion he felt the night he learned of his Gram's scandalous affair. Anger was not necessarily the word that came to mind. Shocked was a more fitting description. Learning that his grandmother had a steamy relationship with a younger man and kept it from her family her entire life was difficult.

"Just like when I started reading Gram's journal, you have to understand, it's hard for us to realize that our grandparents actually..." For the first time in his life, Grayson was at a loss for words. He blushed at the vivid scenes flashing through his head, looking as guilty as a testosterone fed teenager caught with a girlie centerfold under his bed. "Well, it's just hard," he assured Jim, cracking a halfhearted grin.

"Yea, we weren't always old son," Jim returned his smile. "I was a real lucky man. I loved Rosie with all my heart, would've moved heaven and Earth to be with her." His smile faded, his tone became serious. "But I also loved Sam's grandma. She was the light of my life," He stared at the path ahead, dark eyes glazed in tears. "We had no secrets, me and my Emma. She knew about Rosie, but that did not affect our relationship. One had nothing to do with the other," He swallowed hard, the lump wedged in his throat a reminder that he missed his late wife more with each passing day.

"Sounds like you and Sammy Jo's grandma had a special kind of love,"

"The best," Jim wiped the back of his hand across his eye before a teetering tear had a chance to escape. "Some men never find true love. I was lucky to have had that kind of love twice,"

Jim dipped his head toward the house, quickening his pace, Grayson tight to his heels. "About that journal of Rosie's, mind if I read it?"

Grayson nodded with a content grin, the tension in his shoulders slackening. "You know Jim; I think that would make Gram happy. There's a lot she wanted you to know, now you can hear it from her."

The noon high sun drifted slowly behind a puffy, white cloud, casting a shadow across the path they were walking. As a cooling breeze filtered down the mountain, Grayson sensed his grandmother's smile in the pine-scented draft. He pinched his eyes closed and drew a deep breath, gratified for the opportunity to turn the page on Rosaline Worthington's story, giving it the proper ending it deserved.

Chapter 25

A snowy winter surrendered to the promise of spring. Dressed in his best Sunday suit, white shirt and fawn colored bow tie, Jim gazed over the lawn bordering Thatcher Hill Estate. Standing at the picket fence, draped in festive spring garland, the past came back to life in living color. Bright sunshine rained down, a warm pine and lilac scented breeze rustled budding Elm leaves overhead. Despite sunny skies, there was a slight nip in the air, a cool breeze ushering down from Pine Ridge. The remainder of a past journey stretched before him, a cobblestone path strewn with memories as vivid as the sunshine.

The manor was as beautiful to him as it once was. Painted pristine white, the house reflected against sable shutters, four massive pillars supporting a sprawling front porch. Dressed in yellow blooms and white satin, trimmings of an early spring wedding embellished the southern veranda.

For an instant, he imagined a first kiss shared beneath glimmering summer stars and the copper haired beauty who stole his heart decades ago. As the memory took over, Jim's eyes prickled with happy tears, certain that his Rosie would share his joy, watching the past circle back to them. Two people they both loved would begin a life together today; share a future that fate had denied them more than a half a century ago.

Jim's eyes settled on the narrow path just beyond the gate, splitting a lawn of lush green grass, rows of white chairs angled along each side. Elegantly filled urns flanked each side of the steps. Filled with butter colored roses and white daisies, each pot speckled with bright pops of orange poppies, picked fresh from the meadow of Thatcher Hill.

Pulling the gold pocket watch from his vest, Jim swiped his thumb across the crystal face. It was half past four, nearly an hour before guests were to arrive. Tucking the watch back in place with trembling fingers, Jim was as nervous as he had been on his own wedding day. Thoughts of Emma sent a physical pain to his chest. She too would be happy that Sammy Jo had found love.

So much had happened in the past year, the best was his ever-evolving relationship with Grayson. Perhaps more than feeling close to Rosie's only grandson, he felt closeness to the son they lost.

The front door swung open, Martheena scooting through to the porch, decked out from head to toe. A bright yellow dress reflected from ebony skin, her notorious pillbox hat with netted veil perched on silvering hair. Languidly brushing her finger over the sentimental broach pinned to her dress, thoughts of Rosaline reflected from her memory and the last Christmas they shared together. She smiled down at Jim standing unpretentiously at the gate, looking as striking as the handsome picture her late, dear friend had illustrated.

"My, my, Mr. Wilcox, you look dashing," Martheena smiled, shuffling a slow step forward.

Jim shoved the gate open, ambling toward the porch with both hands buried in his pant pockets. "You're quite the sight too Miss Martheena. We clean up pretty good, if I must say so myself." Climbing the steps, he stopped and pivoted, gallantly offering Martheena a bended arm.

She gripped Jim's arm as he led her down the steps, waiting for each foot to anchor to the planks before dropping to the next one. They stopped at the front row of chairs reserved for family, Martheena taking her place in the one closest to the aisle. Before she sat down, she smiled up at Jim. "I figured I'd best get out of the way in there. Madeline and Lettie are helping Sammy Jo, fussing over the final touches. The last thing they need is a blubbering old lady slowing them down." Jim steadied her arm as she sank into the chair, skating her hand over the chiffon fabric of her lap.

Sammy Jo's mother, Madeline, her step-dad Frank, and siblings flew the red eye from California; landing at an airport thirty minutes North of Highland just before dawn. Madeline was ecstatic about her daughter's nuptials, caffeine overload and adrenaline pumping up her excitement. Not wanting to miss a second of the celebration, she arrived at Thatcher Hill shortly after noon.

Frank, Annie and Matthew remained at the farm for a quick nap before the ceremony.

Martheena adjusted the veil on her hat, chestnut eyes shimmering beneath. "She sure is happy Jim," When their eyes connected, her smile deepened. They both knew that Martheena was not only speaking of Sammy Jo.

A gust of air rustled leaves of the Elm, a songbird's whistle gaining Jim's attention. His gaze settled on Rosie's bedroom window beyond, and for an instant, he swore he caught a flash of the past.

"Yep Martheena, I think we're all pretty happy about this wedding," Jim repeated, his voice rich with emotion.

As expected, first of the intimate handful of guests to arrive was Frank and the kids, pulling to a stop in the reserved parking area near the meadow.

"Excuse me," Jim said, turning for the gate. Annie was out of the car and slammed the door as soon as the car rolled to a stop, sprinting up the hill. The younger of Sammy Jo's two siblings, ten years old Annie took after her father's Italian descent, dark hair and olive complexion, but had her mother's flair for energy. Bounding up the hill, she was as pretty as a picture, dressed in a turquoise dress and white strappy sandals, her long hair pulled into a single braid. A little tomboy with feminine frills, her rambunctious energy reminded Jim of Sammy Jo at that age.

"Wow Pops! This place is super cool! Sammy Jo is lucky to get to live here," Shoving her way through the gate with both hands, Annie flung both arms around Jim's waist, nearly knocking him off his feet. "Where is she? Can we see her before she gets married?" she rattled, her face animated with the excitement of a child on Christmas morning.

Jim squeezed her, kissing the top of her head, before motioning to the front door with his hand. "The first room on the right, at the top of the stairs,"

After Annie skipped past him and darted up the steps, Jim turned and met Frank and Matthew coming through the gate. "Did you get some rest this morning?" he asked Frank.

Frank cocked his head to the side rolling his eyes to Matthew. "Are you kidding, not with these two? Between Annie, asking me every fifteen minutes when we were leaving, and Mr. Sourpuss here complaining that he thinks weddings are stupid, sleep was hopeless. I'd had better luck napping behind the brute on the plane that was snoring like a razorback hog."

Jim laughed outright. "I don't think many twelve years old boys like weddings," Grinning at his grandson with a wink he added, "But I've got a feeling you'll change your mind someday son,"

"I was going to ask if I could help with anything, but it looks like everything is under control," Frank scoured the flat, grassy area near the barn and perfectly positioned white tent. Round tables topped with linen surrounded a dance floor, an area at the far end reserved for a band and DJ. Staff professionally donned black and white uniforms, scurrying from table to table, fussing over fresh cut centerpieces of roses and daisies, white china and crystal.

Matthew grumbled quietly, following his dad to the front row of chairs, fidgeting in the seat next to him.

Jim stopped mid stride and spun on his heels, digging the gold pocket watch from his vest. Thirty minutes had passed, his steady pace back and forth at the gate, nearly wearing a bald spot in the grass. Dropping the watch back in his pocket, he tugged at the bow tie cinched at his throat and craned his neck to the side. Nearly all the chairs were now filled, quiet chatter among guests blending with soft music of two fiddlers seated on the porch.

Jim's eyes shot skyward with a silent *thank you* when he at last saw Grayson wandering from the side of the house, like the Calvary. Wearing a black, long tail tuxedo, he looked as charming as Rhett Butler with a debonair smile to match.

Grayson clapped Jim on the back, snorting a laugh. "I'm the one getting married Jim, not you. Take breath buddy," he said, noting beads of perspiration trickling to Jim's temples.

Slowly exhaling, Jim shifted from one foot to the other. "I don't think I was any more nervous the day I married my Emma," he replied, wiping sweaty palms on his suit jacket. "Is this thing about to start? I feel like I'm just about to explode."

"That's why I'm here," Straightening the bow tie at his neck, Grayson tugged at the hem of his vest and leveled his shoulders. His eyes drifted to Lettie Mae's timely saunter from the front door and onto the porch, wearing a creamy yellow floor length gown. She smiled with a subtle nod; her cue to Grayson that Sammy Jo was ready.

"It's show time." Pinching his eyes closed, Grayson took an easy, calming breath. The moment he had been waiting on for a year had at last arrived. "Sammy Jo will be waiting for you out back," he instructed Jim.

With that, Jim stretched out his hand and Grayson took it. "Welcome to the family son," he said, slapping Grayson on the back with his free hand.

"Thanks Pops," Grayson winked and watched Jim disappear around the side of the house before stepping to the open gate.

Whispering guests hushed and the fiddles stopped briefly. Lettie Mae lifted the hem of her gown, gliding to the edge of the porch. After she was in place, the musicians stood and placed their chins against the rests; fingers positioned on the scroll. Drawing bows across the strings, gentle notes laced the early evening air.

A popular country tune painted a visual of Sammy Jo and Grayson's love, conceived and blessed by keeper of the midnight stars. Lettie Mae inhaled deeply, opened her mouth, her soft soprano voice crumbling Grayson's composure.

With a leisure step to the gate, Grayson stopped and slipped his hand in his pocket. Brushing his finger across the gold band that he had lovingly inscribed with their names and wedding date, his heart fell into a steady rhythm. As Lettie Mae sang, he not only heard the lyrics, he felt a calming love, sensing his Gram's nearness. He watched Lettie Mae through a watery haze, waiting for the song to end. After finishing with the last verse and taking her seat in the front row next to Martheena, Grayson slowly made his way down the grassy aisle on trembling knees.

Climbing the stairs, he stood next to Reverend O' Leary, hands clasped in front of him, his eyes glued to the path leading from the corner of the house. His breath caught in his throat in anticipation of a glimpse of his bride.

Jim stepped around the back corner of the house, stopping mid-stride, his breath catching. Sammy Jo stood against a backdrop of lilacs, wearing an ivory satin gown. The neck scooped low, fitted satin clung to her tiny waist, a lacey veil dropped around her shoulders. Copper ringlets framed her face, gentle wisps resembling more a delicate angel than the tomboy he had raised. In her hands, she clutched a bouquet of yellow roses and white daisies, kissed with bright orange poppies that he had planted nearly six decades ago as a symbol of love for Rosaline.

Mouth slackening, he could not get the words out. When he at last took a step forward offering his hand, Sammy Jo took it, her hand quivering. "Sam, you're just about the prettiest darned thing I've ever seen," he said, after a long pause. "Grayson is a lucky man,"

"And I'm a lucky woman Pops. I love him so much," A gentle pine and lilac scented breeze fanned her veil, glints of sunlight catching in amber curls. Transparent blue eyes peeked from beneath soft, ivory mesh. She squeezed her grandfather's hand as the chorus of Lettie's voice faded from the front of the house.

"Well let's get you to that man of yours," Jim said, offering a bended arm. "He's biting at the bit to say I do," Jim's smile was genuine and reassuring.

With slow, steady steps, he escorted Sammy Jo to the front corner of the house. Stopping before coming in view of the guests, he gently lifted her veil and pressed his lips to her forehead. "I love you Sam," he said simply, his dark eyes tearing. "You make me very proud."

Sammy Jo never doubted her grandfather's love, yet seldom heard the words. A man of few words, Jim's deeds were more important than fancy talk.

She wiped a single tear dropping from his eye with her thumb. "I love you too Pops," she replied, kissing his cheek.

Jim tenderly replaced the veil and waited for to hook her arm through his. His mind flashed through a lifetime of memories, from scraped knees after removing training wheels from her bike, to taking his breath away the night she appeared at the top of the stairs, dressed in satin for her first prom date. She had always made him proud, but today he stood a foot taller, his chest puffing like a Bantam rooster.

Music increasingly filled the air, strings of the wedding march drifting from the front of the manor. Jim and Sammy Jo matched leisurely steps, strolling along the grassy knoll. Rounding the side of the house, breathtaking beauty of the bride earned gasps and murmurs from gathered guests, twisting in their seats for a first glimpse. Rising to their feet, family and friends spun toward the gate, Jim proudly escorting Sammy Jo to the entrance. Martheena sniffed and wiped frantically at tears spilling down her face.

Grayson's eyes widened in pleasant surprise, his gaze fixed on his bride with a smile as wide as Texas. Dreams he had of this day did not compare to the stunning vision of his future wife. With a slow, steady smile, he mouthed I love you, everyone but Sammy Jo disappearing from sight. Just as meant from the beginning, it was only he and her, with the gift of a lifetime surrounding them.

Just as rehearsed, Jim paused with each step over the soft grass, guiding Sammy Jo to the traditional wedding march. Leading her down the aisle and up the steps, he gave a final kiss to her hand before placing it in Grayson's palm. As soft string music faded silent, he left the porch and took a seat between Martheena and Madeline in the front row.

The ceremony was simple, the bride and groom repeating personal vows they had written from the heart. After the pastor pronounced them husband and wife, Grayson dipped his wife low in his arms, twisting a lingering kiss over her lips that prompted giggles from the guests, particularly Sammy Jo's younger brother Matthew who's "*yuck*" added to the laughter.

A country remake of "Footloose" vibrated from the speakers, a line of dancers stretching from one side of the reception tent to the other. Sammy Jo positioned in the center of the group, hiked her satin hem in one hand, a trace of her country birthright stomping white western boots to the ground. Dancing three songs straight in a row, she leaned forward panting for breath. As the tune ended, she declined temptation of a wild honky-tonk original.

Worming her way through clusters of chatting guests, she found her husband discussing plans of their honeymoon destination with her stepfather.

"I can't wait for Sammy Jo to see Paris," Grayson said, before catching sight of her. "Taking my little country mouse to the big city," he teased with a wink, anchoring his arm around Sammy Jo's waist as she approached.

Deepening sapphire eyes rolled up to meet Grayson's wink, the corner of her mouth drawing into a grimace. "I hope they have plenty of those little liquor bottles stocked on the plane," she uttered, meaning every word. She had only flown once, and that was to visit her family in California nearly three years ago. Unfortunately, for the flight attendant who carried cool cloths, Sammy Jo spent more time on her knees in the lavatory than she did in her seat.

Looking past Frank's shoulder, Sammy Jo noticed her grandfather strolling up the hill near the house. Excusing herself, she made her way along the trail ending at the picket manor gate. Catching sight of Jim ending his stroll near the well, she studied his slow, intentional focus.

She watched from a distance as he stooped, gathering stems of Poppies in his fist. When he stood, he turned and stared past the meadow of wildflowers. Final rays of a fading sun dissolved into an amber colored horizon hovering above the woods.

Sammy Jo gathered the fringe of her dress in both hands and made her way down the grassy slope. "What are you doing down her all alone Pops?" she called out, the bright orange Poppies in his hand, a telltale sign.

With a full heart, he turned and smiled as she approached. "This has been a good day Sam, I've spent much of my life questioning God, not understanding why," Putting the petals to his nose, he paused, the faint, hazy scent of Earth comforting. "I loved your grandmother with all my heart Sam, never doubted that we were meant to be." On the other end of a heavy sigh, he added, "But, I never understood why I had to suffer the heartbreaking pain of falling in love with my Rosie, now I do,"

As if on cue, an old country tune filtered down the hillside, nothing but meaningful lyrics and a soft spring breeze whistling through the holler. Sammy Jo stepped up to her grandfather, resting her cheek against his chest, his low steady heart beating beneath her. He slipped an arm around her waist and propped his chin on soft curls.

Memories of another time, another life, passed between them. Sammy Jo took a step back and saw remnants of what once was, reflecting in symbolic tears of her grandfather's eyes. "Are you ok Pops?"

He nodded his reply, a watery gaze climbing to the woods bordering the back of the house. All good things in life bear a price. Looking back, he could place no value on the experience shared with a special woman who taught him to love.

He closed his eyes and tipped his head, drawing a gentle, unwavering breath. When eyes of coal opened again, understanding gleamed in the depths, clear insight of the past.

If you don't mind Sam, I think I'd like to take a walk,"

"Would you like me to come with you?" she asked.

"You get on back up to your husband and guests," he offered a slow blink, followed by a tender smile. "I'll be fine,"

Sammy Jo kissed his cheek, assured for the first time in many months that he would be fine. "You know where to find me," Gathering the hem of her dress in both hands, she strolled up the hill toward drifting music.

Jim watched until she was out of sight before wandering toward lilac bordered woods with a handpicked bouquet clasped in his hand. Nestled in the clearing, a special place awaited him, proof of abiding love.

Once again, the heart of Thatcher Hill beat strong with hope and promise, a future always meant to be.

63596755R00187

Made in the USA
Lexington, KY
12 May 2017